TOASTED

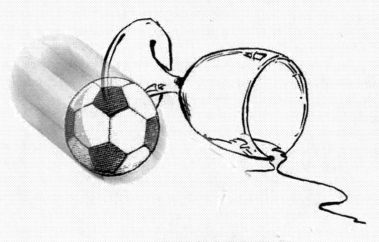

JOSIE GORDON

Lambda Literary award-winning author

Bella
BOOKS

2009

Bella Books, Inc.
P.O. Box 10543
Tallahassee, FL 32302

Printed in the United States of America on acid-free paper

First Edition

Editor: Katherine V. Forrest
Cover designer: Kiaro Creative Ltd.

ISBN-10: 1-59493-157-7
ISBN-13: 978-1-59493-157-4

For my friends

Acknowledgments

While it's true that Michigan's Great Lakes coastlines are dotted with quirky little towns with unique histories and vivacious lives, the dramas of Middelburg and its inhabitants are entirely made up by me. I just borrowed the geography—and even that I tweaked, adding a county and town where there is none. Don't go looking for it on a map. It doesn't exist and never did. There is no resemblance to the living or dead. Same goes for the Episcopal church. Well, it exists, of course, but Lonnie's diocese, bishop, colleagues and parish live only in my head. And yours, friend readers—and yours.

My thanks to my tribe: Rhoda, Trisha, Cindy, Lori, Carla, Devon, Pat, Craig, Jesse, everyone in my family, Casper and Desmond who snore while I type and then demand to play ball, Hattie who naps on my desk, and Tim who makes sure I get my exercise picking up paperclips, and most of all, Jen. I couldn't do it without them. Any errors in this text are mine, not theirs.

Special thanks to all of Lonnie's fans. I've got to tell you, I had the most fun making up the stuff in this book that I've ever had in my writing life. I hope you have as much fun reading it! At www.josiegordon.com I blog when I can and post updates on my writing. Hope to see you there!

Watch for the third Lonnie Squires mystery coming soon!

About the Author

Josie Gordon's first mystery novel *Whacked* (December 2008) won the Lambda Literary Award for the Best Lesbian Mystery of 2008.

This was a happy ending to a rather scary episode: once upon a time, Josie actually found a dead body in the woods. And though every amateur sleuth she has ever encountered in books or on TV would have seized the chance to march right up and investigate, Josie ran like the dickens in the other direction! Later, while waiting for the police, she resolved to write a book in which the sleuth would be as freaked out by finding a dead guy as she was.

Josie loves to sing in choirs, play the Irish whistle, drum, make a mess with paints on canvas (she can't call it "art"), and volunteer with her German shepherds in local hospitals and care centers. She lives with her partner in the woods and loves to spend time where there are more trees than people.

Toasted is the second Lonnie Squires mystery.

You can learn more at www.josiegordon.com.

Chapter One

I pride myself on two things in life. First, serious soccer skills. Olympic caliber. If a torn knee hadn't ended it all, I could've played with Mia Hamm.

Second, genuine compassion for others. Not worth a lot on the soccer field but it comes in handy for my day job. My vocation. You see, I'm an Episcopal priest.

You know how it is when you have two things you pride yourself on—if one goes, you're having a bad day. When both go, well, everyone had just better look out, because you can't be held responsible.

That's how it was that sweltering August Friday as I stood packed into the sticky five-by-five entry of Woman at the Well Episcopal Church with my Committee on Liturgy, all of us held captive by the committee's chair, a supremely irate Bova Poster. Round and sweaty, Bova gripped her bulbous hips. "You're the priest!" The embroidered chickadees on her powder blue tee stretched as she heaved her bosom. "Make! Them! Act! Like! Christians!"

The thing about soccer and compassion, at least for me, is that they go hand in hand and make me a good priest. When I play soccer, I'm patient and wise. When I do well at the job I love, I'm a focused powerhouse on the field.

But I hadn't played soccer in almost four months, since I'd moved here from Chicago's south side, the longest I'd ever gone without a team. Even when I'd torn up my knee in college, I'd had the team. And I needed that camaraderie, the physical outlet of my body cleansed by sweat and effort and stretching beyond my limits. It restoreth my soul.

Without it—well, let's just say when folks like Bova got trying, instead of offering compassion, I just wanted to kick her and the other five members of the committee in the shins—studs up.

This proved how badly I needed to get those last three names for the roster of Middelburg's new women's soccer team. There hadn't been a women's team in town since my old church group, The Well's Belles, had fallen away ten years ago. Except for an occasional reunion game, nothing. If I didn't get a team together and start playing soon—

Bova slapped her hand onto a green sheet tacked in the center of the parish bulletin board. I swear I saw the thin clapboard of the hundred-plus-year-old walls shake. "I! Did Not! Approve! This! Posting!"

I peeled my black clergy shirt away from my breastbone. The church had loads of charm, but no air-conditioning. I wished for another four inches on top of my six-foot height so I could escape the press and feel a cool breeze.

Everyone stared at me. My struggle not to lash out had rendered me silent for several long seconds. *Help, help, help,* I prayed silently as I looked down at the members of my flock and tried for a slightly confused expression. "Can we back up? I'm still unclear about the emergency."

Bova had called me at home, on my day off, screaming

about *An Emergency! The Zaloumi brothers! At church! Need a priest. Now! Life and Death!* I told her to call nine-one-one, dived into my clergy clothes, ran wet fingers through my short black and chestnut hair and nearly broke the land speed record driving to town. I barreled through the church door, my stole in one hand and the bottle of emergency holy oil from my glove compartment gripped in the other—and I'd run smack into the whole committee held captive by Bova.

Bova slapped the offending green sheet again. Hair clung to her damp forehead. "Someone hung an announcement! Without my permission! Make them obey the rules! Like Christians! Not! Like! Wild! Animals!" She whacked the board again for emphasis.

"Hand her a top hat and a whip," muttered the Zaloumi Twin wearing an Old Guys Rule ball cap. I shot him a look and both of their reedy ninety-four year-old bodies bent in unison.

Bova stabbed a finger at them. "They did it! Undermining my authority! Again! Make them stop!"

Frustration coiled in my legs. I really didn't want to be a bitch to these folks, members of my flock. I didn't want to have to bite my tongue either. I wanted to take these quirks of small-town life less seriously. Help them be good to each other.

Kitty Gellar, Senior Warden of the church, cleared her throat and everyone turned. Her bird-thin body looked unflappably cool inside her standard polyester black suit and high-collared blouse. She had lived eighty-some years as an Episcopalian in Middelburg, Michigan, so when she *ahem*-ed other Episcopalians listened. "Father," she said to me, though I hated it when she called me that, "perhaps we could move this discussion to the parish house?"

Next door. Air-conditioning.

"Yes," said mousey commission member Isabella Koontz.

The parish's extravagantly beautiful temporary secretary Ashleigh Moore pushed open the door and the Zaloumis turned to follow.

"No!" Bova punched her hips again and the chickadees nearly

took flight. "I want this solved! At the scene! Of the crime!"

As I watched Bova's chickadees expand and contract, I heard the theme from *Mission Impossible* playing in my head—the old soundtrack I'd heard as a kid watching reruns on lazy weekends with my dad in the basement den. You know the one with the fuse burning fast and short?

Just three more for the team roster, I thought, trying to compose my face so I looked like I was considering the situation at hand. *Three more women in the next ten days and you'll have the Well's Belles resurrected.*

I tried not to sigh out loud and looked again at the flyer, alone in the middle of the empty bulletin board. "This says that starting Sunday we'll offer both bread and wafers for communion and that people can have their choice."

"Exactly!" Bova nodded triumphantly, as if all were now made clear.

I was still lost. "It's Committee on Liturgy business."

"No! It isn't! It's the Zaloumis! Meddling again!"

Eddie and Leon Zaloumi stared back at me with four identical brown eyes. The brothers were meddlers who acted half of my age—which is thirty-four—most of the time. In the three months I'd been at this parish they'd put peeper frogs in the ladies' room and brought me snakes just for fun. Doing something just to get a rise out of Bova—who was easily riseable—would be their MO.

"Did you gentlemen put this here?" I asked.

"Yes, Reverend," the Twins said together.

"Are you still part of the Committee on Liturgy?"

Identical nods.

"But I didn't approve it!" Bova said. "Any of it."

"You know," Ashleigh interjected from her spot nearest the door, "the committee did approve both bread and wafers starting, like, this Sunday."

"No!" Bova's chickadeed bosom bounced. "Bread only! Traditional communion! The way Jesus himself did it!"

Oh for God's sake. My right foot jiggled.

The Zaloumis shook their heads and Isabella winced.

"Want me to print the minutes?" Ashleigh offered, trying again to escape back to the cool offices next door.

"Not necessary," Kitty pronounced. "Father, what was decided at the meeting?"

I shrank about six inches. Kitty was the only person, other than my ex, Jamie, who could make me feel so small so fast.

"I wasn't there." The one meeting I'd missed in the last three months. I'd been trying to recruit a few soccer players after the big women's coffee hour at the Christian middle school.

"There will be no changes!" Sweat popped out across Bova's forehead. "That's the announcement that should be here! I made a flyer!" She bit her lip.

Leon poked Eddie—or maybe the other way around—looking satisfied.

Energy buzzed across my skin and suddenly I got it. The committee *had* decided to offer both, but Bova didn't like the decision. So she'd decided to announce that there'd be no change. She knew Isabella would never speak up against her publicly, and Kitty and I hadn't been to the meeting and if the Zaloumis protested, no one would believe them. So the Twins had pre-empted her with their own flyer. Just like a give-and-go on the eighteen yard line. The defender had no idea what had just happened. So Bova, instead of just ripping down their flyer and going on her merry way, had decided to start a war.

Well, Lonnie, they hired you to reconcile folks of the congregation. How about some reconciling? Thus sayeth the voice in my head.

Or some old fashioned head-knocking. "The thing is," I said out loud, "I'm the one with authority over the worship service." *Supposedly.* "And none of this got run by me."

Eddie and Leon shrugged their bony shoulders inside their matching plaid cotton shirts.

"Um, like, I hear the phone ringing?" Ashleigh waved her squared black fingernails toward the doorway. "And I don't even, you know, get the wafer thing? We don't do that at the CLOSER churches."

Christ the Lord's Own Sainted Elect Reformed churches

5

comprised seventeen of the twenty churches in Middelburg and almost ninety-eight percent of its inhabitants.

"Go." I turned to the board and tapped the silver thumbtack. "If this is what the committee decided, then it stays."

The Zaloumi without the hat pumped a fist.

"No!" Bova gripped the green sheet.

I placed a hand against her arm. "Don't touch it."

"I'm chair. I post notices! They broke the rules!"

"Actually," said Kitty, "you're threatening to break another rule right now."

"Wh-what?" Bova blinked. Like I said, no one messed with Kitty.

"The flyer was posted by members of the appropriate committee. That's allowed." Kitty's voice reminded me of a brick wall. Rough, but no cracks. "So you'd need their permission to remove it."

"But I *am* the committee!" Bova crossed her arms in front of her stomach, squinching the embroidered chickadees into a long kiss.

I looked at the others, hoping someone might cut this poor woman some kindness. Not that she deserved it, but if we all only got what we deserved, where would we be?

The Old Guys Rule Zaloumi scratched his whiskered neck. "Tell you what. I'll flip you for it."

I remembered this was Leon, because of the scar that cut his left eyebrow in two. Left, L, Leon.

He pulled out a quarter and tossed it. "Call it."

"I will not!" said Bova.

"Tails, it stays," said Eddie.

Leon snatched the coin out of the air and smacked it onto his forearm, then glanced at it. "Tails it is." He scooped it back into his pocket. "'Fraid the flyer stays."

No one else noticed that Leon hadn't shown his coin. It could have been heads for all we knew.

Bova looked at me. "This is the problem in this congregation. Lack of reverence. Lack of respect." She pulled her spine straight.

"It's no wonder the whole town—"

"No wonder the whole town what?" My blood pressure boiled at the jab.

"Talks." Bova looked at her feet, half smiling, voice low. "About you being—you know."

My heart leapt into a sprint. Jamie had been in town last spring when I'd almost died in my own front yard. She'd ditched me and returned to Hyde Park the next day, but enough people had seen her and I together. Had someone figured out I'm gay?

"Reverend?" Isabella asked.

I raised an eyebrow trying to look cool. "About my being a woman, you mean?"

Bova shook her head. "Much worse."

I wondered if the others could hear my heart thrashing against my chest in the tiny, hot room.

"For one thing, most days, you don't even wear the right clothes," she continued.

I wore clergy clothes, especially the hot plastic collar, only on Sundays or special occasions. The official outfit did not help people relax.

"And you poked your nose in when Vance got murdered last spring," Bova said. "As if you liked it. And then you took the dead guy's dog home! It's strange!"

"Saving the innocent always is," said Eddie, straight-faced.

"'Specially 'round here," Leon added.

Bova ignored them.

"She caught the murderer!" Isabella said.

"Some say she *brought* the murderer," Bova said.

"Some shouldn't be speaking at all." Kitty crinkled her lips.

Red flooded across Bova's neck. "Well, all I'm saying is that people are saying she moved to town and next thing, Middelburg has its first murder in decades."

Kitty inclined her head. "Anything else?"

I wished she hadn't asked as Bova nodded with importance.

"She lives out of town. In the woods. Alone." Bova scanned the room, drinking in her audience's attention. "And everyone knows about the gay thing."

I felt my knees buckle. *Breathe.*

"What kind of person can do that?" Bova asked.

The room swam.

"To a God-fearing religion professor?" Bova finished.

I blinked. "What?" She'd lost me. "Do what? Are you talking about Guy Rittenga?" He was the only religion professor I knew. "He's married." What did that have to do with me being gay?

"You talked him into giving that speech about gays up at the college's graduation and got him fired!" Bova jammed her hands on her hips again.

So "the gay thing" wasn't about my sexuality! But what was it about? "But Guy retired." I looked around for support but everyone avoided my eyes.

Bova humphed at my naïveté. "That's what he says, probably to save face. But everyone knows they really fired him. Poor Maris." She shifted her weight to one hip. "Why do you think you can't get people to sign up for a new soccer team?"

"Because they are afraid of the Episcopal church," I said. "Don't want to do anything that isn't associated with a CLOSER church. That's why this team will help our congregation's relationship with the town."

"No. Because people don't want to be part of anything you're running," Bova said. "They think you're—" She stopped, looking satisfied.

My heart jumped again. Maybe I hadn't escaped so easily. "They think I'm what?"

"In league with the antichrist," Bova said, enunciating each word with a politician's flair.

Is that all? Laughter bubbled out of my chest. "Are you kidding me?"

"*That* explains it," said Leon Zaloumi. "She lives in the woods. Alone." He tossed his hands above his head. "She keeps a black animal."

Eddie nodded. "She didn't run or scream when we brought those milk snakes in. Snakes bein' allied with the devil 'n' all—

8

this explains it."

"Explains what?" Isabella asked. She was too innocent to know better.

"She's a witch," said Leon. Eddie nodded. The others snickered. Even Kitty smiled.

"This is not a joke!" Red flooded from Bova's neck into her face. "I'm talking about being able to hold my head up in this town when people think my priest is a servant of the devil!" She looked me up and down. "Reverend."

Silence.

Yep, I definitely needed a soccer team to burn off this stress. Sweat dripped down my spine. I tried to latch onto anything compassionate and respectful to say, but the only things floating through my head were four-letter words. Still, being a rumored consort of the devil was better than being outed, at least in Middelburg.

Suddenly, the theme song from Mighty Mouse flew from my pants pocket and cut through the room.

Caller ID: Marion Freeley. Best friend extraordinaire. Coming to save the day.

Phone clock: 1:23.

I switched the ringer off. "It's an emergency. I have to go."

"Shall I tell Altar Guild to accommodate wafers when they set up Sunday morning?" Isabella asked.

Mental note: hug Isabella. "Yes." I tapped the green sheet on the bulletin board. "This stays put. Starting Sunday we'll serve both bread and wafers at communion. I'll order the wafers."

"Already done," said Isabella, patting her temples with a tissue.

Everyone edged toward the exit.

"Wafers taste like stale toast," Bova muttered. "Who would serve that to the Lord our God?"

"Then we'll raise the chalice over them," Eddie said, "and toast the wafers with the wine."

"A toast for the toast," said Leon.

Bova narrowed her eyes at me. "We'll just see what the bishop has to say about all this."

"Enough." Kitty raised her hand as if about to swat a couple of mosquitos.

If we'd had a ball and a goal, we could have worked it out right there, Bova and I, a one-on-one shoot-out. That's the beauty of soccer—clean. Conclusive. As it was I had to suffer a delay of game. "We'll continue this discussion," I said, "*both* discussions—at our meeting Monday morning."

Kitty placed her hand on Bova's arm. "Come along. I'll buy you a nice glass of iced tea."

Chapter Two

"Didn't you just want to kill her?" Marion asked as she tossed Linus's Squeaky Toad across my kitchen. The six-month-old, all-black German shepherd skidded after it. Fifteen years ago Marion had played stopper to my sweeper on the Well's Belles championship team and, though we'd gone years without seeing each other, the close friendship had reignited when I'd moved to town last spring. We were packing a final few things to spend the rest of the afternoon on the beach—Marion free from kids, me free from parishioners for a few quiet hours—and I'd told her about what Bova had said.

"No. I want her to grow up and quit demonizing people just to make herself feel better." I bent to pull on my sports sandals and the beach towel around my neck rubbed my face. It smelled like sunshine.

"Sometimes I feel that way about the whole town."

"Me too." Marion didn't know the half of it. I'd never told her anything about being gay. I'd never told anyone. Jamie had figured it out and pursued me. It was the only relationship I'd had. I missed it, but not enough to talk about the truth. Not around here. Not even with Marion. I loved her and trusted her, but people slipped. And one accidental outing in this town and I'd be out of a job and a home and God only knew what else before I'd even realize what hit me. For now, the situation fit my life just fine. I had a congregation to worry about. A relationship would just demand too much.

Linus trotted back from the living room and dropped Toad at Marion's perfectly manicured feet. Her nails were a cheerful yellow this week. A bright orange and yellow tie-dye caftan draped her ample frame.

"Do you really think that's why I can't get a team together?" I leaned against the sink, watching Linus flop after his toy again. "Because people think I'm an evil influence? I mean, you'd have heard something like that down at the Grind, right?"

Marion shrugged. "People know I'm your friend and they like my place." Marion owned and operated The Windmill Grind Kaffe Klatsch and All Dutch All the Time Café smack in the middle of downtown Middelburg. The Grind had been there for more than a hundred years. Marion had run it for a decade. "Either you don't come up in conversation or if you do—"

"—they'll be nice," I finished. Marion had introduced me to the concept of west Michigan nice. Folks would rather lie than be perceived as not nice, a situation that led to a lot of nasty misunderstandings.

"One or two have tried to save my soul." Marion tossed Toad again. "You know, help me see your evil ways."

I threw my soft-sided cooler at her. "And you didn't tell me?"

"It's part of Star's campaign to trash you. I don't pay attention to her crap."

Star Hannes. Middelburg Town Councilwoman and Social Dictator for Life. Most recently, United States Congresswoman

Wannabe. She'd taken a dislike to me the minute I walked into town and started asking questions about how things worked around here.

I yanked the fridge open. "But everybody else does." I grabbed a few cold sodas from the fridge. "I *have* to pay attention."

"No, you don't." Linus dropped Toad on Marion's toes again. "Don't give her your energy."

"But she's screwing up my chance to form a soccer team!"

Marion held up Toad. "She just wants to make sure you don't compete for her popularity. There's only room for one First Lady of Middelburg and the good councilwoman wants to be it." She hurled the toy into the living room then wiped her forehead. "How hot is it in here?"

"For God's sake, I'm a woman Episcopal priest in a town of CLOSERs. I've lived here three months. She's been here umpteen generations. I can hardly compete!"

"Well, with the Orions attending Woman at the Well and your rather showy capture of Vance's murderer. . ." She took the cold sodas and held them to her temples. "You gotta admit, you upstaged her both times."

True. Christopher and Elyse Orion brought some respect to my little church. They'd moved to Middelburg shortly after I'd arrived in May, bringing their multibillion dollar gaming research company and their openly gay teenage son. And though Woman at the Well had almost split over issues of inclusivity—in fact, I'd been hired to reconcile the parish—the Orions chose to attend our Episcopal church because at least we wrestled with the issue. The CLOSER churches wouldn't even touch it.

And I had captured a murderer on stage in front of practically the whole town. Been in the local headlines for nearly two weeks. Got interviewed on the Grand Rapids TV stations—more airtime than Star.

Add that to what Marion didn't know and no wonder Star was out to get me. When I'd discovered the killer, I'd also discovered Star's plot to sabotage a community celebration, so that she could then fix the mess and become an even bigger local hero. She figured that would cement her election victory this fall. And I'd told no one, except Star. She knew I had evidence I could whip out against her any time I wanted.

However, if she really was the source of these nasty rumors about my evil influence on Guy Rittenga, it gave me the power to shut her up. This made me feel so much better, I dropped the bag of baby carrots I was going to pack and grabbed some Three Musketeers bars instead. *Soccer team, here I come.*

"Can't believe you eat that stuff and complain about my cooking."

I held up a bar. "Low fat. Plus these I can stop eating." Marion was a heck of a great cook and though I'd always been fit, my metabolism had slowed way down in the last few years. My belly rounded like never before and I'd actually spotted puckers in my thighs just a few weeks ago. I looked again at the bars, then tossed them back into the fridge. *Carrots it is.*

"So, with this wafer and bread thing—you gonna cut your Sunday morning bread order?" Marion's bakery at The Grind provided the communion bread for my parish and almost every other church in town.

"No. Just tell Josh to hide it from the Zaloumis when he delivers it. They're pro-wafer and there's no telling what they'd do to get under Bova's skin."

Marion snorted. "This is why I gave up Christianity." She fingered her pendant, a silver spiral sun.

"You didn't really give it up. You added to it."

"Yeah," Marion stood. "A little Buddha, a little Krishna, a whole lot of Gaia." She waggled her head side to side. "Girlfriend, ain't no one in this burg gonna let me call myself a Christian."

"Call yourself whatever you want."

"Not in public." Marion only shared her hodgepodge of beliefs with me, her husband, and a few of the Belles. As far as the rest of Middelburg knew, she was a nice CLOSER woman. It was better for business.

I glanced around the kitchen for anything else to toss in the cooler. "We're good to go."

Marion floated on her four-inch heeled sandals into my living room and, as always, I marveled at her grace. Heels like that, I'd tip over for sure. "Just call me an undercover smorgasbord of faith." She tossed her towel over her shoulder. "Though I can't say I think much of smorgasbords." Her nose wrinkled. "Probably something that Loaves and Fishes lady would cook, though." She dabbed at her face with her towel. "I can't believe people are paying good money to hear her talk about cooking."

She was talking about Cousin Donna Hancock's Loaves and Fishes Culinary Ministries, a moveable megachurch feast showing in town this weekend and next. I'd never heard of it—that sort of thing hadn't played well during my years in south Chicago. But evidently Cousin Donna's popularity had exploded in the last few years in towns just like this one. Women flocked from hundreds of miles to her sold-out shows.

"Donna doesn't just talk about cooking," I said. "She demonstrates. And prays. Besides, the show's a benefit for the recreation center we both want. So don't knock it." Turned out Elyse Orion had gone to high school with her, and as soon as Star found out, she'd strong-armed Elyse into convincing the cook to do a benefit for Middelburg's new recreation center.

"Just as long as people don't all stay home and cook instead of coming to The Grind." Marion snagged Linus's leash from its spot by the door and he ran up to her and sat. "Perfect little angel," she cooed as she hooked him. "Let's go."

"Nothing can compete with the Grind." I grabbed my car keys, turned off the oscillating fan that kept the old cottage from becoming a furnace, and held the door open for friend and dog.

Marion wiped her face again. "Don't worry about Star Hannes and her anti-Lonnie contingent. You'll get your team. All of us soccer junkies are counting on you. You got until the thirteenth, right? And only three more people to sign?"

I nodded then looked around. My skin didn't feel right. Had we forgotten something?

She slapped me on the shoulder. "So let's go. This'll be just what you need, a good dose of the Earth Goddess." She spread her arms wide. "And blessed be *The Simpsons* because only my promise to rent that show made my boys promise not to wreck the house while Mommy has some private time. Let's go!"

I lingered, still feeling that strange draw to the house.

"Come on."

Whatever wanted me could wait. I pulled the door shut and sure enough, my cell phone sounded its generic ring from inside the house.

Marion thrust a finger at me. "Do *not* answer that!"

But I had to look. I always had to look. What if it were a real emergency with a parishioner? Or my mom and dad? Or my sisters?

I jumped through the door and checked the caller ID. "It's Colleen." A former Belle, a utility player off the bench, and good friend of both of ours. "Maybe she found someone to add to the team!"

"Lon, thank God you answered." Colleen sounded squeezed with panic. "It's D.J."

Her eight-year-old son, a soccer prodigy with a very old soul. "Is he okay?"

"D.J.?" Marion asked. She often took care of him when Colleen had to work late.

Colleen explained the boy had injured himself playing forty miles away in Grand Rapids. "He's probably got a groin pull, but I've got to go to the hospital."

"You want me to come with you?" I asked.

"What happened?" Marion asked.

I held up a finger so she'd wait silently a minute.

"No," said Colleen. "But I need you to sub for me this weekend. At the Loaves and Fishes show. From three to nine tonight and tomorrow morning until three."

My face must have fallen because Marion panicked and grabbed my arm. "What happened to him?"

"I don't think I can do that," I said.

"Go!" Marion said. "Go on! Gaia can wait."

I shook my head at her and covered the phone. "She wants

me to work security at the cooking show."

Marion's eyes widened. "Don't!"

"Please," said Colleen. "You just offered to come to the hospital. Well, do this instead. It will give me huge peace of mind. I can't just ditch on Char—she had such a hard time finding people to begin with."

"I—uh—" I wished I had a solid excuse at hand. But Char was another former Belle, left fullback, running security for the event. She'd pumped the whole Belle network for help, but I'd said no, I couldn't give up both days off in one week.

"Please!" Colleen's voice squeaked. "Just this weekend. So I can focus on D.J." *Ouch.* "Besides," Colleen said, "you're the only friend I have who hasn't got kids, so you're actually free to do it on such short notice." *Double ouch.*

"She can find someone else," Marion said.

"Please, Lon."

I felt her pain. I mean, hadn't I spent the last two weeks trying to scrounge up a women's soccer team only to be told no over and over? And wasn't Colleen a friend? A former Belle? She'd even signed up to play on my new team. She didn't think I consorted with the devil.

"Plus, the place will be loaded with women," Colleen said.

For a terrifying moment I thought she meant I could look for a date there.

"For potential soccer players," she concluded.

"Right!" I laughed my relief. "Maybe I could finish the roster." That would be a load off my mind. Besides, who wanted a date? Jamie had only been gone three months. And really, an evangelical cooking school? Not the likeliest of sources.

"Ah, crap," said Marion, leaning over and snapping off Linus's leash.

"The New Well's Belles! You can do it!" Colleen cheered like I was her kid running up and down the soccer pitch.

Yeah, I thought, *I can do it.* Even with Star doing her damndest to turn the town against me, there'd be hundreds of women there from nearby towns. Probably three who'd want to play soccer.

God was handing this to me on a silver platter.

"Traitor!" Marion hollered when I agreed.

"Tell Mare she's full of it," Colleen said with a half laugh. "I know she was in there this morning helping set up the stage kitchens."

"Oh, was she?" I cut a glance at Marion.

"What?" She spread her hands wide in mock innocence.

"Just wear khaki slacks," Colleen said. "Char will have a security tee for you there. Tomorrow you'll want to dress up a bit for the breakfast reception, but you can change later."

"No reception," I said. "No way."

Marion clutched her chest as if having a heart attack. "Not the reception too!"

Hobnobbing with Middelburg's movers and shakers was more than I could handle in my current mood. "No."

"Lon," Colleen said. "How would it look if everyone who is someone around here showed up, including the pastors of all seventeen Christ the Lord's Own Sainted Elect Reformed churches, but the troublemaking new priest of that Episcopal Church didn't?"

Probably like I was off somewhere dancing with the devil.

"Don't go!" Marion wailed. "There'll be mimosas from plastic cups! Unidentifiable cheese foods!"

Those dangers aside, Colleen had a point. Just maybe I could have a little chat with Star, convince her to back off—or else.

I took a deep breath. "I'm in."

Chapter Three

Frontline Church of Christ squatted near the freeway, well outside of Middelburg, in the midst of blueberry and cornfields. I'd never been in it, even though I drove by it every time I traveled between town and home and I'd nearly throttled its founding pastor, Brady Wesselynk, at least a half dozen times. He annoyed me so much because in a way, I admired him. Like me, he wasn't Dutch, hadn't grown up here, and wasn't a member of the Christ the Lord's Own Sainted Elect denomination. But unlike me, Brady was a happy-handshaking ultra-conservative in a "God wants you to be happy and wealthy" kind of way. He'd managed to earn a place of power and respect in Middelburg and support throughout west Michigan. That he'd planted his expensive and expansive complex here made locals proud, and they waxed lovingly about him, especially when he let local schools and community groups use the church's professional quality soundstage for events like tonight's cooking show.

Frontline's long drive wound past acres of manicured lawn, sportive fountains, and professional grade softball fields. A scrolling neon sign urged me to "Remember the power of CPR—Christ's Power Released." I gritted my teeth.

Be nice. There are lots of ways to do church.

A vast banner welcomed me to Cousin Donna Hancock's Loaves and Fishes Culinary Ministries. The Christian fish symbol lay on a platter surrounded by ill-drawn parsley, with a sliced loaf of bread and two glasses of red wine standing nearby. It looked like something the Zaloumi twins would dream up on a slow day.

The black parking lots exhaled shimmering waves of heated air. Orange sawhorses closed them off, but I followed the arrows to the central gate. Quite a setup. We never locked the doors at Woman at the Well, just the sacristy closet to protect the communion wine.

I felt a whole lot better about things, though, when I saw who stood in the guard's booth by the yellow gate.

"Hey," said the gatekeeper. Barely over five feet with tight chestnut curls, a khaki sheriff's deputy uniform, black combat boots and a contraption around her waist that looked like Batman's utility belt, Red Carson swaggered up like a linebacker. "You got an invitation? And I need a photo ID." She pulled her dark glasses low on her nose and looked over them. "'Cause you look suspicious to me."

"Priest. Armed and dangerous, that's me. No invitation." I held out my wallet. "But here's the ID."

She waved it away and checked me off on her list. "Sweet of you to fill in for Colleen last minute. How's the kid?"

"Haven't heard. Didn't sound too bad."

She pointed in the direction of the fartherest ball field. "Show volunteers in parking lot K." Then she swung her arm back toward the main entrance. "Those doors are open for about another five minutes, then it's lockdown until the show starts."

"Seriously?" That seemed a little much.

"These fans of Cousin Donna's are like rabid dogs on a bone.

A few minutes ago, a lady tried to get in here to park. I told her no parking except for security until five o'clock. Guess what she did?"

"What?"

"Offered me two twenties!" Red pulled her damp curls behind her ears. "So I said no, thanks, and she still couldn't park here and she called me a *bitch*, right here in this church parking lot!"

"Lightning didn't strike her down?"

Red laughed. "Talk to God about that, will you? I expect a little more support from the On High. A crack of thunder, at least!"

"Well, you'll have the crack security team on the inside for support."

She wrinkled her face.

"I've been practicing." I snugged my shades and put on my best Sydney Bristow impersonation. "Excuse me, ma'am, but could you lower your cookbook and back away from the spice display? Ma'am, back away from the turmeric, please!"

"Very reassuring." Red patted some contraption on her belt. "But I have a taser, so you call me if you need backup. When the show starts, Don and I will be working inside too." She wiped sweat from the sides of her nose. "How's it going with the soccer recruiting?"

I tried to look optimistic. "Still need three. You sure you don't want to sign up?"

Shaking her head, Red hit the button that raised the yellow gate. "No way. I do enough running around after people in fields. And after hours, it's just the cars and me. Nice and quiet. No back talk."

She and her brother ran a garage on the southwest end of town, out near where I used to stay summers with my Great-Aunt Katherine. "Well, if you change your mind. . ."

"Once you're in, follow the signs past Fellowship Hall A toward the Green Room. And hey, great haircut." She waved me through.

I worried about my hair a lot since I'd had to cut it short

21

after a nasty head injury last spring, so the compliment sparkled through me as I drove to Lot K. I passed a massive RV resting near the church, person-high script on the side proclaiming it the property of "Cousin Hancock's Loaves and Fishes Culinary Ministries."

The main doors to Frontline Church, six wide, hissed and slid as I approached. Ostentatious air-conditioning pricked goose bumps from my damp skin. In the three-story high lobby of smooth brown brick and glass, noise bounced off every surface as people bustled around vendor booths, arranging their wares.

I checked my watch—3:37, seven minutes late and counting—and turned past the crystal nail file booth (Never Needs Sharpening! Lasts a Lifetime!). Colored banners hung from the skylights. Display cases announced prayer groups, Bible coffee hours, teen prayer lock-ins and kiddie rainbow salvation classes. My head swam. An especially enormous banner hung above and across the main entry: "Prayer is the Key to the Morning and the Bolt on the Night."

I wondered if I should have locked my car in the Frontline parking lot.

I finally spotted a poster-sized map of the church hanging above the drinking fountains and plotted my course down a hall adorned with smiley faces and a burgundy sign welcoming me with "No Perfect People Allowed!" Contemporary Christian art, all of it original, hung on the walls. I paused in front of one so abstract I couldn't identify the subject. Maybe once the show got rolling I could come hang out here and enjoy them. It beat listening to recipes for Practically Perfect Pumpkin Pie, or whatever Cousin Donna had on her docket.

The sudden bang of an opening door drew my eyes to the far end of the hall. My former left fullback, Char Maarten, hurtled toward me. "You're saving my butt, Squires." She threw her arms around me. "But now I can't find the boys. That's six security people missing! I can't do this without them!"

"Really?" I mean, sure, Cousin Donna Hancock, home-cookin' and prayin' guru extraordinaire, had a following among the Christian meat-and-potatoes crowd, which is essentially what populated Middelburg. But they'd never seemed like the type to go nuts for a celebrity, despite Red's story.

Char grabbed my arm. "They were frothing at the mouth in the ticket line last week. Tickets went on sale at ten o'clock that Friday morning and Marion called me at five thirty when she opened the Grind to say people were already lined up around the block! By the time I got there at seven, there were hundreds of them. Some had driven in from Iowa!"

Impressive.

"And when the first dozen saw me, they started pounding on the plate glass. The whole thing could've shattered! They pounded and chanted for hours before the sale even started!"

I tried to look compassionate, but failed, and grinned.

"It is not funny," Char said. "It scared me. I called Robbie and, God love him, he brought his housemates Josh and Paul over just to stand there and look big. They stayed until the crowds died down. The whole house-load is working for me tonight. I owe them pizza for life if I ever find them!"

Poor Char. Her jet-black wisps fell loosely around her ears, brushing her cool metallic earrings and her perfectly made-up face. Wearing jeans, sandals and a crisp white blouse, Char looked every inch the artist and businesswoman she was, except for the squint of anxiety around her eyes.

"Tonight," she said, "there will be one of you for every forty of them. I just hope it's enough. Mandy Tibbetts, that's Cousin Donna's manager, assures me that unless I worked crowd control at a Beatles concert in the nineteen sixties or at a Filene's Basement Clearance sale, I'd never seen anything like what we're going to see when those doors open at four forty-five."

Suddenly the vision of me facing down forty sturdy Midwestern women hell-bent on getting the latest recipe for Gospel Goulash or whatever it was Cousin Donna Hancock concocted wasn't so funny. "A lot of screaming, sweating and fainting?"

Char stopped and leaned in to whisper. "Women stampeding anyone and anything that stands between them and vendor specials."

"Are there a lot of those?" I whispered back.

"Everything from potholders to pots, spices, dishes, personalized wooden spoons, and God knows what all. They do giveaways before the show. And there's goodie bags. One on each seat."

"So everyone gets one. What's the problem?"

"Mandy told me that if even one coupon is missing from a goodie bag, the woman could rip your heart out."

"Come on."

Char's eyes widened. "Mandy says they're even worse about the food prizes. Cousin Donna raffles off every dish she makes. It's her trademark."

"But wait. Didn't they come here to learn how to make the dish? What's the big deal?"

Char shrugged. "Don't know. Maybe having a guru-cooked meal is a big deal for this crowd. After the ticket fiasco, I believe what Mandy tells me."

An idea struck me. "You know, this will be great training to get you back on the pitch."

Char looked annoyed. "I told you. I'm thirty pounds heavier and two businesses busier. No." Then she smiled. "Bet you can't guess who my snottiest customer was on ticket day?"

Too easy. "Not Congresswoman Wannabe Hannes?"

"She wanted four tickets. When I told her the limit was two, she said those who sacrificed to get into line early should reap the rewards and those who hadn't should reap as they sowed." Char gestured dramatically in perfect imitation.

"Very Biblical," I said.

"Soon it was a campaign speech, and I had ten women jammed into the office demanding extra tickets because they'd sacrificed so much. I thought I was going to have to dial nine-one-one for tear gas!"

I laughed.

Char rubbed her temples. "When I agreed to run security, I thought it would be helping old ladies find their seats."

Scuffing noises at the lobby end of the hall announced a posse of beefy young men, all wearing flip-flops and various versions of baggy pants, sport sunglasses and black security tees. My self-image sagged. Even when I got my tee, there was no way I'd look as badass as them.

"Hey, Mom. Hey, Rev Lon." Char's son Robbie waved. "Sorry we're late. Will forgot his ID. and we had to go back."

"All of you?"

They eyed each other like it was a trick question. Typical college boys on summer break—tan, bleached blond, muscles, oozing testosterone. "Well, yeah," Robbie said.

"Then we had to talk our way past the cop," added a very tall redhead with tattooed forearms.

"Guys," Robbie flipped a hand toward me, "this is Reverend Squires. She's cool."

"Hey," I said, my self-image restored. I nodded at the only other one I knew, Josh who worked at The Grind both in the kitchen and as delivery guy.

In true young-man-meeting-strange-older-woman-priest fashion, they mumbled and looked away. The one wearing a black ball cap even blushed.

Robbie swung his arms around his mother and kissed her cheek. He was the young male version of Char, husky, red-cheeked and black-haired, only his was gelled into little spikes. I guessed his heart was as big as his mom's too, otherwise, what would he and all his friends be doing at a Christian cooking show on a Friday night and all day Saturday?

"It's nice of you guys to give up the next two weekends to help your mom," I said.

Their silence and steady stares caught me off guard. They reminded me of the Zaloumi Twins just last week, when they ceremoniously presented me with a live bat they'd trapped in their farmhouse attic.

Something was definitely up with these boys.

Chapter Four

Char led us through the doors at the end of the hall marked Authorized Personnel Only. A sign like that would never work at my church. With Episcopalians, everyone would think they were authorized.

We walked down some halls and past a lot of doors. I was lost until we turned through a door labeled Green Room. Applause broke out from the women there.

"Rev Lon!" one of them shouted. I high-fived my way through eight of my former soccer teammates. I'd played with them when I lived here summers with my great-aunt. The Well's Belles, 1993 church league conference champions, still hung together after all these years. Romee, our keeper, as Dutch as they came, sporting several fiery tattoos that you only saw in the locker room. Bets and Annika and Gaby and Luce, midfielders who now had seventeen children between them. Rika, Julie, Trix and Brenna, who I didn't know as well off the pitch, but loved anyway.

I did a quick calculation—Char's crack security force was entirely made up of fifteen middle-aged women and college boys.

Romee had her mussed blond locks wrapped into a hair umbrella, the kind you usually see on toddlers. Multicolored rubber bracelets dangled from her wrists, and she bounced in her bright yellow Chuck Taylor hightops. "How's D.J.?"

"Colleen hasn't called."

We stepped into the Green Room and someone whistled.

"Sheesh." Josh tipped his Red Wings ball cap back. "A guy could live in here."

Or a priest. The Green Room made a nice efficiency apartment, kitchen on one wall, flat screen television on another, and in between sat comfy chairs, a sofa and a dining table for eight.

"You'd impress the ladies," said a low voice behind me. I turned expecting James Earl Jones, but saw a short skinny guy who looked about thirteen years old. "Turn on the mojo." His face gave no promise of whiskers, but his head burst with chocolate curls. He wore metal-rimmed glasses and a porkpie hat, looking like a cross between Gene Hackman in *The French Connection* and Eddie Haskell. "Hey," he said when he noticed me looking. "I'm Will."

"None of you clowns can live here with me," Josh said. "You'd mess it up for sure."

The boy wearing the black ball cap gave him a shove. "You never share anything."

Josh shoved back.

"Boys, please, this is serious."

"Sorry, Mom," said Robbie. "They're animals."

Jungle sounds ensued.

Char walked across the front of us like a sergeant with an unruly squad, clipboard in hand. "People! Focus!"

Like a gaggle of elementary-school kids we segregated ourselves—over-thirty-something women on the right, twenty-something college boys on the left. Char passed around a sheet for us all to write names and cell numbers, promising to distribute copies before the show.

"There's already trouble," Char said, glaring at the clipboard. "I've just learned of a previously unscheduled knife giveaway at five forty-five."

We blinked at her.

"At five forty-three every woman in this place—that's roughly five hundred and fifty of them—is going to run from the Cook's Compressor Bags booth, which has a scheduled giveaway at five thirty-five, down the north hall and across the lobby into the south hall to the Clean Cut Knives booth. Will there be enough of you there to control a crowd so close to so many potential weapons?"

Around me the group shifted.

"Five hundred of them," Romee said, "dozens of knives and fifteen of us? Interesting game plan." She grinned.

It certainly won't be boring.

"Not even all fifteen of you," Char said. "Because other areas of the venue need to be staffed at all times." She pulled packets from the clipboard and began to pass them around. "Here you'll find schedules, floor plans and the basic plan for where each of you needs to be when. Let's have a look, see if you have questions, and figure out what to do about this knife thing. Start on page seven, personnel assignments."

We all flipped through our pages and I found my name and notes.

Preshow: Lobby Station Krystal Kleer Nail Files
(ALERT! Giveaway at 4:55!)
Show: Backstage Left, Food Escort.

Hmm.

"What if you shifted me from the Lovely Linens booth for that knife thing?" asked Annika VanTassel, Belle right midfielder. She had four-year-old triplets and could handle a high level of

28

chaos.

"Not possible," Char said. "Lovely Linens is raffling off a gift basket at five fifty, the final pre-show event. That's the last place I want to go thin."

"I could probably leave cookbooks for a bit," said Trix Raymer, Belles' right fullback. "They don't make good weapons."

Char bit her lip. "Maybe."

"But what if someone sneaks up during the knife giveaway," said Romee with a not-quite-straight face, "and makes away with the signed edition of Cousin Donna's latest?"

Gaby flipped a hand up. "I'll do it. The spices won't assault anyone if I'm not there."

"No," Char said. "That's a particularly volatile spot between spices and non-stick cookware."

"I could go," I said. "I'm on the nail file booth, but that giveaway is a lot earlier."

"Good," said Char. "From five twenty on, you're my extra knife person."

Char walked us through the entire two-day schedule packet, then told us we'd be using cell phones instead of walkie-talkies because they were quieter. She made us all hold ours up, obedient soldiers.

"Set on vibrate," Char said. "Check battery levels. Confirmed they are powered up? Thumbs up to affirm."

Buttons were pushed and thumbs went high in the air. Shared looks among the boys at the ridiculousness of the whole thing. I raised my hand and asked if we could introduce ourselves. Robbie explained he and the others all shared a cottage at Five Points, the tiny college and seminary located in the wooded dunes about a mile southwest of town.

Paul was a blond who wore a hemp choker with black beads, scruffy jeans and brown Birkenstocks, no socks. He looked like a hippie version of JFK.

The tattooed one, Jeff, towered over the rest of us, red hair hanging in his eyes, mod plastic-framed glasses reminding me of the ones my mother had on in the photos from the 70s. He had an ornate cross drawn the length of his left forearm and maybe a Bible verse too—I couldn't quite see. Spindly hairy legs stuck out of cavernous holes in his baggy, many-pocketed tech shorts.

Josh I knew. Dark blond locks almost joined his scruffy whiskers. Well-tanned and well-muscled, he practically glowed in his black shirt and khaki tech shorts.

The one with the black ball cap introduced himself as Xander. He had the same dark blond hair and beard as Josh, the same tan, muscles, tech shorts and tennis shoes. If I didn't know Josh, the only way I'd be able to tell them apart would be by the color of their baseball hats. But then, young men always looked alike to me. Only Will, the tiny one with the voice of God, stood out.

"Doors open at four forty-five," Char said. "Giveaways until six. Show starts at six thirty." She reached into a box and tossed me a black tee. "Uniform." She stretched her arms wide. "This is the Green Room. Romee will bring the winners of the drawings here to claim their food prizes." She explained how each dish would be raffled off. "Mandy Tibbetts tells me they've had a growing problem with false claims, so she'll check everyone's IDs before escorting them back."

"Got it," said Romee.

"Lonnie will take the food prizes from Cousin Donna and escort them here."

My heart raced. No one had put interaction with the talent into my job description. "She's bringing it to me backstage?"

Char looked at me like I was daft. "She doesn't leave the stage. You go out to her and get it."

"Onstage?" Inside, my stomach started lacing up its running shoes.

Romee put her arm around my shoulders and squeezed. "Stage fright?"

"Come on, Lon," Char said. "This is your gig. You handle food and drink in front of a crowd every single week. Wearing a long robe. This'll be a piece of cake compared to that."

Presiding at a Eucharist in front of a few dozen people was not the same thing at all and I wanted to say so, but my mouth had gone dry. What if I spilled a tureen of gravy or dropped a plateful of green bean casserole?

Next, Char led us down the hall about ten feet and through a door into the dark. A short set of stairs carried us up into the black backstage. A metal box on the wall glowed with colored lights. Next to it, thick ropes ran from the floor up into the utter black abyss overhead. Thick black curtains blocked light from the stage except for a narrow crack where it didn't quite meet the wall.

"This is stage left, where Lonnie will be during the show." Char pushed the velvet curtain aside and we followed her onstage to a beautiful reproduction kitchen. Cherry cabinets, granite counters and stainless steel appliances gleamed in the stage lights. Marion had certainly done a nice job setting it up.

"Everything here meets Cousin Donna's specifications. Special wiring installed, utensils purchased of appropriate materials and colors. Things triple-washed to ensure sanity—"

Romee nudged me and I suppressed a giggle.

"I mean *sanitation*." Char glared at us. "Cousin Donna is an exacting professional culinary artist."

I glanced behind the counter, expecting hanging wires and messy stacks of stuff. At least, that's how it was behind the altar at Woman at the Well. I hid tissues, throat lozenges, a cup of water, an extra microphone battery pack and any extra bulletin notes to be announced. But none of that here. Cousin Donna's private domain was neat as a pin.

This, of course, made me like her less.

Char pointed to the echoing auditorium, three levels high. Hundreds of seats, each with a pink plastic shopping bag, brimming with goodies. I could hardly believe it was a church.

"Each seat has one goodie bag," Char said. "One person, one seat, one goodie bag. They are not identical, but all have the same retail value." She stopped at the edge of the stage and faced us. "If someone complains to you that they received a sample of chardonnay finishing salt when they would have preferred Celtic sea salt, simply tell them there is nothing you can do. They are welcome to trade, of course, provided both parties agree."

Char reached under the papers on her clipboard and pulled out a strange-looking thing, part pink cardboard, part bra strap. "This is a seat saver," Char said. "Specially designed by Cousin Donna herself." She showed how it slipped over the back of a seat. "Each woman writes her name on one, places her saver like so, and can leave to spend money at the vendors without fear of losing her seat." She carefully replaced the saver on her board. "Those of you in the auditorium make sure no one moves the savers to get a better seat."

"People do that?" Annika asked.

"According to Mandy Tibbetts, it's the number one reason for bodily injury and ejection from the show."

Chapter Five

"There are injuries?" asked the tall tattooed redhead. I'd forgotten his name already.

"They eject people?" That deep voice. Will.

Suddenly, everyone looked more interested.

"It's like hockey," said the boy with the black cap.

"It's like soccer," said Romee, again bouncing.

Char sighed and led us to stage right where she showed us the giant fishbowl from which raffle winners' names would be drawn. Then she pulled a stack of blank entry forms from her blazer pocket. "These are like gold," Char explained. "Each goodie bag has one. Brady Wesselynk assures me his staff stuffed, checked and triple-checked that each bag has only one. So if anyone comes to you complaining they didn't get one, don't believe it. But if someone rips theirs, or makes an error and can trade you the damaged one, they can have a new one." She gave each of us two.

I stuffed mine into my pants pocket beneath my car key.

"Last thing," Char said, sweeping aside the stage right heavy black curtain like Toto exposing the Wizard of Oz. "The backstage prep kitchen." An oven, microwave and fridge crowded the small backstage area.

"Smells great," said Will, reaching a hand toward the oven door.

"Don't touch that, young man!" The solid female voice came from the dark corner of the wing, followed by a woman who looked like a cross between the quintessential 1950s mom and the sort of girl you'd see on a pinup calendar in a car repair shop canoodling with a jackhammer. Pedal pusher jeans hugged a super model figure, bright white Keds shone on tiny feet, a red bandana swept her dark hair up with just the right touch of recently-bedded-messy, and the red-and-white checkered blouse burst forth with an impressive cleavage. No one failed to notice the small gold cross nestled there.

She held out a hand to Will. He took it, licked his lips.

"That is Brandy-Braised Praise the Lord Moose Jubilee, the moose killed and canned right here in Michigan," the woman said, offering her hand next to the tall tattooed kid. "You can, of course, substitute beef, if moose is not readily available." She moved on to the guy with the black ball cap. "Or pork." She shook Josh's hand. "Or any other large, substantive piece of meat." She lingered a bit in front of Robbie. "I love a good piece of meat, don't you?"

She had just turned to the guy who looked like a blond JFK when Char stepped forward, a Momma Bear protecting her cubs. "Everyone, this is Cousin Donna Hancock."

Cousin Donna finger-waved to all the boys and nodded toward us women. Romee finger-waved back. Annika poked her to behave.

"That stew is the grand prize of the evening," the cook explained, "and no one must touch it except me and the winner."

34

And me, I thought.

"No one must touch any of the preprepared food." Cousin Donna stuck out a hip and propped both hands against it, a pin-up girl sort of pose. "Not the Moose Jubilee. Not any of the ingredients for the Sunny Spirit Salmon Spread, or the sauce for the Wonder of Wonders Green Bean Casserole." She licked the corner of her mouth. "Did I say I'm so thankful to you all for coming to help out with my little cooking show? I just couldn't do it without you."

None of the guys had started to drool yet, but it looked like it wouldn't be long.

"I'm glad to know there are so many of you," Donna said. "My fans can get a little out of hand." A slow smile curved across her face as she looked up at the guys from under mascaraed lashes. "And sometimes, you know, I need a hand myself." She walked up to the kid who looked like JFK and tapped his chest. I thought he might keel over. "You are?"

"Paul," he said, his cheeks patched with red.

Donna walked the line of guys again, tapping each boy on the chest like pushing buttons to get toys to speak. She didn't bother with us. Romee nudged me and rolled her eyes.

"I'll remember all your names," Donna said, evidently forgetting she'd never even heard ours. "If I need any help before the show, I'll know who to call. But in the meantime—" she sidled up to the oven and spun like a model from *The Price is Right*, "if any of you touch any of my appliances or foodstuffs or cookware associated with the performance," her eyes narrowed, "unless explicitly instructed to do so by myself or my staff, you will not only be out on your butt, but liable to trespassing and attempted larceny charges."

Smoke might have curled from her mouth and nostrils. Maybe her eyes flashed red. I couldn't be sure, because as soon as she finished her warm and homey face returned and she sashayed past the boys one more time, tapping Paul on the chest again.

She turned to Char. "Mandy usually keeps an eye on things backstage until the show begins, but she's gone out for koosher salt." Donna glared at Char. "Evidently none can be found in this town. I don't know where she's gone or how long she'll be, but the moose cannot be unattended for even one second." She smiled again at the boys. "I'm going to my trailer now."

Donna left and Char sighed. "Who am I going to put on the moose?"

After more reconnoitering than it takes to scramble a team wall together to block a direct kick, I wound up on moose duty, but only until Mandy Tibbetts returned from the kosher salt expedition. So I had a quiet time until just before the doors opened. The worst thing about babysitting Brandy-Braised Praise the Lord Moose Jubilee was that it gave you time to think. And what I thought about was what Bova Poster and Marion had told me about the rumors around town involving me. No wonder my parishioners acted so tense with me. I would too if I was getting crap in the community about my priest. How was I going to help them learn to love each other if they thought I'd done something to wreck their social lives? Tomorrow at that breakfast reception, I was going to find Star Hannes and deliver unto her a rock solid piece of my mind.

Exactly how, I wasn't so sure.

Help, help, help, I prayed and my cell phone vibrated in my pocket.

"Lonnie, hun, it's Mom." As always, my mother sounded chipper, singing her words over the hum of some household machine in the background. She never just talked on the phone. She called when sewing or doing laundry or sometimes even vacuuming. This sounded like a blender.

"Hey, Mom," I half-whispered. "Can I call you tomorrow? Or Sunday afternoon? I can't talk."

"Lonnie, sweetie, I can't quite hear you over the breadcrumbs. I'm making macaroni casserole for your father and he does like his homemade breadcrumbs."

"I'll call Sunday," I nearly shouted.

"Okay. I didn't really have much to talk about. But what did I want to tell you? Something important. Let's see, what was it?"

My mother didn't get listened to much at home, so over the years she'd developed the habit of having long conversations all by herself. Sometimes I could be on the phone for twenty minutes and other than a few well-placed "uh-huhs," I didn't say a word.

"Oh," she said, "I know. Your father wondered if you could recall the actors who played the doctors and the nurse on the show *Emergency!*"

"Only the doctors and the nurse," my father yelled from somewhere in the background. "Not the paramedics. I know that."

God forbid my father call and ask me himself.

"Who'd he bet?" I asked.

"Siggy, down at Hot Wheels," Mom said. His buddy from the sports bar in Oak Brook. My mom and dad watched Chicago sports there. I could still barely imagine my mom in a sports bar, but it was something the marriage counselor had suggested when they got back together nearly a dozen years ago and they'd kept it up. Only recently, Dad had started betting on my trivia abilities—he said it paid out better than the Bears.

I sighed. "Robert Fuller played Dr. Kelly Brackett, Bobby Troup played Dr. Joe Early and Julie London played the nurse."

Mom repeated this to my dad.

From the direction of the auditorium came a strange rumbling swoosh. I wondered if one of those big electric lines to the stage kitchen had a short. I stood.

"He says you have to know the nurse's name too," Mom said, "or he won't make the team."

I peeked past the side curtain to the stage and auditorium. All peaceful, but the noise grew louder. "What team?"

"Tell her it's the trivia team at Hot Wheels," I heard my father tell her. "Tournament. Big prize money."

"I can't remember," I said.

Suddenly, in the back of the auditorium, doors flew open and the cooking school groupies swarmed down the center and side aisles, flailing purses, arms and wide-brimmed hats like a plague of matronly locusts.

"It's fifty bucks!" my dad shouted. "I need the nurse's name!"

The crowd slowed as women edged their way into rows. One gray-haired woman charged to the middle of about row fifteen, then started climbing forward over the seats in the other rows to bypass the crowd. Another woman pulled her down and wagged her finger, scolding her.

Where were the boys? They were supposed to be in here monitoring this first tidal wave.

I edged a bit onto the stage so I could see better. The six guys stood at the back of the auditorium, cowering out of the way. No one stood up front where battles over seats had already begun. No one except me.

I took another step onto the stage. Star Hannes stood in the center of the completely filled front row, talking to the women sitting there. She pulled a billfold out of her purse.

Oh, no. She was not going to buy herself the best seat in the house. Not after this woman sacrificed to get herself that seat. *No way. Not on my watch.*

Chapter Six

"Mom, I gotta go."

"Okay, dear. Goodbye."

"Lorraine!" my dad yelled from the background. "Fifty bucks!"

I walked to the front of the stage, watching Star but replaying the opening credits of *Emergency!* in my mind. The tri-tone buzz of the station bell, the departure of the trucks of Station Fifty-One. The close-up on each main actor. And Julie London played—

"Nurse Dixie McCall!" I hollered at my mom. "Love ya!"

I hung up and leapt off the edge of the stage like a paramedic entering a collapsed building. "Star!" I got stuck for half a minute behind three women jumping up and down in the aisle squealing over their goodie bags like toddlers with Christmas stockings, but still I struggled toward a flash of grape linen suit. "Star!"

"Lonnie!" Romee came up from behind me, squeezing past

the still squealing women. "I've got it covered up here. Get back to the moose!"

"Star's bribing people for seats!" I pressed forward.

Romee grabbed my shoulder. "Did you leave the moose alone?"

"Yeah, but Star!" The corner of a cookbook jabbed me in the ribs.

"Get back to the moose!" Romee shoved me gently toward the stage. "I'll get Star."

"There!" I pointed over the head of a thin woman clutching a shrink-wrapped Cousin Donna cookbook to her breast.

Romee disappeared into the melee as I pushed through the frenzy to reach the stage. I leapt up just in time to see Star wrapping her own seat saver over the first row center seat. Around her the crowd swirled—with their seat savers in place the women were all flocking back out of the theatre for the giveaways.

I wanted to jump down and rip that seat saver right off that chair, but Romee closed in on her. She could handle it. Back to the moose.

I pushed aside the heavy curtain to backstage right and there stood Cousin Donna, hands on ultra slim hips. *Uh-oh.*

"Did I not say that this kitchen area was not to be left unattended for one second?"

"Yes, but—"

"The only butt involved here is yours, lady, and it's on the line if anything goes wrong with my dishes. What's your name?"

"Lonnie Squires. I was only gone a few seconds. The fans—"

"Well, Lonnie," said Cousin Donna, "if that is your real name—I'll remember you." She turned to leave, wagging her hips, then suddenly turned back. "Do you have a way to contact other members of the security team?" When I nodded, her face turned all beatific again. "Give me the contact list. In case I need anything. I like to know who's where during the show."

I pulled the copy Char had given me from my pocket. I'd get another later.

The stage door behind us opened and the thin-suited woman

40

I'd seen banging on the trailer door earlier huffed up the stairs carrying several grocery bags.

"Where the hell were you?" Donna's eyes glowed, beatific giving way again to smoldering.

"I got lost in that other town. Holland. The roads don't make sense there."

"Well, this person," she waved a hand under my nose, "left the kitchen unattended while you were gone."

The woman, who I guessed was Mandy Tibbetts, Cousin Donna's manager, barely glanced at me. "I'm sure everything's fine." She handed Donna a small brown bag. "Kosher salt." She hefted her large brown bag but Donna made no move to take the burden from her. "Bud Light." Juggling purse and bag, Mandy reached into the bag and pulled out a bank envelope. "Five hundred in cash for the week. And—" She pulled out a smaller envelope. "This was left at the front office for you."

Donna grabbed it. "Fan mail!" Her fingers worked furiously at the seal.

"It's almost showtime." Arms still full, Mandy herded Donna toward the stage door.

"This first." Donna's grin faded as she read. Maybe not the fan mail she was expecting. But then she folded it into her jeans pocket and fluttered her lashes at me. "Such wonderful people you have here in town, Lonnie. You are so blessed to live in such a Christian atmosphere."

"Yes," I said.

She placed her hands on my shoulders bobbing her head as she spoke. "Thank you so much for your help. Mandy can take care of things back here from now on." She shooed me as if I were a pigeon. "Go. Go. Go. Win yourself a tea towel or something."

A shove in the direction of the stairs and I found myself in a brightly lit hallway slapping dust off my rear. *Bizarre.*

I looked toward the Authorized Personnel doors that kept this area clear of frenzied women. *Well*, I thought, *knife giveaway, here I come.*

The rest of the preshow flashed by. We all survived the

dreaded knife giveaway, as well as the rush on the fifty percent off sale at the moisturizer booth, the free samples of jams and salsas, the collecting of names for the fishbowl drawings, and the return of all the ticket holders—hair askew, goodie bags laden, sensible shoes scuffed—to their seats. I did glimpse a kerfuffle involving four young women and two of the Belles over accusations of seat saver manipulation, but no blood was shed. Just before the show started I saw Star and her buddy Mimi Manser sitting front and center with Elyse Orion. I liked Elyse and hoped Star's manipulative charms didn't dazzle her.

Sparkling lights cued the audience to applaud and scream as Cousin Donna strode onstage. She wore a powder blue clingy jersey wrap dress, somehow looking both like Mama Cleaver and a Hollywood starlet. After a long prayer during which you could have heard a pin drop, she began her first dish, Great-Granny's Paraclete Parfaits. She whipped around the fake kitchen, cheerily spinning locally grown blueberries in a prechilled stainless steel bowl. As she made granola from scratch she chattered on about traditional meals bringing families together again, describing how husbands' and children's eyes would light with happiness and love for the Lord when presented with this easy-to-make-in-minutes dessert.

Not much for me to do until the first food lottery, so I hunkered in a corner by the glowing light board to work on Sunday's sermon. One of my tricks of priestly survival was to never leave home without a lectionary—the book of week-by-week scripture readings—and a notebook.

I almost laughed out loud when I saw that the gospel for the week was the loaves and fishes passage from Matthew. Another score for the divine sense of humor.

Lots of people remember how Jesus uses just a few fish and loaves to feed thousands of people in that story. But tonight, the early part of the story caught me. The part where Jesus is tired and asks people to leave him alone, but they hound him anyway, so he goes to a deserted place. They follow him anyway.

I could imagine how that felt. Maybe he wanted to tell all

of them to act like good Jews and go away. Maybe he wanted to curse them. But he didn't. Instead, he saw that they looked hungry and so he fed them dinner. I couldn't imagine myself having that kind of compassion. But maybe, once I got my soccer team going, maybe then I could imagine myself with that kind of open heart again.

I peeked back onto the stage in time to see Donna set the parfaits in the fridge "to chill for twenty minutes. And then," she said, "all four parfaits will go to one lucky winner!"

The auditorium exploded in applause. My stomach pirouetted. That would be my cue.

Next, Cousin Donna pulled out a bowl of deboned salmon, explaining it had been caught in a local lake and smoked in the garage of Middelburger Berend Berkoop. People hollered as if she'd announced Brad Pitt was in the house. After a few minutes of whirring and spooning, Donna produced a fluffy pink spread. "Next, the homemade crackers, starting from good old-fashioned white bread. Just darn those anti-carb, whole-grained spoilsports!" Looking shocked at her own use of the word *darn*, she covered her mouth. The audience laughed and applauded. The bread would slow toast in the oven, she said, "and in a few minutes we'll have tonight's loaves and fishes." She waved an oven mitt like a magic wand. "Sunny Spirit Salmon Spread with Tasty Toast Points!"

I had to step back to hide my laugh. Somehow the vision of Cousin Donna waving a hot mitt appeared in my head next to that of Jesus miraculously multiplying loaves and fishes and it cracked me up. Too bad I couldn't use it in a sermon.

When Donna brought out the four fully chilled parfaits on a platter, you'd have thought someone had opened the Ark of the Covenant. Like in *Raiders of the Lost Ark* when the light shines and angel choruses sing?

"And now," cried the cook, "who will draw the lucky winner of Great-Granny's Paraclete Parfaits?"

On the other side of the stage, the tall redheaded tattooed guy stepped up to the fishbowl. Nodding to the audience who applauded wildly, he snaked in his long arm.

"Just one now." Cousin Donna shook a finger at him. "Even if some of these ladies have bribed you with promises of a dozen cookies. Only one lucky winner can have the parfait and eat it too!"

Cheers from the auditorium.

Goofy as this whole thing was, it *was* kind of fun. And Cousin Donna certainly knew her audience. I'd never seen the stoic Dutch women of Middelburg so whipped up about anything. As a general rule, Dutch folks don't do frenzy.

"Wanda Mueller!" yelled tattooed guy into his hand mike. Somewhere from the audience came a shriek like a hawk spotting its prey.

Cousin Donna clapped crazily. "Wonderful, winning Wanda!"

Wanda, a fifty-something heavyset woman I vaguely recognized from town, ran down the central aisle toward Romee who stood with her arm raised.

"Darling, that lovely security lady right there will bring you back to our special café room where my runner—" Donna gestured to me, and with a deep breath, I stepped out onto the stage, "will bring you your prize. Enjoy to your heart's content. Later in the show we'll have you back to tell everyone how much you just loved that dessert! All-righty?"

I took the winner's name slip and the tray with four parfait glasses from Cousin Donna and turned back. *God*, I thought, *please do not let me trip.* Panic surged after I stepped into the dark wing from the bright stage because I couldn't see, but then I felt the reassurance of something I did know—soccer. Find your body, your center, your balance. I settled into my legs and knew I wouldn't misstep as I headed down the stairs and across the hall into the Green Room.

You'd have thought Wanda Mueller had never eaten a dessert before from the way she squealed. I handed her the winning raffle ticket. "Want this for your scrapbook?"

"Do I get to eat them all?" she asked.

"I guess." Romee tapped the refrigerator. "Or you can store some in here to take home later."

Wanda looked skeptical. She wore a cardigan that had been cut from a sweatshirt and was heavily embroidered with multi-colored birdhouses. Even though it was ninety outside, she'd come prepared for the chilly air inside Frontline. "How do I know they won't get eaten? I don't want to spend the rest of the show back here guarding them."

"Do you think someone will bother them?"

"I paid twenty-five dollars and stood in line six hours to see this show and you're going to force me to sit back here to protect my prizes? You're security. One of you do it."

"We have assigned stations," Romee said.

Wanda looked unmoved.

Romee rolled her eyes. "I'll call the head of security and express your concern. We have to get back." We left Wanda eyeing her prize and stepped into the hall. "You think we need someone back here?" she asked.

I shrugged. "Call Char and explain the situation. It's up to her if she wants to move someone or not. There will probably be lots of leftovers that need protection."

When I got back to the wing, Donna had begun "a really fun little recipe" called the Holy Night Tuna Cup. She cut flatbread into squares, dampened them with water, pressed them into a muffin tin then filled them with tuna and garnished with cheese and tomato. The Holy Night part came when she cut little cross shapes out of the flatbread scraps and stuck them on top.

"Normally," she said, "you bake these beauties for about half an hour," and suddenly, Mandy Tibbetts, now wearing a slinky little black dress and enormous red hot mitts, entered from the other side of the stage carrying a steaming muffin tin. "Thanks to the magic of show biz," Donna said, "we have a platter of them ready for our next lucky winner!"

Imagine the wild shrieks from the house when Donna announced that three lucky winners would share the six tuna cups. The boy with the black ball cap drew winners and I carried the cheesy cups to the Green Room. Paul stood outside the closed door.

"You here to guard the prize food?" I asked.

"Guess so." He opened the Green Room door for me.

Three excited women puddled around me as Wanda sat in front of the fridge, arms folded. I placed the tray on the table between the new winners and gave each their raffle ticket. Their handwriting looked just like them, loopy and precise. They all had straight hair below the shoulder like mine used to be, chic glasses, and a simple silver cross necklace. Out-of-towners probably. Still worth asking them about soccer. I'd bring the next prize-winner back, then ask them all at once.

"Would you like to share?" one of them asked Wanda.

Wanda pursed her lips. "I'm not sure one parfait is worth one of those. What is it anyhow?"

I left them negotiating and returned to the stage just in time to see Donna pull the fully chilled Sunny Spirit Salmon Spread from the onstage fridge. She chatted her way through the arranging of the hot toast points, exclaiming the virtues of the "inviting little triangles that will remind your guests of the Triune God."

Oohing and aahing.

Soon, Josh appeared to draw the next winner. He read the slip and grinned at the audience and in his best game show announcer voice proclaimed, "and the winner is . . . Guy Rittenga!"

An anemic smattering of applause and I stepped onstage to retrieve the slip and the food. I shaded my eyes and spotted Guy moving down the aisle, grinning from ear to ear. I'd noticed a few other men in the audience before the show, but hadn't seen Guy.

"Congratulations, Guy!" Cousin Donna clapped madly. "I'm always so grateful to see someone of the male persuasion interested in learning about cooking and keeping a Christian home. What about it, girls?" She spread her hands toward the audience. "Don't we all wish we had someone at home like Guy to cook for us?"

It was like a gift from God—I could ask him about what Bova had told me at church.

Thank you, thank you, thank you I prayed as I walked off the stage with Guy's winnings.

Behind me Cousin Donna went on with the show. "And speaking of men, how many of us have had to face the challenge of making something truly appetizing from some wild animal our loving husbands shot and brought home to us?" Applause. "Well, next up, Brandy-Braised Praise the Lord Moose Jubilee."

Bowl of salmon spread and winner's ticket in one hand and plate of toast points balanced between arm and chest, I pulled open the door to the hallway just as Paul yelled, "Hey! You can't be back here!"

I pulled out of his way as he blew by, headed for two women dressed in running tights crouched just inside the door at the end of the hall that led to the parking lot. I figured they'd turn, apologize, and leave, as most nice Midwesterners would, but no. One of them hauled back and slugged the kid in the nose!

He slammed into the wall and slid to the ground.

Then they turned and looked at me.

Chapter Seven

I checked my watch as I always do first thing in a crisis: 7:22. Then I yelled, "Hey!"

The women pushed past the collapsed kid and ran into the Green Room.

I set down the spread and toast and pressed my cell to call Red. "Tresspassers in the Green Room," I shouted. "Help now!" Then I burst through the door after them.

The three Holy Night Tuna Cup winners sat at the dining table, mouths agape, as the women in running suits held out hands demanding the uneaten. Wanda Mueller stood against the refrigerator, arms folded, shaking her head slowly.

"Ladies." Everyone looked at me. "Move to the couch and have a seat." I was spoiling for a fight.

One of them lifted an eyebrow at me. "What? You're gonna make us sit?"

Never take that tone with a soccer addict who hasn't played in three months. *Never.*

I lifted my hands. "Just do as I've asked."

"We drove more than three hundred miles and stood in line forever to get tickets to this show," the other woman said. "We didn't get seats." She thrust a thumb at Wanda. "She got four parfaits. She can share. It's Christian."

Wanda shook her head. "My parfaits, fair and square."

I took a step forward to make them sit when Paul came in, a bloody trail leaking from his nose. He pointed to the first woman. "She punched me!"

The tuna cup ladies gasped.

"We want a tuna cup from each of you," said the first woman to them.

"And two parfaits," said the other to Wanda.

Wanda squared her body. "You think you can make me move?" She grinned. "Try it."

Whoa. A mild-mannered Middelburger tough-talking some strangers? West Michigan nice evidently went out the window when free food was at stake.

The Green Room door opened again. "Here's Guy." Romee stopped and assessed the situation. "I'm calling the cops." Guy stood beside Romee, amazed at the situation.

The first woman leaped forward and grabbed two tuna cups while the other attempted to push Wanda from the fridge. Wanda, like the proverbial mountain, could not be moved. Paul ducked as the first woman ran out the door. I dove at the other, but missed and slammed into an armchair. Wanda lashed out with a leg and tripped the other woman so she fell into the open arms of Guy. Both of them tumbled into the hall, but he held onto her. Wanda dashed out of the room after the first woman and the missing Holy Night Tuna Cups. "Watch my parfaits," she screamed as she went.

Moments later Red and her partner Don Loomis arrived, leading thief number one by the arm, Wanda puffing beside them. After a second of silence, everyone applauded Wanda and

Guy. Don took the handcuffed culprits away and Red took names then led Paul aside for a statement.

Guy lowered himself into a seat at the dining table with the others. "So where's my salmon spread with toast points?"

I about swallowed my tongue when I realized I'd left it in the hall where anyone could have stolen it, but mercifully, it was still there. I handed Guy his winning raffle ticket with a flourish. His handwriting, I noticed, was messy, almost illegible, typical professor stuff.

"I'd like to talk to you," I said, "before you return to your seat. It's urgent."

He waggled bushy gray eyebrows. "Let me settle from the excitement. I'd like to enjoy my prize food and these ladies' company."

"I'm stage left. The door just across the hall. Please. It will only take a few minutes."

He agreed and turned to his dish. All the others cooed over Paul's nose and generally celebrated the defeat of the dark forces of evil.

There's nothing like a little good-on-evil scrimmage to stoke your adrenaline and make you feel like you can conquer the world. Thanks to the crazy ladies, I even had a nifty sermon idea. The whole feeding the five thousand thing—Jesus didn't do it all alone. He asked his disciples to feed the people. They thought it was impossible, but they did it anyhow. With a little teamwork, miracles occurred. Everyone had enough.

It seemed like a message my Committee on Liturgy needed to hear.

Even better, I felt like God had handed me just what I needed. First, a chance to talk to Guy. And second, Wanda Mueller. The way she defended that refrigerator, then took off after the thief! She might look ample, but she'd make one hell of a good defender on the soccer pitch.

For a while I worked on my sermon, half listening to Donna talk about the Lord as she did something to her moose meat. Then I heard the stage door open and saw a silhouetted figure stumble in. Guy.

My skin itched with anxiety as I moved toward him, finger to my lips. "Thanks for coming," I whispered. I wanted to get him back into the hall before we caught hell for making noise backstage.

He mumbled something and leaned against me hard.

"Let's go back out." I jumped as his hand grabbed at my T-shirt. He said two syllables I couldn't make out. "Guy?"

He turned toward the light board and in its pale rays I could see his face beaded with sweat, saliva at the corner of his mouth. He coughed once and his next breath came in a rasp.

"Here, sit." I took his pulse as he slumped against the wall. Or tried. I felt nothing like the regular beat we all know so well. More of a flutter, no rhythm. No strength.

Holy God, he was having a heart attack.

I grabbed my cell. Time: 8:17.

I dialed 911. "I'm calling help, Guy. Hang in there."

He flapped his hands loosely in front of his face, his head lolling. I waved the bottom of my shirt toward him, trying to help him get air as I explained to the operator as quietly as possible what I was seeing. I hung up and pressed my hand against his forehead. "Help's coming." He nodded, his face lopsided.

Stroke?

"Can you walk?" When his hands flapped again, I helped him stand. His breath came raspy and rapid and his feet dragged, tipping inward. I got him down the steps and into the hallway before he tripped over his own feet.

"Holy shit," said Paul as he rounded the corner from another hall, fresh toilet paper wadded in his nose. "Should I call a doctor?"

"I did." I pointed toward the Green Room. "Get a wet towel."

Guy moaned and curled up, clearly holding a pain in his belly, drool running from his mouth. He flapped a hand as if to grab hold of my arm, but it fell flat.

"What, Guy? Do you want to get up?"

He moaned again, rolled his eyes, and suddenly lurched toward the restrooms down the hall.

"Here, here!" Paul skidded up and dropped two wet towels.

"You need some help?" Wanda stood at the ready.

"Paul, go outside." I wiped Guy's forehead. "Flag down the ambulance and direct them back here." I looked at Wanda. "You aren't a nurse or anything, are you?"

She shook her head. "Secretary. Got nothing to offer."

Guy moaned again. Said something.

I handed her my cell, gave her Char's number, and told her to go around the corner to call Char and update her. I didn't want her to upset Guy.

Wanda glanced at the Green Room. "Watch my parfaits, will you?"

"GO!"

Guy curled up again, moans interrupted only by the rasping of his breathing. He tried to move an arm, but his elbow barely flapped.

I wiped his face again. "Hang on, Guy. Help's coming."

Just as I heard the siren in the distance, Guy vomited once and lurched into a seizure.

Paul led the paramedics in about the same time as Wanda, Char, Romee, Julie, Will and Josh all showed up. Char directed Julie up to the stage to take over for me, then sent Romee back to her station. She huddled with me as the paramedics bent over Guy's shuddering body. "What happened?"

I told her what I'd seen. The boys murmured to each other and backed away.

"Heart attack?" Char asked one of the paramedics.

"Stroke, I think," he said. "Hypersalivation, tachycardia, bronchoparalysis. Clear loss of use of extremities. We'll get him to Tri-Cities."

Suddenly there was a loud beep and the two men turned to Guy. To all of our horror, his heart had stopped. They began CPR.

I'd been trained, of course, on a dummy, but in that moment

I learned that nothing prepares you for the crunch and suck of doing that kind of violence to a real human being. Everything about it made my skin crawl. Guy, his eyes half open and unfocused, his flaccid hair askew, his usually dapper attire now scrunched and wrinkled. Men pushing him so hard his limbs jumped, landing in a new unnatural place each time. All of us backstage in a megachurch. Surreal.

I looked at the others. Char held her hands clasped to her chest. The boys stood against the wall with huge eyes. Wanda paced about five feet away.

After they wheeled Guy out and drove away, silence pulsed around us until Cousin Donna's voice drifted out from the stage. "Add a little brandy," she said, "but only after you've done a taste test. With a glass." The air rumbled with laughter.

Chapter Eight

Of course, I called Guy's wife and met her at the hospital. She wasn't my parishioner, but I felt someone ought to be there and I wasn't sure, given the scuttlebutt, if they were still on good terms with whatever CLOSER church they'd attended before last spring. When Guy went into toxic shock and multiple organ failure, Maris asked me to pray with them. Her dark hair streaked with gray, gold bracelets dangling from each wrist, cotton blouse and skirt flowing easily around her, Maris held her husband's IV'd hand while I prayed.

At 2:14 in the morning, Guy died. I stayed with Maris a few minutes—she cried then laughed that he'd died at some woman's cooking show. He should have stayed home to watch sports, like normal men. I'd seen plenty of newly bereaved skating the surface of their fresh grief. Eventually, reality would knock her to her knees. I told her to call me anytime.

As I drove out of the Tri-Cities Hospital lot, my security T-shirt smelled of sweat and sickness and tears. I hadn't known Guy that well, but he'd exuded vitality and confidence and he'd delivered a speech in support of inclusion that may have cost him his job. I felt like we'd lost a good one.

I was sad, it was dark, and I was headed back to my little cottage in the dark woods without Linus. The radio played only rock out of Grand Rapids, which did nothing to soothe my sharp edges, so I checked my phone, which I'd turned off in the ICU. Message one was my mom burbling over crowd noises to confirm my dad had won his bet and to promise to visit soon. I was too tired to even contemplate that. Message two was Char announcing a special security briefing at eight a.m. I moaned. Maybe three hours of sleep? Message three was Marion. "Char told me what happened. Come sleep here. No matter what time."

Perfect. My dog was there. People were there. And it was much closer to Frontline Church than my house.

When I tapped gently on the Freeleys' front door, Marion stood there in a brilliant orange kimono decorated with foot-long red and white koi, her arms wide.

I fell into the hug and detailed the whole thing over six flaky homemade kraklingen and a mug of steaming Dutch cocoa, then collapsed into the bed with my pup. I'd barely sunk into sleep when Linus bounced his chunky too-big paws onto my chest and licked my nose. Marion's kids, Cameron and Mitchell, shoved him away and thrust a plate of poached eggs and dark crusty bread onto my lap.

"Mom's gone." Cameron crawled onto the foot of my bed and slapped the quilt smooth over my feet.

"She works five to three on Saturdays," Mitchell added, standing against the wall and watching the crowd on the bed. "It's busy at the Grind."

"Boys!" Denny's voice came from down the hall. "You forgot her coffee!"

Cameron zipped away. He returned holding a large coffee mug, placing each foot intentionally in front of the other as he brought it to me.

"Thanks." I took the mug from him and shoved Linus's nose out of the way. "Hot. Dangerous."

"Your clothes are clean," Mitchell said. He leaned against the wall, then pushed himself off. Repeated this twice. "You want me to get them?"

I did, and after a shower and another cup of Denny's strong coffee, I looked and felt like I'd slept a full night. I kissed all the boys in thanks, including Linus, and headed for Frontline, the eight o'clock security briefing, and the dreaded breakfast reception before six more hours of Cousin Donna-land.

People filled the Green Room—the security team, Brady Wesselynk, Red and her bear of a partner Don Loomis, Mandy Tibbetts, and Star Hannes. Red and Don's uniformed presence made everyone nervous, I could tell. Being with a cop was the only time I saw people get more nervous than when they were with me. Cop power outdid priest power every time.

"Paul won't be joining us this morning," Char said. I hadn't noticed him missing from the crowd. "Pain from his injury."

Some of the guys sniggered and I imagined Paul's pride hurt as much as his nose. After all, he'd been flattened by a woman.

"I appreciate everyone else coming early. In light of last night's events," Char twirled her pen over her clipboard, "we need to speak together for a few minutes."

"Excuse me," said the tattooed redhead. "Shouldn't we have a prayer or something?"

Everyone shuffled their feet and looked at me. Always having to pray in every group was one of the downfalls of being clergy. Everyone acts as if our presence takes away their ability to speak to God.

"Creator God," I began, my sleepy head groping for words, "in the face of a death like Guy Rittenga's, we can't even pretend to understand the depth of your world and your ways. But we trust in the goodness of all your creation. Bless Guy Rittenga, his family, and us as we suffer his loss. Amen."

I looked up and the boys all stared at me like I'd landed from

Mars. *Oops. Forgot.* No respectable CLOSER person would ever admit to not understanding how God worked.

"Thanks, Reverend." Red hitched her utility belt. "First off, we want to let you know that there'll be a lot of rumors flying around today. And since we'll want to talk to some or maybe even all of you, we want you to know that no one is in trouble."

Everyone shifted. "Then why do you want to talk to us?" asked the redhead.

"Well, Jeff," said Red, who *would* know all their names, "just to fill in the picture."

Don unfolded a piece of paper from his breast pocket. "Professor Rittenga died of heart failure following a severe neurological crisis brought on by overwhelming septicemia." He folded it again. "There's a lot more such medical jargon,"—he pronounced it *jar-gone*, "but bottom line, he died following an infection. Something he probably had for a while and it just exploded last night."

"The important thing to remember," Star's voice pulled every head in her direction, "is that the professor's death has nothing to do with the cooking. Or Middelburg." She raised a finger like a sword. "The benefit will go on!"

Ah, so that was her concern. An ugly death with a lot of media coverage. She didn't want it to dirty her. Well, knowing Star, she'd soon find a way to turn it all to her advantage anyhow.

"That's not what I read online," said Will. Everyone looked at him and he warmed to the audience. "It's all over the Internet, that Professor Rittenga took one bite of Cousin Donna's cooking and dropped dead." He looked across at me. "A few sites even said that a priest was already here to do last rites and wondered how she knew he was going to die."

"What?" How the heck had I shown up in some version of last night's events?

"I read one," said Xander, "that said Middelburg lacked proper sanitation. Another said this church contains poison."

"That's a reprehensible lie!" Brady thrust a hand upward as if reaching for God himself. "This church has state-of-the-art equipment and exceptional standards for safety at all levels. Our excellence reflects the greatness of the Lord."

Silence.

"A sudden death at a cooking show, even if there's no reason at all to believe it's related to the cooking, is bound to attract media attention," said Red.

"Though it is curious to find our own Reverend Squires once again linked to a mysterious misfortune in Professor Rittenga's life." Star's smug look clarified her delight in this curiosity.

"In a few minutes," Char said, "several hundred women are coming in here and they'll have heard the rumors. Right now, let's focus on best serving them."

"There'll be press too. They're likely to ask you questions," Don said, "since you're official and all."

"Do what you can to stop rumors from spreading," Red added, glaring at Star. "We'll probably grab each of you for a few minutes, just to confirm what you saw or didn't see during the day yesterday."

The door slammed open and Cousin Donna Hancock, in pedal pusher blue jeans and a blue-and-white gingham shirt with matching hair bandana, burst into the room then posed, holding the door at the end of a locked arm, as if waiting for a spotlight to hit. Finally, she spoke. "Where is she? I want to see the woman who—!" She stopped and, like a mummy risen from a tomb, pointed a finger at me. "YOU! You left my premade Sunny Spirit Salmon Spread unattended for the good Lord knows how long yesterday. You are the one and only reason this happened!"

"Ms. Hancock," Red started.

"*You* are the sorry excuse for security," Donna said, spittle gathering at the corners of her red lipsticked mouth, "the sole flaw in this usually perfectly orchestrated program, that forced my people to have to admit to the newspapers that no, the food was not under the watchful eye of staff the whole time because *you* left the backstage kitchen unattended! *You* have ruined me!"

She stepped toward me, fingers curled into lethal weapons and I backed against the refrigerator. Red stepped forward, inserting her body between ours, hand on gun.

"Donna!" Mandy flushed.

Donna whirled. "You are no better. Thought you'd keep this little meeting from me? Well, if you hadn't forgotten the kosher salt, this moron wouldn't have been keeping an eye on the kitchen to begin with."

Moron? "Now, hold on," I began, but shut up when Red shot me a look.

"Now Ms. Hancock." Don shifted his burly shoulders as if preparing to wrestle an alligator.

Donna whirled toward the deputies. "And you people! A town that doesn't sell kosher salt. What sort of Podunk Nowheresville is this cow pie community anyhow?"

Hackles bristled across the room. You can say just about anything in public in Middelburg as long as you don't question Jesus as the one and only way to salvation (which is what got me into trouble most of the time) or insult our town.

"Ms. Hancock," Red began. "We've just instructed the security team to reassure anyone who asks that there is absolutely no reason to believe that the food you prepared here last evening can be connected with Dr. Rittenga's death."

"We know that, ma'am," said Don. "It was an unfortunate coincidence. That's all."

The not-so-happy-homemaker digested that a second, then smiled at him. "Call me Cousin Donna."

Don blushed to the roots of his blond buzz cut.

"I'm so grateful," Donna said, "that you know what really happened to that poor, unfortunate man. However, you know the media. They can't wait to trash a celebrity, especially a Christian one." She batted her eyes as if trying to prevent tears. "Is there anything we can do about that?"

"What if we just test the spread," I said, "and the toast. Prove that it's safe."

Star smiled at Donna. "Nothing like a scientific report to stop those rumors."

I barely processed the fact that Star agreed with me because

Donna leapt toward me. I dodged, but all she wanted was the refrigerator. She yanked it open and stood gazing. "Where's the spread?" She looked at me. "Did you take it to the hospital?"

I shook my head.

"The salmon spread is gone?" Red looked over Donna's shoulder. "Obviously Guy didn't take it home with him."

"But we don't need it," Don said. "The lab report proves that."

"Weird," I said.

"Is it?" Star gazed straight at me.

Cousin Donna clapped her hands and grinned. "You mean someone stole it? Someone stole one of my dishes?" She turned to Mandy. "You hear that? Someone stole the Sunny Spirit Salmon Spread!" She spun a full circle. "Are the Tasty Toast Points gone too?" They were. She raised her hands to the skies. "My fans stole my food! Like a work of art! It's a Loaves and Fishes miracle!"

"What about the thieves?" I asked.

"Thieves?" Cousin Donna whirled on Mandy, who squirmed in her button-down Oxford and blazer. "There were thieves and you didn't tell me?"

"I released them at the town limits," Don said. "The boy didn't want to press charges if they just drove away."

"Besides, they were gone before Guy ate his prize," I said.

I could practically see the wheels turning in Red's head. "I'm not sure it's important, really," she said. "Don's right. No one actually thinks the food was involved."

Donna clasped her hands to her breasts. "And someone coveted my food enough to steal it!" Expansive sigh. Then she pointed again at me. "Make the papers print that!"

"Excuse me," Mandy said, touching Donna's shoulder "but the breakfast reception has begun. We need to get you there. To meet your fans."

Mandy surely understood her client. At the mention of fans, Donna's temper melted. "My wonderful fans are actually breaking in! And stealing food! It's a sign, don't you think? Of stepping up to a whole new level?"

"Let's just focus on today," Mandy cooed. "It's Boundless Blessing Turkey Day."

"And Wonder of Wonders Green Bean Casserole," Donna said, her voice perking up.

Mandy led her out the door, Donna yammering all the way. "Of course, we still have to find the Sunny Spirit Salmon Spread, don't we? To prove I'm really innocent?" Star followed.

Red caught my eye and we both raised our eyebrows: *nutty*.

"Actually, ladies," Char said, "we all need to get to the reception. Boys, you're in charge of crowd control until they open the auditorium doors."

As we walked toward the breakfast reception, I stewed about the rumors the guys reported seeing on the Internet. My stomach lurched. How had I gotten tangled up in speculations about Guy's death?

I smelled Star Hannes at work. Anything to deflect negative attention away from herself or her causes.

What was I going to do about it?

Chapter Nine

Red and Don hadn't exaggerated the hyped-up energy of Cousin Donna's fans or the ferocity of the TV crews on the scent of a scandal. After I saw someone pointing me out to a camera crew, I ducked and dodged my way to the reception. Even there reporters had set up front and center. I should have known. Star was going to give a speech. She wanted cameras rolling.

"A toast to the woman who made this all possible," Star said and everyone raised a glass. The perfect symbol for how things went in Middelburg—Star said jump and people did. Standing up on the dais, the councilwoman looked regal in a persimmon suit of summer-weight wool, with matching pumps, creamy off-white blouse and string of perfectly matched pearls. "To Elyse Orion. Without her willingness to convince her old friend, the magnificent Cousin Donna Hancock, to do this benefit, we'd be far short of the funds we need to complete the new state-of-the-art Middelburg Family Recreation Center!"

Elyse stepped forward and the women clasped hands. The green microfiber of Elyse's cardigan clashed with Star's fruity suit, and I appreciated a woman who could dress up in jeans. Her blond curls bobbed when she spoke. "The real heroine is Cousin Donna Hancock who pledged two weekends of her busy life to help us out. She is now a friend to everyone in Middelburg!" Elyse sounded and looked like *Gone With the Wind*'s Melanie Wilkes. She clapped her hands furiously.

Cousin Donna stepped forward and posed like a well-trained beauty queen, slightly turned, one leg in front of the other, smile unwavering, head cocked, a small wave for the crowd who cheered, but not too robustly, as robust cheering in a church could be impolite and if there was anything Middelburgers were when gathered in a church, particularly with television cameras rolling, it was polite.

So we all stood politely as Star reviewed what we already knew—how construction had begun in May after Christopher Orion had donated a third of the cost of the proposed center, as a "good neighbor" gift to his new community. Since then, the building had gone up with astonishing speed, "thanks to a strong work ethic and Dutch efficiency."

Star thrust her glass forward again. "And I have several other exciting announcements. First, many members of our community will escape the horrors of an unfit body by joining one of the many league teams forming to take advantage of the new center. The deadline for team rosters is Wednesday, August thirteenth." She caught my eye. She knew damned well I didn't have my soccer roster together. "Second, the city council has named a new director of the Middelburg Recreation Center, my husband, Gil Hannes!"

I nearly gasped out loud as everyone around me applauded. Gil, a stringbean of a guy dressed in a suit, shirt, tie and shoes of the same shade of brown, stepped up beside Star and Elyse and waved. His pencil-thin mustache twitched over what might have been a smile. I'd seen him once or twice around town, slinking in and out of the Breezin' Brew coffee shop with a stack of newspapers. Star tended to keep him out of sight.

"His office will open next week, the first in the new facility." Star raised her glass, a triumphant grin stretching her face. "The locker rooms open in late September for outdoor exercisers and the rest will open November first! Congratulations, Middelburg!" The crowd applauded again.

November first. Just days before the election in which Star hoped to gain a congressional seat.

I could hardly stand it. A weedy divorce attorney running the recreation center? Didn't anyone in town see a problem with a councilwoman's husband getting a plush new city job? I stomped to the linen-covered food table, stabbed three pigs-in-a-blanket, and dropped them onto my plate. I grabbed a flute of champagne and spotted one of my soccer players, Belles' right winger Julie Stantvoordt and her husband Rick, huddling near a potted ficus.

"What's with the three pigs?" Julie stabbed her fork at my plate. "You'll suck at soccer." When I rolled my eyes, she shrugged. "Okay," she said, "then what's with Gil as the rec director?"

I shook my head. "Star's long fingers are everywhere."

"Star took quite a stand in support of Donna," Rick said, "what with the cameras rolling during her speech."

"No risk," I said. "Lab reports say no poison."

"The rest is just media hype," Julie said. "I'm already tired and it isn't even nine a.m."

"So." I glanced over the crowd. "You guys see any likely candidates for the soccer team? Deadline's coming and I need three."

Rick's eyes widened. "Please, Lon. Please make the team happen. Get her out of the house to burn off some steam."

Julie elbowed him in the ribs.

"I'm trying." I wiped the pig-in-a-blanket grease from my fingers.

"Well, let's find you some players." Rick set his dishes in the potted plant and rubbed his hands together. "Lots of women to pick from." He pointed toward Mandy Tibbetts, who was wandering around looking dazed. "Her?"

"Not local," I said.

"No endurance," Julie said.

"How do you know?" Rick asked.

"She came into the post office to sign for a package yesterday. Ran half a block from her car and was all out of breath."

"Okay." Rick studied some more. "What about her?" He pointed out a knot of men in faded suitcoats and khakis speaking with a lone woman in a bright blue blazer. "She looks like she has endurance."

In that crowd you'd need it. "Is she at the college?" I stuffed my last pig into my mouth.

"That's Pia Hakksen," Julie said. "She's some sort of Great Lakes diver, so maybe she has good lungs and legs. Go ask her."

The diver had the broad-shouldered lanky look of a swimmer, a deep tan and sun-bleached blond hair refusing to stay in place around her ears. "Does she make a living at that?"

Julie shook her head. "She does something with the science department up at Five Points."

Uh-oh. "The people at the college aren't too happy with me right now. Or so I hear."

Julie made a face. "Then settle that too. Tell them you had nothing to do with Guy's speech. Maybe they can help put that wild story to rest."

Maybe. And maybe this Pia would be up for it, even bring along a friend. Then it would just be a matter of time until folks loosened up about my parishioners and me.

I gave my plastic plate to Julie. "Wish me luck."

"Luck."

Hi, I don't believe we've met, I practiced as I crossed the room. *Sounds stupid. Sorry to intrude, but . . . just as stupid. A friend of mine mentioned that you might be interested in joining a women's soccer league.*

I looked down at my shirt to be sure I hadn't spilled anything and forced myself to smile as I stepped up to the group.

"...science's inability to technologize that which is

65

transcendent and chaotic," said a bearded man.

"I'd like to hear more," said a flabby man with a Beethoven-esque shock of dull gray hair, "about how it's in keeping with the Five Points mission." His small eyes darted over me, then back again. "Reverend Squires, isn't it?"

I didn't know him but no surprise that he knew me. Everyone in town knew the latest newcomer.

"Lex Brenninkmeyer." He didn't offer his hand. "Provost of Five Points College and Seminary."

The ice in his eyes frosted me, but I smiled anyway.

He had to be nice, of course, so he introduced me to two biology professors and Governor of Laboratories Pia Hakksen. Then we all stared at each other.

I suppressed the desire to run. "I wondered if I might speak to you privately," I said to the woman.

Her bright blue eyes shifted to the provost and back. "I don't know you."

Okay, this was a mistake. Still, we were here so I might as well press on. "I'm recruiting for a women's soccer team and I wondered if you, or perhaps anyone you know might—"

"No." She blinked at me.

Now she was just being rude. "No one you know plays soccer? A mom who wants to learn more about her kid's sport? Kinesiology profs? Anyone?"

"Pia." The provost looked pained. "Why don't you finish this conversation with the reverend elsewhere and rejoin us when you're able?"

She blinked at me again. "Follow me." Her back rigid, she led me across the room to stand in front of a large watercolor of The Empty Tomb. There, for the first time, emotion flooded her face. "Are you trying to get me fired too?" She glanced toward her colleagues, then backed up two steps.

I understood. Now a huge potted palm stood between her and them. "Of course not," I said. "Why would talking to me get you fired?"

"Because of what you did last spring. First, talking Alec

Manser out of seminary."

Alec had been tangled up in that whole mess surrounding Vance's murder. He'd taken his new wife and gotten out of town. I didn't blame him.

"Second, Guy's gruesome death."

"I didn't do anything to him."

She scowled. "You deny putting him up to that chapel talk?"

"I didn't put him up to anything. Guy came to me with a speech about Jesus and inclusive love. He wanted to run it by a liberal theologian and said I was the only one in town. I gave him a few things to read and the next thing I heard, he'd retired. That's all."

Pia blinked, but I saw her soften just a bit.

"What does this have to do with getting up a soccer team anyhow?" I asked.

"You're obviously a bad influence," she said. "Turn the Episcopal church liberal, talk a religion professor into supporting gays. What next? Corrupt the mothers of Middelburg's children by playing soccer with them?"

The TV camera crew headed our way and I stepped beside her against the wall, well behind the palm. A rough plastic leaf scratched my cheek.

"Alec Manser wasn't truly called to the seminary. I just helped him sort out his real vocation from what his parents wanted him to do." I'd also helped him sort out his secret marriage and their surprise pregnancy, finally convincing him to tell his family the truth. Though it had all happened before I ever met Alec, his parents somehow blamed me. Mimi hadn't spoken much to me since.

"Maybe. But Mimi is Star's second-in-command and her husband Cal is our VP for Ideology. And we all want to keep our jobs."

This would go nowhere, I could see. "Okay then. Sorry I bugged you." Besides, I wanted to get out of here before that crew got any closer.

But Pia didn't move. "You know, not many of us really think

you put Guy up to that talk," she said. "He'd mentioned his idea to a few people. How the unfair treatment of gays, of anyone who believed differently than the CLOSER church line, failed to live up to Jesus' vision. No one thought he'd go public. I mean, that's suicide at Five Points."

"Did they really fire him?" I could almost not believe it, even here.

Pia nodded. "Absolutely. They cut some sort of deal to keep him quiet about it and got him out."

"But why cut a deal?"

She blinked as if astonished at my innocence. "Do you think the college wants people to believe that they forced out a beloved religion professor because he welcomed gays into the church? How would that look in the liberal media?"

"It would look good to some people. I guess it depends on what sorts of students you want to attract."

She nodded. "Yes. Also what sort of *donations* you want to attract."

"Are you telling me Five Points attracts liberal students and liberal money?" Now that was a surprise.

"Not really."

"You've lost me. Wouldn't conservative donors be pleased if he was fired?"

"Yes, but not if it made the papers. Not in this changing political climate. That would reduce the publicity payoff for being connected with the college."

College politics sounded even more conflated than church politics—too baffling for me. "So do you actually know they fired Guy, or is this a rumor too?"

Pia looked at her shoes. "He disappeared from campus right away."

"No one even called him to see how he was doing?"

"No." Pia looked up at me. "E-mails are monitored. Town is so small, people see where you go, who you talk to. It's too risky."

"You aren't kidding me, are you?"

68

She shook her head. "You know, a lot of us agree with what he said. But we keep quiet. We need our jobs too much." She looked at her feet.

My foot started to jiggle as I forced myself not to scold her. We all make compromises to keep the money coming, I knew. "So how did I get attached to the mess?"

Pia studied me long enough for me to notice the streaks of gray in her blondish brown hair. "Easier to blame you," she said with a rueful smile, "than to believe one of their own would, after all these years, get up and preach about the need to welcome gays as children of God."

"Then love can work magic everywhere, huh?" I tried to smile.

She nodded. "When the rumors started, people jumped on them."

"Outsider as scapegoat."

She nodded. "I'm sorry. Actually, I would play if I could. Indoor soccer would help me keep in shape over the winter."

"You dive in the big lake?"

"In the dark cold waters, yep." She smiled. "Ever seen a shipwreck face to face? Sitting where it landed eighty or a hundred years ago after the ice cracked its hull?"

"Can't say I have, no."

"It's cool." Her eyes fastened on someone behind me and her face hardened. "I'm sorry," she said in a suddenly harsh tone, "but the answer is no."

A meaty hand slapped me on the shoulders. "Reverend Lonnie Squires! Now if this isn't a meeting orchestrated by our good Lord himself." That booming voice—Brady Wesselynk, Frontline's head pastor.

"That's putting a positive spin on things," came Star's voice.

I stretched and turned, feeling the blood pump hard through me. I was in just the right mood to talk to these two. I hoped the potted palm was big enough to hide the carnage.

Brady pumped my hand, then Pia's. As always, he wore sharply creased khakis and a Ralph Lauren shirt—this morning a light pink dress shirt under a navy jacket and tie. "So glad to welcome you to my humble home away from home," he boomed. "Frontline Church of Christ." He grinned, exposing big square recently whitened teeth.

Pia cleared her throat. "I have to get back," she said, and practically bowing she retreated to her colleagues.

"So," Brady said, smoothing his hair against his temples, "how are you on this fine morning of the good Lord's creation?"

Star arched an eyebrow. Her shoulder-length hair swept away from her face, curled below the ears to just touch her blazer collar. It had recently been refoiled—I saw red highlights mixed in with the auburn and blonds. Had she gone from three colors to four?

Star didn't like my silence. "First the tragic downfall of a respected religion professor. And now his untimely death." Her lips jerked into a quasi-smile. "Lucky for you they say he had an infection, or else they'd be asking exactly what you have against the poor man."

Brady nodded. "True."

"Look, both of you." I was in no mood for their crap. "You need to drop the game, now. Leave my parishioners alone. Leave me out of your creepy townie intrigues. I won't try to stop you from doing your thing. Leave us alone to do ours."

Star's eyes narrowed. "You think I care about you or your church?"

Brady looked confused. "We must all love our neighbors."

"That's not what she's talking about." Star snapped like a terrier and the big man recoiled. Then she leaned in close to me. "Seriously, how did you convince Rittenga to give that talk? Did you do it to score points with the Orions? Because of their son the gay?"

"His name is Bill."

Star's face filled with conspiratorial knowing. "They chose your church, out of all the churches in town."

"Woman at the Well is the only open congregation in town. And I had nothing to do with Guy giving that talk." I wanted

70

to grab them both and knock their heads together. "Come on! You're the two most influential people around here. You have an obligation to get the truth out there."

Brady nodded. "You shall not bear false witness against your neighbor."

"Right," I said. As a rule, I couldn't stand it when he flung Bible verses, but I'd go with this.

"By swearing you had nothing to do with it," Star said, "aren't you slandering Guy?"

"Whoever secretly slanders his neighbor, him I will destroy," Brady continued. "Psalm 101."

"No, no, no. I didn't do anything," I said.

"If you're innocent," Star said, "I fail to see your problem."

"When my parishioners get treated with suspicion and hostility, I can't work effectively."

Brady slung a big arm over my shoulders. I gritted my teeth. "Hear you can't even get a soccer team together. Through Jesus, the forgiveness of sins is proclaimed to you, Lonnie. Acts 13:37."

"That's lovely, but it's not my sins I'm worried about," I said. "It's the crappy way this community—your community—treats my congregation. Because of rumors about me."

Brady winked at Star the way my parents used to when I was twelve and I was about to rip into him when the Lord sent an angel to intercede on my behalf.

Chapter Ten

"Just the three lovely people I hoped to run into," said Elyse Orion as she walked up to us. She gave my hand a little squeeze. "Reverend, how are you this morning?" Her blue eyes shone with such genuine concern, I wanted to bless her then and there.

"A bit overwhelmed," I confessed.

She nodded, but not the way Brady nodded when he faked listening. "Long night for you."

"Yeah."

Elyse smiled at Star and Brady who managed to smile back. Just like two bullies on a playground when someone with more power, or in this case, more money, arrived on the scene, they backed right down. No one wanted the billionaires mad at them.

"I've been speaking with Donna," Elyse said, chipper as a puppy, "and there are a few things that must be addressed." She turned to Brady. "Are you agreed that the benefit performances must still go on next weekend, regardless of the publicity?"

Brady smoothed the hair at his temples, evidently relieved he hadn't been asked for more. "Sure, of course."

Elyse turned to Star. "And are you still willing to extend your hospitality to her throughout the week, as planned? I still regret that our little renovation has kept her from bunking with us."

I laughed at the thought of anyone "bunking" in the Orions' lakeshore mansion.

Star stretched her face into what she probably hoped was a pleasant smile. "Of course. Anything for your friend is an honor."

Elyse smiled. "All settled then." She turned toward me, curls bobbing. "What do you make of the missing salmon spread?"

"It really doesn't matter," I said. "The police aren't—"

"Aren't what?" Red Carson stepped up beside me. Around the reception hall, people glanced our way. What was a uniformed cop doing with the councilwoman, the pastor of the church where the death had taken place, and the priest who'd supposedly cost the deceased his job? I could feel their questions spinning, itching across my skin.

But then Elyse smiled and leaned forward, offering her hand to Red for a quick squeeze and like magic, everyone in the room returned to their own conversations. Once again, Elyse reminded me of Melanie Wilkes—if she said something was okay, it was.

"Thank you for coming," Elyse said to Red.

"I got a message this was important?" Red questioned me with her eyes.

"We simply must prove," Elyse said, "that Donna's cooking had nothing to do with this unfortunate tragedy."

"Whoa." Red raised her hands. "There is no question of guilt! There is no crime. The man died of overwhelming septicemia."

"Nonetheless," Elyse said, "the media is insinuating that her cooking caused it."

"Doing what the liberal media does best," Star added. "Damaging the innocent."

"And it's important *to me* that we protect her reputation," Elyse said.

Ah! Everyone shifted as they understood the situation. The billionaire had a request.

"Right now, no official problem exists," Red said. "What if we find the spread and it turns out something was wrong with it?"

"Perhaps it would be better to act biblically and turn the other cheek," Brady offered. "If something wrong is discovered, there will be an investigation."

"Worried it's poisoned with something from the church?" Star asked.

The big man puffed up. "Of course not!"

"If something's wrong with it," Elyse said, "well, then, of course, the source must be found. Others might get sick too!" She chewed her lip, then, "Perhaps the salmon?"

"Berend Berkoop has been smoking salmon for seventy-five years," Star said. "No one in this town has ever so much as belched from it!"

She must have recommended Berend's salmon for the show.

"What about the cream cheese or onions?" Brady asked. "The toast?"

"Tainted toast?" I asked.

Star pointed a lacquered nail at me. "You had charge of the backstage prep area before the show and you left your post."

Heat flushed through me. "I only left for a minute." Pressure built in my throat. "And I did it to stop you," I lifted a finger toward Star, "from pressuring other women out of their front row center seats."

Star drew a big breath, but before she could respond, Red cut in.

"Let's all just relax. Right now, no one is blaming any of you—or Donna—for what happened to Guy."

"Not good enough." Elyse's curls bounced. "Cousin Donna is a culinary artist of the highest quality. We simply can't leave suspicions about the safety of Cousin Donna Hancock's Loaves and Fishes Culinary Ministries lingering out there."

"True," said Star. "Safety, after all, is the backbone of these United States. Safety and freedom. That's why I support this investigation." She turned to Red, cocking a perfectly tipped nail in her direction. "The police will simply have to—"

"Oh no," said Elyse. "No, indeed."

Star swallowed hard. She didn't hear *no* very often. I just loved Elyse Orion.

"I have come up with a better way," said Elyse. She turned to me and held out her hands like a model displaying a prize. "I want to hire *Lonnie* to prove Cousin Donna Hancock innocent."

"*No!*"

Star and I said this together and with exactly the same tone of horror. Probably the only time we'd ever agreed on anything.

"I appreciate the thought," I said to Elyse, "but I can't. I have this today, and a sermon to write for tomorrow. A week full of committee meetings. Plus, I have a women's soccer team to recruit."

"Besides, she is a priest," Star said. "She's not trained to deal with mysteries."

"Actually," I said, only because I loved pushing the councilwoman's buttons, "I'm extensively trained in mysteries. The mystery of grace, for example, or of God's radical love. How about baptism and communion and marriage and—"

"All right, all right." Star showed more frustration than usual. "We get it."

"My husband believes you are a superhero amateur detective," Elyse said.

"Oh for goodness sake!" Star crossed her arms.

"You disagree with Chris?" Elyse asked, smiling dangerously.

I flashed Star a goofy grin. The only reason Christopher Orion thought I was a superhero amateur detective was because I saved him from the sabotage that Star herself had orchestrated last spring. Without Star, I'd be nothing and she knew it.

"No, of course not, Elyse." Star sighed. "I'm just so distraught over Guy's death. A religion professor at the college, such a longtime member of this community."

"And of Sixth Christ the Lord's Own Sainted Elect Reformed Church," added Brady.

"Tell Chris I'm flattered," I said to Elyse.

"He'll be delighted to hear you've taken the case. You can work on it all week, while Donna's here in town!"

I raised my hands. "Elyse, no. I'm not taking any case. I don't take cases."

"You know," Star said slowly, indicating she was thinking and that could only be bad for me. "As the one who left the prep area unattended and started this whole thing, I think you should."

"The press started this whole thing!" I said. "By misrepresenting facts."

"Don't you think people would find it strange if you refused to help? Why won't our great local amateur detective help investigate the true cause of death of Professor Rittenga?"

"Now hold on," Red said. "There's no question about the true cause of death."

"Unless," Star said, and the glint in her eyes made my skin crawl, "could it be you don't want the missing food found?"

"Wait a minute—" I said.

She spread her hands as if offering up the obvious. "You *were* one of the last people to have access to the food before Guy ate it."

"Wait, what?" I couldn't believe it. "Are you insinuating that I poisoned Guy?"

"Of course not," Star said. "Just warning you how it could look if you don't help."

She was, of course, much more interested in how she could spin it if I failed. Plus this would sink my chances of getting a team together. I'd be running around on a wild goose chase. Anger burned in my chest.

"It *would* look a bit strange," Elyse said, "you refusing to help."

Red hitched her utility belt around her hips and said nothing.

"Please, Lonnie," Elyse said. "I want to hire you to help. I invited Donna here and I just feel so responsible!"

"But the spread is gone."

"I do want to emphasize *hire*," Elyse said. "I could help you recruit players!" Her curls bounced. "A soccer team seems like such a sweet idea and if I helped you—" She nudged Star. "If Star and I helped you out, we could surely recruit enough players for your team." She smiled. "Would that free up enough time for you to have a look-see into Cousin Donna's nasty problem?"

I'm not sure what made me happier, Elyse's offer or the crushed look on Star's face. Star would never cross Elyse Orion. If I agreed to do this fool's errand, I'd probably get my team and trump Star at the same time. Too good to be true.

I'd just walked into one of God's Surprise Parties, as my Aunt Kate used to call them. A non-crime. An innocent woman, who just wanted someone to help clear her reputation. I could relate. As ridiculous as it seemed, I suddenly knew God was handing this to me so I could get women's soccer going in this town. *Thank you*, I prayed.

"Okay," I said. "I need three more players, plus alternates, by the thirteenth. And I'll look for the spread."

Elyse clapped. "It has to have gone somewhere!"

"Sorry to interrupt, ladies." Char Maarten appeared from behind the potted palm. "And gentleman. But security places in two minutes."

"This is all just splendid," Elyse said, her hands aflutter, then landing on my forearm. "I so look forward to your sermon tomorrow, dear."

"Just a second, Brady," I said as the big man turned. "I want to talk trash with you."

"Excuse me?" A rosy flush ripened his big cheeks.

"Did your custodial staff clean the Green Room last night? Was the trash emptied? Could the salmon dip have disappeared that way?"

Everyone turned to look at him, a big mule caught in the headlights. "I—uh—well, I'm not sure of the schedule of—I'd have to check with—"

"Lonnie," Char said. "We need to go."

I patted Brady's arm. "I'll be backstage left all day. If you could find out and let me know before the show ends, we'd all be grateful."

"I will," he said, glancing at Elyse. "I sure will."

Chapter Eleven

"So," Char asked as we walked toward the backstage, "did I hear you agree to find the missing salmon spread?"

I felt a new bounce in my step. "What you heard was Elyse Orion guaranteeing I'd get a team together if I looked. So, heck yeah, I'll look."

"Well, after you left last night, Paul stayed outside the Green Room, even though his nose started to swell," Char said. "Maybe he saw something." She tilted her head with a thought. "Or snuck it out himself. Those boys are always looking for food." Before she scooted off to check on the others, she gave me the address where Paul and the other guys shared a house, just off campus up in the dunes.

From backstage, I peered past the curtain to watch the audience enter. No stampedes for the best seats, no bags swung at unsuspecting heads. Guy's death had subdued them. But still, there were no empty seats either.

The house lights dimmed, so I swung away from the curtain just as my cell vibrated.

"Every woman has her price," Red said. "Didn't the thing with Vance teach you to keep out of police business?"

"Hey, no crime, so no criminal. You said so yourself."

"Stay out of it, Lonnie. You don't want someone swinging a shovel at your head again."

Energy bolted into my legs and I shook my feet one at a time. It's a quirky thing about me. Don't tell me not to do something and expect me to obey. I see that sort of thing as extra motivation.

Plus, Red was using scare tactics to make me obey.

"Low blow," I said.

"Sorry." She paused. "But listen, Father Brown, if someone did steal that dip, just remember he or she may not want to be exposed."

Cousin Donna took the stage—the applause thin compared to last night. I tiptoed down the steps into the empty hall. "You think I'm in danger from an hors d'oeuvres thief? And who is Father Brown?"

"No one wants their sins made public, Lon."

"It's fish spread!"

"Doesn't matter. It's breaking a commandment. Could be a lot of social consequences. So tread lightly on that."

Good reminder that the world of Middelburg was not the world I'd lived in. "And Brown?"

"Know G.K. Chesterton?"

"Great Anglican writer," I said. "I haven't read his detective stories."

"Better read up if you want to be a priest and an amateur detective," Red said. "Pick up some hot investigative tips. But don't expect me to play the dumb cop. Or the bully cop. Or the love interest."

My pulse danced again. "What are you then?"

"Your friend," she said. "But not a fictional character."

"Me either."

"And don't let them treat you like one, like their own private fantasy of a clerical detective. Middelburg is backward, but it isn't some flowery English village. Real people. Real fear. Real desperation."

I heard muffled laughter from the audience. Donna was warming them up like yesterday's braised moose stew.

"So, we walking tomorrow after church?" I asked. We did most Sundays.

"Perfect time to practice identifying trees by their bark," she said, "before the leaves drop."

"It's August!"

"It's west Michigan. You'll see red in the trees in a week."

At the auditorium end of the hall, the Authorized Personnel Only doors eased open. I watched as a hand appeared, then an arm. Someone was quietly sneaking back here during the show.

"Lon, you there?" Red asked.

"Wait," I said, ducking back into the doorway. "Someone's coming."

A wide hip appeared, then all of Wanda Mueller popped into view. She helped the door close slowly so it barely clicked. I heard her steps come toward me, toward the Green Room.

"Everything okay?" Red asked.

I didn't answer. I wanted to see what Wanda was up to. She had been exceptionally concerned with food stealing.

Wanda rolled through my doorway and nearly knocked me up the stairs. I dropped my cell.

"Whoa!" Wanda said too loudly.

I put my fingers to my lips and pointed backstage and grabbed my phone. I could hear Red's voice buzzing through the speaker. "Lonnie!"

"I wanted to talk to you," Wanda said. "Privately."

I held up a finger so Wanda would wait. "Sorry about that," I told Red. "It's okay here. Gotta run."

"Don't do that again!" Red said, irked. Which made me feel strangely good.

Wanda seemed taller and wider than I remembered. She

looked angry, brow furrowed, upper body leaning over me. "Is it true," she asked, "what the news says? That professor died right after eating her food?" She jerked her head toward the stage, her heavy blond brows furrowing even deeper. "I gotta be worried about anything?"

"No," I said. "The medical report indicated he had a massive infection that overwhelmed his body."

She stared at me. "And it didn't come from the food?" As hulking as she was, she didn't send out aggression vibes, more like big, strong, don't-mess-with-me vibes. Nothing west-Michigan-nice going on here. I liked her.

"You aren't feeling ill, are you?" I asked.

"Feelin' fine. Thanks."

"You get your extra parfaits home okay?"

She kept staring, but in that way a little kid does—not judging, just being there with you. "All three. Gonna serve 'em to my book club tomorrow afternoon. If you're sure they're safe." Her mouth tucked up a bit at one corner. "Wouldn't do to kill off the book club, no matter what crap they make me read."

I smiled too. "No. Hey, did you stay in the Green Room after Guy—after I left?"

"You betcha. With all that hullabaloo going on, who was gonna watch my parfaits?"

I nodded. "Yeah, smart move. So, did you happen to notice what happened to the Sunny Spirit Salmon Spread and toast last night after things wound down?"

She looked a little startled. "What? It's gone?"

I nodded.

She furrowed her brow again. "I moved it, after the ambulance left. Pretty obvious the professor wasn't gonna want it again, but someone might. And that stuff, it sits out, it goes funny." She barely smiled again. "Maybe it already was funny?"

Here was a chance to prove it safe! "Did you taste it at all?"

"No, I did not." She shook her head squarely. "I wouldn't want no unauthorized tasting of my parfaits and even if a man is sick in the hospital, he deserves to have people leaving his salmon spread alone."

I tried to hide my disappointment at her honesty. "So, you put it in the fridge?"

"Found foil in a drawer, covered it up. In case he came back and wanted it."

Wow, I thought. *A truly nice person.* "So, hey," I said. "You ever play soccer?" She looked sideways at me and I knew she thought I was kidding. "Honest. I'm recruiting women for an over-thirty women's team." Her eyes narrowed and I panicked. "Oh! Oops, sorry if you aren't over thirty!"

"Thirty-eight," she said. "You really see me running up and down a field?" She held her hands out to display her girth.

"I saw you guarding that refrigerator with a devotion and agility that I'd admire in any member of the defense. Or even goalie."

She chewed on that and slid a glance at me again. "Seriously?"

I nodded. "And if you have any friends who might like to play, have them call me."

Wanda nodded once. "Okay, yeah. Sure. Put me on the list. I'll try it out. As long as it doesn't conflict with my book group."

She produced a pen and business card and wrote her home info on it. Wanda Mueller worked as an administrative assistant at Dutch Clean Carpet Care. "I'd better get back, then."

"Oh, hey," I said. "When did you leave the Green Room last night?"

"I hung around until the last prize, some lady from Iowa who won the moose stew. The ladies with the Holy Night Tuna Cups came back and got their stuff and we all admired the moose stew, then we all pretty much left together. That salmon spread was in the fridge then. The boy who got socked in the nose was still at the door when I left. Maybe you should ask him."

That was the second person who'd pointed me to Paul. Guess I knew where I was headed when the show ended.

Chapter Twelve

Cousin Donna Hancock's Loaves and Fishes Culinary Ministries ran smoothly enough to be dull for the rest of the day. Prize winners grinned, ate their food, and gave glowing testimonies to the power of Christ and Cousin Donna's blessed cooking. During the intermission after the presentation of the Wonder of Wonders Green Bean Casserole, Char let me leave my post to use the bathroom and look for Brady to see what he could tell me about the custodians.

It wasn't hard to track Brady down—I just followed the echoes of his braying laughter through a maze of shiny corridors to a brightly lit high-tech meeting room. He sat on the edge of a table, holding court with a cluster of seventy-something men in patterned polo shirts, khaki shorts and high white socks.

"Hey, Reverend," he said with a wave. The men turned in unison, like synchronized swimmers, to study me. "We got a cooking school widowers support group here."

I smiled at them all. I didn't see a cup of coffee, a cookie, a sports section, not even an open Bible on the tables.

"Just, you know, telling stories," Brady added.

"Could I talk to you outside for a minute?" I asked.

He excused himself with a "women are crazy" shrug to the others and followed me to the hall.

"We've got a first-rate staff here at Frontline, you know." He slapped the wall beside him. "All solid Christians."

"I'm sure. Did any of the solid Christians on your cleaning crew take the salmon spread?"

"No." He shook his head. "No way, Jose."

"You sure about that?"

He nodded once. "They said so."

"If they admitted stealing the spread, would they lose their jobs?"

Brady squinted at me. "Of course. Thou shalt not steal."

I felt like flinging a little Bible. "Jesus said we should forgive seventy-seven times."

"I quoted the Ten Commandments. Foundational law," Brady said.

"'The law indeed was given through Moses; grace and truth came through Jesus,'" I said. "Gospel of John."

He blinked. "Lon, I have to tell ya, my crew is upright. They didn't take the spread."

"Do you have to believe them because otherwise it would look bad for you?"

Brady flushed. "I believe them because they confessed to something else. They aren't proud. Okay. They didn't even go in the Green Room last night. In fact, they haven't been in there since cleaning up after church last Sunday." *So there*, his cocked head added.

He saw this as a good thing? "What did they clean last night?"

"The auditorium. The public lavatories and where Guy got sick, of course. But they didn't take your spread."

"You know, Brady." I looked up and down the hall and his gaze followed mine. "We all want our churches to look good in the public eye."

"As representatives of the good Lord," he said, smoothing his hair back from his temples.

"Exactly. And I'm glad to be able to report that your employees are not thieves. That they keep the place spotless. All that."

"Well, thanks, Lon." He tucked his hands into his pants, clearly ready to call this conversation quits.

"But you've been so worried about people thinking you employ thieves or that Guy got sick here, you sort of overlooked the obvious."

He screwed up his face. "What?"

"That Guy came in sick. And maybe left germs all over the place." His jaw dropped as I turned to go. "I'd get that Green Room cleaned up if I were you."

"Right you are, Reverend." He waved a finger in the air. "Right you are. I'm on it. We've got state-of-the-art cleaning materials. Antibacterial everything. No germs in this place, no sirree."

I wasn't interested in his Cleanliness-R-Us speech. "Just let me know if you find the spread."

The rest of the day flowed by. Precisely at three, Cousin Donna's show ended with everyone standing, swaying, hands clapping or raised toward the ceiling in a rousing rendition of "Gather Around for the Table is Spread." The notes echoed in my ears as I made my way through the crowds and outside. My skin still held the chill from indoors so the blistering heat felt good as I crawled into my car.

I sang along with John Denver about meadows in Canada as I drove away from Frontline and checked my messages. My mother had called six times, but left only one message. I pushed the buttons to retrieve it, but still wished I could join John's men and ponies on their long, lonesome ride.

"Lonnie, honey, it's Mom. Please put 'call Mom' at the top of your To Do list, 'kay? Love you! Bye-bye."

Like my mother had ever kept a functioning To Do list in her life.

Next I checked in with the Freeleys to make sure Linus wasn't driving them nuts. Denny said the pup kept his boys busy, so he had no problem keeping him a few more hours. It helped him out while Marion was at work.

I swung west down Main Street toward Central Park, where the farmers' market had just begun to close. A few tired folks were still loading the remains of the day onto well-used pickups for transport back to the farms. Sometimes you can get stuff at super discounts this time of day, if you were willing to have a few bruises on your fruit.

Fifteen minutes later I had a canvas tote full of fresh apricots, peaches, plums, tomatoes and corn on the cob. I'd also succumbed to Salted Herring's Homemade Candies booth. I didn't go for the salted licorice fish that had made Carice van Peperstraten her fortune, but she had great homemade malt balls. Blueberries I'd get from the guys across the street. I felt better knowing I'd eat healthy later—mostly—and headed off toward the boys' house in the dunes.

Lake Michigan glittered dark blue and choppy underneath the clear sky. Sailboats tilted in front of the breeze and the beach undulated with swimmers. Soon the road turned away from the shore, following the stable backside of the dunes as it wound up toward Five Points College and Seminary and the surrounding neighborhood.

John and I sang about living in danger as we climbed the narrow one-lane road up the dune. The beech forest that held the sand stable rose straight up to my right and fell away straight down to my left. Three deer stood in the valley below me, painted with shadow by the late afternoon light. They watched me, ears pointed to the sides, clearly used to noisy cars and music. Of course, a thousand students went to school up here.

At the top of the dune, a vast, grassy expanse unfolded, dune tops linked along the lakeshore. I passed the left fork toward campus and headed to the Five Points neighborhood. The lakefront houses squatted like thick giants, clutching at the golden dune grass and gazing out toward the watery horizon. Beemers, Land Rovers and H3s clustered in these driveways but as the road snaked back down the shadow side of the dune, it was Fords, Hondas and beat-up Subarus that filled the drives and lawns in front of lopsided porches and peeling woodwork. My '88 Honda wagon and I fit right in.

The boys' house rambled across a not-too-well cut lawn, the wraparound porch filled with a lumpy fabric couch and some plastic chairs that might have come from a classroom. A can of chewing tobacco sat on the railing near the stairs and cigarette butts littered the ground behind the gangly holly bushes. Window air conditioners whirred in several places and I hoped someone would hear my knock.

Jeff answered. He'd lost no time getting home from Frontline and getting comfy, wearing nothing but shorts ripped from old sweatpants. Tattoos colored his skinny, hairless upper body. I particularly liked the Native American shaman reaching upward around Jeff's pierced left nipple. Someday I wanted to ask him how that fit with the Bible verses inked into his arms.

"Hey, Reverend," he said. "Still wearing the uniform!"

I hadn't changed from my black security tee and slacks.

He stepped aside so I could enter. From the foyer I could see back into a kitchen, its counter littered with half-empty soda cans and open bags of chips. To my right, seven beanbag chairs faced an enormous plasma TV hooked with wires to three different gaming consoles. Even with no one there, it beeped and blinked. It reminded me of the ICU. "Is Paul around?" I asked.

He grinned. "Yeah." He loped back into the kitchen. "Hey, Geiger!" he yelled. "Door, man!"

I heard thumping from upstairs, then Paul cascaded down the curved stairs to my left. He wore scruffy cutoffs, his hemp choker, and was also bare-chested. He practically skidded to a stop when he saw me. He glanced back up the stairs, and then ducked in greeting. "Hey, Reverend." He brushed the tip of his

88

nose lightly with his fist and I saw the purpling under his left eye. He stared just past me, into the empty living room.

"How are you feeling?"

"Fine." His body angled away from me, like I'd seen Linus do when a bigger, meaner dog approached. Not submissive, but none too thrilled to see me.

Fair enough. This was his place. "I need to ask you a few questions about last night."

He shrugged, glanced at me, then back at the bean bags. "I don't know anything."

Ah. I'd worked with enough kids in my former life at the Episcopal school to know that when a young person tells you he doesn't know anything before you even ask him something, well, he knows something. About what, no telling, but something he doesn't want to share.

Staying vague seemed the best route. "A man died last night," I said.

"I know." Sigh. From deep within the house, male voices rose in shouts of agony and protest.

"NFL preseason," Paul explained.

I looked at the dark plasma in the empty room behind me.

"Oh, they're watching the big TV," he said.

The big one? This one would hardly fit in my cottage's living room. "You don't watch?"

His eyes drifted toward the stairs again. "I got homework. Summer school." He looked miserable.

"You want to sit down?" I asked.

"No." He brushed his nose again. "I gotta get back."

He sure didn't want me here. "I need to know if you saw someone remove the salmon spread and toast points—the food Dr. Rittenga won—from the Green Room last night."

He looked surprised. "It's gone?" When I nodded, he seemed to think about it. "No. I guess someone might've snuck it out. I wasn't searching people or anything."

I felt like I had to ask it directly. "Did you bring it home? It's okay if you did," I added quickly. "You aren't in trouble. I just

89

need to find it."

"I haven't got it."

That felt like an evasion to me. "You know where it is?"

"No."

"Did you take it and give it to someone else?"

"Reverend, I do not steal. Plus," he said, his eyes hard now, his face slipping into a near-sneer, "I could care less about shrimp dip."

"Salmon," I said. "Spread."

He shrugged. "It's pink. It's fish. Whatever." He rubbed the end of his nose again. "Can I go?"

I sighed. I'd hoped the spread would turn up here and my case—such as it was—would be closed. "Yeah, but can you grab the others to talk to me for a sec?"

Paul bolted up the stairs two at a time, bellowing, "Door!" then disappeared. Jeff peered around the kitchen doorway.

"Oh, hey Reverend, you still here?"

"Can I talk to the rest of you guys?"

He ambled toward me, stuck his fingers between his lips and shrilled a whistle that could shatter glass. It worked. Four more boys tumbled into the hall, all in various states of partial nudity appropriate to a summer afternoon.

"Hey, Rev Lon." Robbie grinned, giving me a high five. "Whazz up?"

"Guys, here's the deal," I said. "I need to find the salmon spread that Professor Rittenga won last night."

"The stuff that disappeared from the refrigerator?" Josh asked. His blond hair rumpled under his red ball cap.

"Yeah. No one's going to get into any trouble, but they want to run some tests, make sure nothing in the spread made the professor sick."

Robbie shrugged. "I haven't seen it."

"I thought he had an infection," said Will, in his deep voice.

"That's what the police think, but Cousin Donna wants to be sure everything is as safe as she thinks it is."

"You can check out the fridge." Jeff ushered me forward.

"Proceed at your own risk!"

I looked doubtfully at the counter stacked with dirty dishes and old food containers.

Josh bobbed in front of me. "Don't make her do it! Not nice."

"You just don't want anyone checking out your stuff," said Xander.

"You're just pissed 'cause he shoved you on your ass the other day for helping yourself to his mama's lasagna," said Will.

Xander thrust out his chest. "Doesn't want anyone touching his stuff ever." He shook his hands by his face and danced on tippy-toes mimicking a little kid. "Don't go in my room! Don't touch my books! Don't eat my cake! Don't touch my mom's frozen lasagna! You guys!"

Everyone cracked up, but Josh shoved him. "Don't frickin' touch my mom's lasagna."

"Dude!" Xander shoved back. "She sent back enough to feed us all for a week."

"Be a Christian," Will said. "Share."

"Do not touch my lasagna," Josh said. "Or I'll kill you."

The grins wavered a little bit at Josh's tone. This boy was serious about his mom's lasagna.

Josh lightened things up again quickly. "Rev Lon sees much more of this kitchen and I'll lose my job at the Grind for sure. And just 'cause you people live like pigs."

Pig noises all around.

"Like you keep the basement a pretty palace," Xander said.

"Fun as this is, guys," I said, "I probably should let you get back to the game. If that spread turns up, don't eat it." If they had brought it home, it was probably long gone. Still, a little fear might shake it out if they did have it. "Or if you find out that someone did eat it, make sure they bring whatever's left to me and I can help them get the right medical treatment."

"How about that big lady?" Josh said.

"Yeah!"

"The one who tackled the skinny chick!"

91

"She ought to play for the Lions!"

"I already talked to Wanda," I said. "She hasn't got it."

"Or already ate it," Will said.

Things disintegrated from there, so I made them promise they'd call me if they thought of anything else. Josh walked me to my car. "They aren't bad guys. Just no respect for personal property."

I laughed.

"You really got no idea where the spread went? Not out in the trash or anything?"

"No."

"Weird."

"Yeah. If you think of anything that might help, call." I settled into my car.

"Or I'll catch ya when I drop off the bread Sunday morning." He thumped twice on the roof. "See ya."

As I drove back toward town, I figured I knew three things:

One, I didn't think any of the boys had the spread.

Two, Paul had a secret, but then what college boy didn't?

Three, I was very glad I didn't live with six college boys.

I yawned as I pulled into Freeleys' driveway to pick up Linus. Past four o'clock. Time to go home and take a nap before dinner and sermon-writing. Denny opened the door before I could knock, finger to his lips. "They're passed out in the living room," he said. "Come see." He tiptoed with surprising lightness down the hall.

There they were, his two sons and my adolescent long-legged black German shepherd, stretched out in three parallel lines on the floor, sound asleep in front of an episode of *The Simpsons*. It was actually one I recognized, an early one, where Bart, who has been hit by a car, visits hell. I watched as Satan told him to lie, cheat, steal and listen to heavy metal music. Even when I was in high school, I thought how crazy it was that some people thought music could send you to hell. In fact, it was that sort of thing that inspired me to be a priest. Through Woman at the Well and chapel in college, I'd learned a more loving way, and I wanted to share it.

But what I really wanted to do now was lie down beside them and nap in that same loose, limp, lazy way that we all napped during summer vacations from elementary school.

"You want to watch an episode or two?" Denny settled himself on the couch and gestured to the recliner. "Might inspire a sermon."

I sat. "I love you people," I said and fell promptly to sleep.

Chapter Thirteen

Next thing I knew, someone was puffing warm damp air against my cheek. I moaned "no" and the thumping of a too-big tail against a coffee table made me sit up quick. "Shhh!" I grabbed Linus's loose scruff and pulled him toward me. On TV, Bart and Lisa sang karaoke to the theme song from *Shaft*. Without waking anyone, I grabbed the pup's stuff from beside the door and tiptoed out.

I loved the drive home. Town gave way to small grassy dunes, big beech woods, and eventually, blueberry fields. I loved looking out for deer or turkey, skunk or possum, red-tailed hawks or turkey buzzards. Once a bald eagle seasoned the view. Today, though, I saw only crows. And as I got close to home, I felt my stomach twisting up with fear.

I have a lot of ways to deal with my demons. I started developing them when I was a kid and my family blew apart and sent me to spend summers with my crazy, autocratic Great Aunt Kate. Fear, anger, loneliness—I guess we all have our defenses against the things that haunt us. You'd think I'd have some extra-special demon-defying powers as a priest, but honestly, I don't. In fact, when it came to defying fear, pretty much I had Linus.

Linus sat in his front seat the whole way home, his still stocky puppy body curved behind his suddenly long front legs. His adult-sized ears flopped sideways from a still-tiny head. One chunky paw rested on my forearm while I chattered away about the troubles of the weekend. "And when we get home," I said, "you check it out, okay, boy?" He looked at me with sober copper eyes.

Someone needed to check it out. It had been two days after all.

I pulled into my cottage's gravel drive and dust clouded around us. It hadn't rained in weeks and everything was crusty and dry. I loved this funny little rental. From here I could bike to a well-hidden township beach on Lake Michigan and see a million stars at night.

I got to spend my days in town with people and my free time out here with trees, blueberries and God. Still, every single time I arrived home, my stomach lurched.

Calm down.

My fear about coming home hadn't let up much since the attack last spring. On TV, when people get assaulted they bounce right back to normal routine. Not me. Even though the person who attacked me now lived in jail, I still got nervous every time I walked through my own front yard. I knew my vulnerability. I'd almost died here.

My fear infuriated me. I hated that some whacko had stolen my peace. Plus, it felt like lack of faith. But there it was.

I let Linus out of the car to run around. The goofball adolescent didn't look like much of a guard dog, but once he'd barked at just the right time to save my life. I figured he'd probably do it again if the need came up.

Unloading the car, I studied the nearby trees and the front

door. My potted azaleas had shriveled in the heat, but otherwise nothing looked amiss.

In the blueberry fields across the way, a dozen or so guys hunkered into the towering bushes, pulling the dusky berries and dropping them into big yellow buckets. We waved at each other. I'd taken them all an industrial-sized cooler of lemonade last month when I first saw them. Since then Linus and I had visited them—him on leash, of course. It made me feel safer to have them watching my house.

I opened the cottage door and let Linus run ahead to check it out. He bounced on the couch, ran into the kitchen and stuck his nose in his water dish. Then, face dripping, he dashed into the bedroom where I heard him leap on and off the bed. After he was done jumping, he ran back into the laundry area, then back into the front room where he thrust his head into the bag of his stuff I was holding and emerged with Squeaky Toad. Which he squeaked at me.

That would be my sophisticated security system reporting the all clear. My stomach untwisted. That particular demon went back into hiding, at least for the moment.

Barely twelve hours later, I wrestled my demons again, this time at church. Every Sunday, I got an attack of the nerves. Performance anxiety, really. I had to stand up, say what I thought about the Bible and life, risk having people walk out or quit church or God only knew what. I had only done this preaching thing for a few months, and it still scared me every week.

It reminded me of my first season of college soccer. I knew I could do it as well as anyone, but I had pregame jitters something awful. So now, as then, I developed a sequence of pregame rituals to calm myself down.

I arrived at church two hours before the eight thirty service, finished up my sermon and walked through the quiet, empty sanctuary. Specks floated in the pale yellow slants of sun and everything smelled like old polished wood. First, I checked the service book from which I'd read the prayers to make sure all the large-letter pages were in order. Next, I made sure the chalice and small plate, or paten, had been set by Altar Guild the night before, and sure enough it stood gleaming on the credence table behind the altar. Next to it, two cruets of communion wine stood full. Next to them sat a large paten. When Josh brought fresh bread from The Windmill Grind bakery, someone from Altar Guild would place it here, ready to go. But today the paten was already half full, with wafers to be used in communion for the first time.

I went through the door in the panel wall behind the altar into the sacristy—sort of the storage room for all things liturgical. I made a mental note to restock the home communion kits after the service today. I needed to put the leftover consecrated wafers into them and put a new one in my car. I'd used my emergency one at the hospital the other night with Guy. I pulled my white alb from the wardrobe and decided against putting it on yet. The unair-conditioned church was still cool with the fans blowing the light morning air, but I'd heat up fast in this plastic collar, long shirt, pants, socks and an alb on top. Holding my alb in one hand, I grabbed my green stole with the other and carried them back through the sanctuary.

Soon everyone—with their quirks and passions—would come together to be church, to be a community at this table, for this meal. That was the best part of the whole thing for me.

Satisfied that I was ready, I headed across the lawn back to my office. Josh pulled up in his old Subaru. He held up two fat brown loaves and the flat priest host.

"Any news on the missing shrimp dip?" he shouted.

"Salmon. And no."

He shrugged. "Good luck today." He headed for the church to deposit the loaves.

At 8:20, I stood in the cool of the parish house commons, tying my cincture around my alb at the waist and feeling terrific. Almost everyone had gone to the church to take their seat, but Bova Poster and Isabella Koontz stood with me settling into their own robes. They were my LEMs this morning, the Lay Eucharistic Ministers who would do the liturgical readings and help serve communion wine. Woman at the Well didn't have a big congregation and I certainly could have served communion myself, but they liked to keep the service moving. Besides, having two lines, with the priest giving bread to all and two people serving wine, was the way they had always done it, thank you very much. Even though these women had battled each other the last time I saw them together, this morning they presented a united front, straightening each other's robes, reminding each other about the touchy short in the pulpit microphone.

"Ready?" I asked. We faced each other. I saw that Isabella had smeared her lipstick when she pulled on her robe. I was just debating how to tell her when Bova jumped in.

"I'm going to check myself in the mirror," she said, grabbing Isabella's sleeve. "Come on. You too."

Cantankerous Bova in an act of kindness. No demons here.

After I checked a mirror too, the three of us walked across the lawn to church. Bets Alderink finished the organ prelude just as we entered, so I barely had time to say hi to Patrice and Rochelle Koontz, Isabella's daughters and today's acolytes. Normally we had three, but D.J. Brink had stayed home to nurse his groin pull.

"I don't know when to hit the sanctus bell!" eleven-year-old Rochelle whispered as we formed a line. "D.J. always does that!"

"I do," said nine-year-old Patrice, who stood a full head taller than her older sister.

"Never mind about the bell," I whispered as the processional hymn started. "We'll do without this week. Now go!"

And so we entered: two acolytes in red robes and white cottas (Rochelle carrying the silver-plated gospel and Patrice carrying the cross), the eight-person choir, then Bova and Isabella, then me. Once at the altar, I blessed the congregation and together we prayed, "God, to you all hearts are open, all desires known, and from you no secrets are hid."

In that case, I prayed in my head as the congregation continued the spoken prayer, *if you could help me find that salmon spread, I'd be grateful.*

98

Next, we sang the *Gloria* and I followed with the collect of the day. "Defend your church because it cannot continue in safety without your help," I read and really meant it, thinking about little Woman at the Well, the congregation fighting themselves, getting mistreated by other folks in town. The lessons and psalm went smoothly. Neither Isabella nor Bova stumbled over any unpronounceable biblical names. The sequence hymn, *Savior, Like A Shepherd Lead Us*, got everyone's blood going. By the time I read the gospel, the heat had begun to cling to all of us.

Keep it short, I thought as I stepped up to the pulpit for the sermon.

"This week's gospel reading gives us a heck of a story. Imagine this. You've been working night and day, loads of overtime. Traveling to meetings. Barely seeing your family. And finally, blissfully, vacation comes. Ah." I stretched out my arms and sighed, relaxed. "Where you headed? A warm beach? Mountain forest? Cultured European city? Disney World?"

People laughed.

"There you are, relaxing. Resting. Recharging. It's everything you want your vacation to be—for about half a day. And then it starts—phone, e-mail, text messages. Folks from work who need just one more thing. One thing from you that's really important. Crucially important to them. You turn your machines off, but then the hotel phone starts. You go to the pool, but then a messenger shows up with faxed documents. Please, a co-worker cries, just this one more thing."

I paused to let that sink in.

"How would you feel?"

Another pause. Mumbles in the pews. Good.

"I'd feel hounded. No peace and quiet. People whining, clamoring for attention, for you to solve their problems. Most of us would probably want to scream—*leave me alone!*" My voice echoed as I paused.

"This is exactly what happens to Jesus in this story. He wants some time to rest, but the crowds won't let up. And does he tell them to go away? He turns back and gives them what they ask.

He heals them. But here's the kicker."

I paused and leaned forward over the pulpit. "Even that wasn't enough. Because as soon as he heals them, they want more. Can you imagine that? It's like having people from work actually follow you on your vacation, and after you're done doing the things they want you to do, they slap you on the back and say, 'Dude, I'm hungry. Buy me dinner, will ya?'"

Laughs.

I gave them a few seconds to think about it, and felt my own blood boil as I imagined it myself. I knew how ungracious I would be if that happened. "It would be perfectly just of Jesus to say, 'Folks, I told you not to come. You got yourselves into this mess. I already healed you—when are you going to learn some boundaries?' But no. He hands a few loaves and fishes to the disciples and says, 'Feed them.' The disciples think he's lost it, that he's asked them to do the impossible, to divide limited resources much farther than they can possibly go. But the bread and fish do last. Everyone is fed. Much remains left over. They'll be eating fish sandwiches for a week." A few more laughs.

The heat and humidity hung in the room, so I zipped toward my conclusion.

"And so, in the New Testament, people behave badly, whine, demand, and show no compassion for their teachers and what justice do they get? Miraculous food where no food should be. Health where only sickness should be. It's a good lesson for us all."

Please, Lord, I thought, *let my Committee on Liturgy be listening. Let everyone who's been crapped on by someone in this town be listening.*

"When people around you treat you badly, when they simply ask too much of you, demand more than any polite person would ever dream of demanding, try to meet them with a generous heart. Even when your resources are at their lowest, meeting people with a generous heart opens the doorway to miracles. And you just never know what will happen then. Amen."

We sped through the prayers of the people and the passing of the peace and announcements. Isabella and Ivor Koontz brought forward the gifts, a tiny cruet of wine and paten of bread. While the collection plates got passed, I spread the purificator, or white linen, as a sort of placemat for communion. I folded the green veil that draped the paten and chalice and set the paten to one side. It contained only the priest host, a flatbread about the size of a slice of softball, the one I'd hold up to break before the congregation at the moment of consecration. I set the pall—the piece of linen-covered cardboard that helped balance the whole thing—on top of the folded veil. Bova stepped forward to take the platter from me as I moved everything until it was just so.

I didn't realize anything was amiss until after The Lord's Prayer and the breaking of the bread and folks had come forward to the rail. I grabbed the paten the Koontzes had brought up and started distributing bread until Kitty Gellar whispered, "Wafer, please." There were no wafers in my paten, so I turned to the larger one still sitting on the credence table. It held only the second loaf of bread. I glanced quickly around and caught Bova Poster's eye just as she looked away from me, a look of tight-lipped satisfaction on her face.

Somehow she had stolen the wafers!

How dare she remove the wafers set by the Altar Guild? How dare she ignore not only the committee's decision but mine as well? Who the hell did she think she was? The priest?

Right there in that sacramental moment, my anger demons let loose and started whirling inside me. I turned back to Kitty, apologized, and kept going with the consecrated bread. I tried to focus each time I said "Body of Christ," but I was so furious I could hear my heart pounding over my own words. My head buzzed through the postcommunion prayer and when I ended the service with a shout of "Go in peace!" I was feeling none too peaceful. Parents whisked their kids over to the parish house for Sunday school while I stood at the door shaking moist hands with everyone, just *waiting* to pounce on that interfering witch. But she never came by. She must've used the side door.

At the parish house, most of the adults milled around drinking coffee while the week's snack time hosts set up food and punch. After a half hour, the kids joined us and we all hung out munching on homemade windmill cookies, cheese, lemonade and iced tea. Bova was nowhere to be seen. I nodded and made chitchat, but my brain whirled with the nasty things I wanted to say to her when I saw her at tomorrow's committee meeting.

I'd just taken a bite out of my second cookie when I felt a tug on my alb, down around knee-level. Gary Alderink, Bets' four-year-old, gazed up at me over flushed cheeks.

"You look handsome today," I said as I knelt.

He straightened his black and white checkered vest and stood with one shiny black shoe on top of the other. "Are you a princess?" he asked, deadly serious.

"Why do you wonder that?"

He pursed his lips in concentration and gently touched the end of my sleeve. "All this pretty lace."

I almost never noticed the intricate lace that trimmed the edges of my alb. I looked at the vine details for the first time.

"Princesses have lace," Gary continued. "And flowers all around them. And sit on a throne."

The altar had fresh flowers every Sunday. And during the LEMs' readings, I did sit up front in a highbacked chair of dark wood with royal blue velvet cushions.

"You're very observant," I said.

He nodded.

"You notice things that not everyone else sees." I wished I could ask Gary to help me track the missing salmon spread. "All those things you noticed? The same clues lead to two different answers. They could mean someone is a princess, but they could also mean someone's a priest. Like me."

He nodded.

"Someday, would you like to come sit in the big chair at the front of the church?"

He smiled wide enough to display all his tiny square baby teeth. "Yes!"

"Great. Tell your mom I said come by any time during the

week and I'll give you a tour, okay?"

"Yes!" He scampered away and I wanted my frustration with Bova the Wafer Thief to go away. A magic kid like that—I didn't want her poisoning my whole day.

I knew I'd feel better after I talked it out with Red, but when I got home I found a message saying she had to cancel our Sunday afternoon walk. I played with Linus, hurling a tennis ball with all the emotion I could muster, but still felt aggravated, cheated, disrespected—a long list of offenses that made me want to pop out of my skin. So, I biked the four miles to the beach.

The silvery singing sands of the eastern shore of this lake are probably the best-kept secret in American coastlines. The smaller beaches, like this one, were often completely empty even in summer. Today, the water tossed with a brown chop, little mixed waves poking in all directions, flapping gently at the sand. I kicked off my sandals and walked toward the water, the fine sand singing beneath my feet. It's almost like the *shoop shoop* of nylon windpants, but more melodic and more solid at the same time. The first time I'd heard it, when I was thirteen, it seemed like one more uncool, weird thing about this place. Today, it reminded me that not everything in my life was completely out of tune.

I left my towel in a heap and waded, then dove into the warm water. It cooled my sand-broiled feet and my steaming scalp. I floated, my heart beating in my ears, watching the cloudless blue, feeling the pat of many waves against my skin. The water held me just when I needed to be held. All the nastiness in my blood seeped away. I felt pretty sure that at tomorrow's Committee on Liturgy meeting I would not kick Bova Poster in the shins.

"Thank you," I prayed aloud. I missed my usual hour with Red, but floating like this with God was pretty good stuff too.

I got home about four and the caller ID on both phones said Red had called. When I tried to call her back, I got her voice mail and left a message. I'd just stepped out of the shower when the phone rang again. My skin prickled and I toweled hard as I checked the phone.

Private caller. Sometimes Red came up that way, depending

on which phone she called from, so I picked up.

"I'm calling to let you know you won't get away with this!"

Not Red. "Happy Sabbath to you too, Star."

"It isn't enough that you failed to find that spread before something else dreadful happened, but you had to dupe poor Elyse Orion into promising she and I would recruit your soccer players. You can rest assured I'll tell her we owe you nothing!"

I tossed my towel onto the hook and walked through the kitchen to my bedroom. The heat felt good on my still-damp skin. "I don't follow you."

She sighed. "No one tells you anything, do they? I almost feel sorry for you. Don Loomis found your salmon spread for you."

Red's partner had beaten me to the spread. I tried to sound happier than I felt. "Well, that's good news. Now you can have it tested and prove Cousin Donna's innocence once and for all."

"We can't test it. Don ate it."

I sat on the bed and tried not to laugh. "Ate it?"

"He ate it early this afternoon, right after church. Didn't want anyone to know he'd taken it from Frontline, so thought he'd destroy the evidence."

"Well," I said, trying to keep the chuckle out of my voice, "then he's the evidence. Nothing's wrong with the spread."

"Wrong, detective. Don Loomis is dying!" Star paused. "Just like Guy Rittenga. And it's all your fault."

Chapter Fourteen

After stowing Linus in his puppy crate, I drove as fast as I dared north to West Olive's Tri Cities Hospital. I parked in the clergy spot next to the ER entrance, flashed my clergy ID and got a nurse to lead me straight to Red, who sat in a little alcove with Brady Wesselynk and a blank-faced woman of about fifty. The woman looked just like most Middelburgers her age, pedal pusher jeans, a pink jewel-necked tee, blond hair stiff with spray, no makeup. She sat utterly still. The immediate impression was that she wasn't even conscious, though her watery blue eyes were open.

Brady stood and offered me his massive hand. "Lonnie, this is Lynn Loomis." I remember that the Loomises attended Frontline, which explained Brady's presence here.

"I'm so sorry to hear about Don," I said.

She didn't move. She stared at a door marked Do Not Enter.

The portal to the ICU and the world of doctors where her husband lay. Where Guy had lain just two nights ago.

I sat next to Red, who looked grateful, and joined the silent waiting.

Time both expands and contracts in that kind of place. You can be stunned at how the hours scramble together and alarmed at the stretched ticking of every second. Waiting for the worst does that.

Eventually, though, the Do Not Enter doors swung open and a long dark woman in scrubs approached. Each of us caught our breath.

"Mrs. Loomis," the doctor began. "We've had to put your husband on a ventilator."

Red slumped beside me. I had to fight the urge to touch her hand.

"He—he can't breathe on his own?" Lynn whispered. Her pale face didn't fold with grief, her steady hands didn't move from her knees.

"No," the doctor said. "The incoordination has progressed swiftly to paralysis, including bronchial paralysis."

"He's paralyzed?" Brady asked, face flushed. "From an infection?"

"We have him on broad spectrum antibiotics, trying to knock out whatever is doing this to him," the doctor said. Her nametag said Dr. Lucinda Lopez. She had a kind voice. "At first it presented like a stroke, but there's no evidence of that." She checked a folder. "Now it presents like an overwhelming bacterial infection, akin to Toxic Shock Syndrome. His kidneys are failing. And although a differential CBC indicated a raised white blood cell count level, there is no variance in the levels of differing white blood cells."

"What does that mean?" Brady asked.

"That it doesn't seem to be an infection," Dr. Lopez said. She closed the folder. "The good news is that his heart, though thready, is still beating on its own."

"What—what now?" Lynn asked.

"I honestly don't know. We've been caught behind this thing

the whole time, responding to each new symptom, barely able to run a diagnostic before another new symptom develops." I sensed the frustration in the doctor's voice.

"Is this what happened to Guy Rittenga?" Lynn asked.

"I didn't work that case," the doctor said, "but of course, everyone is considering the similarities." She offered a small smile. "Remember, though, Mr. Rittenga was already unconscious when he arrived and his heart was much weaker. It gave out before his symptoms progressed as far as your husband's have. And we don't know if Professor Rittenga suffered the same early symptoms. We just don't know enough."

"Would something in that spread make this happen?" Brady asked.

Dr. Lopez checked the folder again. "The food is in the lab, along with the contents of his stomach. So far, no indication of that. We're running out of tests. Barring that, we'll have to assume an environmental cause."

Brady lost his color so fast I thought he might keel over.

Lynn rose slowly. "I'd like to see him now." It was not a question.

The good doctor nodded. "I'll take you right back."

"I'll wait here." Brady looked queasy as Lynn straightened her spine and followed the doctor through the Do Not Enter doors.

Red stood too and signaled me to follow, leading me to a buzzing candy vending machine. "So is this all over town already?"

"Dunno. Star called me, practically accused me of killing Don. What happened?"

Red's eyes darkened. "Evidently he found the salmon dip in the Green Room fridge Friday night. No one was around, so he thought he'd help himself. Knew we were looking so decided to destroy the evidence by eating it in front of an NFL exhibition game."

I closed my eyes. "God. Why didn't he just say, 'Hey, I didn't think anything about it and took it. Here it is. Sorry'?"

Red rubbed her neck. "I told you whoever took the spread wouldn't want to be found out." She gazed down the hall. "What a mess."

"I wish they could tell us something concrete."

"Nothing yet. Rittenga's autopsy didn't pinpoint a cause of death. His organs shut down one at a time, he had respiratory failure, but his heart gave out so fast, it's hard to compare. Don's a lot stronger." She hitched her thumbs in her gunbelt. "A lot stronger. Turns out the professor had terminal cancer of the liver."

That perked me up. "What?"

"Yeah. I found out earlier this afternoon. Fairly advanced. Probably only had a few months to live."

"He was dying?" Guy had looked haggard, a little yellowish, but I figured that was the result of a life lived in books and libraries and classrooms. "I didn't know."

"Even more interesting, his wife didn't know. She insists Guy didn't know or he would have told her." She paused. "What do you think?"

"Well, it's possible he knew and didn't tell her. People do keep strange secrets for even stranger reasons." I remembered what Pia Hakksen had told me at the breakfast reception yesterday morning about professional suicide at the college. "Maybe he did know. Maybe that's why he gave that controversial talk in May. He could take the risk and it wouldn't matter."

"Would he risk getting fired and losing benefits?"

"But he wouldn't *just* get fired and he knew it." I told her what Pia had told me.

Heavy steps echoed as Brady walked toward us. Red turned. "Any news?"

Brady looked like hell. His hair stuck up behind his ears and his lids hung heavy and gray. "I just can't get over it. Two men, sick unto death. A cooking school with poisoned food in my church."

"We don't know the food was poisoned," Red said. "The men have other things in common."

"What?" he asked. Pale patches formed in his big red cheeks. "Not the church? Not Frontline?"

"They were both there Friday night," Red said.

"But so were you two!" Brady's eyes danced between us. "So was I. And six hundred others."

"Maybe a pesticide—" Red began.

"No!" Brady shook his head.

"Or a cleaning product."

"Everything is child safe." Brady's hands jerked around, unable to find a way to smooth things out. "It can't be the church." His eyes lit on me. "You touched it. You touched the spread." He grabbed Red's shoulder with one hand and pointed to me with the other. "Maybe she has a disease. An infection. Maybe she's a carrier."

"Now, hang on," Red said.

Brady turned to me. "Not that I'd blame you." He scanned me as if looking for an open sore. "For Jesus reached out his hands and touched the leper."

I could see it now. Rumors throughout town that the lady priest's very touch was leprous and made full-grown men drop dead in their shoes. It wouldn't matter if we served wafers or bread at communion because no one would show up!

"Brady," Red said. "What you suggest is very unlikely. Lonnie is not Typhoid Mary."

"And there's no proof to link it to your church," I added, which I thought was more what Brady wanted to hear, but had the opposite effect.

"Oh, God!" He spun, his hands flung upward. "It's the church. My church!" He gripped his hair. "How did this happen? What's going to happen next weekend? Will more people die?" He looked at us with wide eyes. "We have to cancel the show next week!"

"Whoa! The docs have to figure out what's going on first," Red said. "Maybe it's just coincidence."

Brady glanced down the hall. "I should go and be with her." But instead of moving that way, he took my hand into his two

109

massive ones. Evidently he'd forgotten that a few seconds ago he thought I was unclean. "I know we don't always see eye to eye. But as my sister in Christ, I hope you'll help me."

The big guy looked so pitiful, I felt sorry for him. "If I can."

"What if people shun us? My church is this community's largest and fastest growing gate by which souls can enter the light of Christian righteousness. But righteousness does not make one immune to evil worldly influence." He blinked back tears. "If evil has befallen my church, help me." He squeezed my hand, and I struggled not to try to yank it away. "Promise me that you'll figure out how it happened and help clear my name. Before next weekend."

There it was. Church, souls and righteousness aside, he wanted me to clear his name.

Now this was a nifty turn of events. Brady had pretty much sided with Star when it came to messing with my reputation and my congregation's reputation all over town, but he wanted me to help save his sorry butt.

"Promise me!" He yanked my arms.

"Brady, no one will think badly of you if it turns out that some weird bacteria got into—"

"Yes they will! In Christ's name, I'm begging you, Lonnie. What would happen if we became the *Infected Church*?"

Down the hall the silver doors opened and Lynn Loomis emerged alone, then disappeared around the corner into the waiting alcove.

When Brady turned back to me, his eyes jittered so much that I feared he might be the next one in the ICU. "You figured out that whole thing with Vance TerMolen," he said. "You can figure this out. I have faith."

"I've told you—told everyone—that was as much dumb luck and good soccer skills as smart detective work."

But like everyone else, he didn't listen. "I have faith in you." He looked like he meant it.

"All right, I'll—" *Help however I can*, is what I was going to say before he cut me off with a vigorous handshake and toothy grin.

"God bless you!" He patted Red's shoulder then loped back down the hall, turning once to wave. "I'll rely on you!" He paused to smooth his hair and his pants before turning the corner to join Lynn Loomis.

"He pats my shoulder like he wants to pat me on the top of the head," said Red. "Annoys the hell out of me."

We looked at each other and burst into stifled laughter—a break we both needed.

"You're in a hell of a spot," she said, wiping her eyes. "Trying to save an evangelical cook who specializes in saving people along with jams and jellies. Agreeing to help the pastor who stirs up righteous fervor against you. And pissing off Star Hannes just when she's gunning for someone to blame for this colossal public relations disaster three months before her election."

"Not to mention my Committee on Liturgy at war over communion hosts."

She looked at me like I was kidding.

"For real. Don't ask." I noticed the crow's feet at the corners of her eyes looked deeper, longer than usual. "You okay?" Don was her partner, after all.

"I guess."

"What's your gut tell you?"

She shrugged. "Lynn said he complained that his mouth felt funny, that his tongue was stiff, and his throat felt thick after he ate the spread."

"Sounds like an allergic reaction," I said, hopefully. "Anaphalactic shock? Is he allergic to fish? Cream cheese? Something else he got into today?"

"Then one side of his face went all slack and they both figured it was a stroke, so they started driving here. By the time they arrived, he could barely sit up. He slurred his speech and couldn't stop salivating." She looked at me.

"That sounds exactly like Guy." I felt like we were overlooking something really obvious.

"Lonnie?" Red waited for an answer to a question I hadn't heard.

"Sorry. Thinking. What?"

"I said, Don's not as old as Guy, and he's in better shape. Still." She jerked her utility belt up around her waist, "it's a damned stupid thing to do. A stupid stupid way to—"

She didn't finish the sentence, but we both heard her final word hang in the air.

Die.

Chapter Fifteen

Some people think that priests have such a fine relationship with God that they spring out of bed each morning, ready to face the day and do the Lord's work.

It doesn't work that way, especially on Mondays. Even less this Monday, when first off I had to face the Committee on Liturgy.

But, I told myself as I tossed Toad for Linus out in my front yard, it would be a good meeting. I'd name the crap that went on in the service yesterday for what it was and demand that we reach a solution. Period. The committee was a team, damn it, and we were going to act like one or people could be replaced.

I reminded myself of my junior high coach. But they had behaved like junior high schoolers, so I didn't much care.

Linus gave me a minor heart attack when instead of chasing Toad for the umpteenth time he decided to bolt across the street and into the blueberry fields to hang out with the men working there. A few of them jumped into the flatbed loaded with yellow plastic pallets, unsure of the black animal with flashing white teeth galumphing toward them. But by the time I caught up with him, the sight of me—a woman priest—running pell-mell down the tall rows of berries, leaves clutching to my hair and clergy shirt, made everyone laugh.

I had to change my clothes, thank you, dog, so when I finally got to church, I was already late for the Committee on Liturgy meeting. I banged up the porch and into the reception area.

Josh sat on the corner of Ashleigh's desk, a smile plastered across his face, arms outstretched as he animated some story. Ashleigh sat with her arms crossed, watching him. Both froze when they saw me.

"Hey, Rev Lon," Josh said.

"They're in there." Ashleigh pointed to the first meeting room, the tall wooden pocket doors already closed. No sounds came from the room. Well, at least they weren't killing each other yet.

I handed her Linus's leash. "Can you run him up to my office, please?" I stretched my shoulders and spun each ankle once, getting ready for the field. "And hold my calls."

"Sure." She scratched Linus's ears and the thin silver bangles on her wrist clattered. "Some reporter from the Grand Rapids newspaper called. Said he'd call back."

"Just keep taking messages." I didn't want to talk to any of them. They shouldn't want to talk to me. I had nothing at all to do with any of what had happened to Cousin Donna, Guy or Don. I turned to Josh. "Did you need something?"

"Oh, uh, no. No." He blushed and jumped from the desk so fast I realized he hadn't been waiting to see me at all, but had been here to see Ashleigh. Cute. "Text ya later, Ash."

"Right." She waved as he left.

"Didn't mean to drive him off," I said.

She rubbed Linus again. "I'm dating Tom VanderHill. From Holland. Josh knows. But I think he still has a little crush." She crinkled her nose at me. "Have a fun meeting."

Oh, to be twenty again.

Well, I couldn't avoid this any longer, so I slid the pocket door aside and stepped into the meeting room. The rectangular table seated fourteen. Bova sat at one end. The Zaloumis sat at the other. In the middle on one side sat Kitty and Isabella. I sat across from them. "Would you like to move in a little closer?" I asked Bova and the Zaloumis.

"If you'd sat down here with me, they'd have to move down here." Bova didn't look much inclined to move at all.

Time to get this team together. "Move closer if you want to be part of this meeting."

Kitty's eyes focused on me in a new way. Isabella flushed. Eddie and Leon stood up and moved. Bova fidgeted.

"I'm not kidding, Bova," I said. "After what you pulled in the service yesterday, I'm this close—" and I used my thumb and forefinger to show her how close I was, "to yanking you off this committee and from the LEM roster."

She heaved her oversized orange T-shirt, embroidered with humming birds, into the seat next to mine.

"Thank you," I said. "What happened in worship yesterday is never going to happen again. We are a team, people, charged with enriching the lives of this congregation. I will not have petty game-playing going on around the sacrament."

The guys stared at the table. Isabella took a note. Bova stared into space, her arms crossed in such a way that her bosom appeared even larger.

"Coffee?" Kitty asked and slowly uncurled her tiny body from the chair. "It's decaf, so probably safe."

Everyone but Bova raised a hand. As Kitty stepped around the room, I continued.

"Now, what needs to happen so that we can work together for something bigger than ourselves?"

No one looked at me.

"Okay," I said after the silence got too long. "What exactly happened in the service yesterday?"

More silence. They all knew. No one would say anything. They were all too damned nice. Good Lord what I wouldn't give for someone from the east coast to call it like it was, shout a bit, then offer to buy everyone a drink.

"We need to start with some honesty," I said. "What happened in the service yesterday?"

"For one thing, we only had two acolytes instead of three," Bova said. "And neither of them rang the sanctus bell."

Isabella practically leapt from her chair in defense of her daughters. "Lonnie told them not to worry about it because D.J. was gone. You heard her tell them that."

"I could've brought my peashooter," Leon said. "Rung the bell with that."

"Me too," Eddie said. He pulled his John Deere hat lower on his brow.

"Cream?" asked Kitty, holding up the half and half.

"I am talking about the wafers!" I shouted. Everyone froze. "Where were the communion wafers? I want it named. Here. Now. Out loud. Where were the wafers?" Fire might have blown from my throat the way they all leaned away from me.

Kitty set down the cream and tottered to her seat, folding her hands neatly on the table. But she said nothing.

"They were set by Altar Guild," I said. "I saw them."

"The Holy Spirit moves in mysterious ways," Bova said, her nose tilted at too uppity an angle for my taste.

"What?" Leon asked. "You claiming the spirit ascended 'em into heaven? Just to please you?" He and Eddie rolled their eyes together.

Bova just pursed her lips at them.

"Bova, why did you take the wafers?" I asked.

Her eyes and mouth formed three perfect 'O's as she gasped. "What? Are you calling me a thief?"

"No. I just want to know why you took the wafers."

"You are calling me a thief. My own priest! I have never—" Huff. "I can hardly—" Puff. "How dare you?"

"Are you saying you didn't take the wafers?" I asked.

She turned away from me.

"People. If we're going to help this church move forward, to come together as a congregation, to build a healthy, open presence in this town, we have got to be honest with each other. Forget being nice! Just be honest!"

The Zaloumis sipped their coffee. Kitty didn't move. Isabella bit her lip.

"Because if we can't, the committee is a danger to the church."

"She took the wafers," Isabella said. "While you were preaching. I watched her do it as she passed back to her seat after the gospel reading."

"Thank you." I turned to Bova.

She slapped the table. "Fine. I took them. I wrapped them in the extra purificator, so I didn't treat them disrespectfully. Why do you care? Have you ever tasted them? They're thin and dry. They stick to the roof of your mouth. Like old cold toast."

"I had a girlfriend tasted like that once," Leon said.

Eddie cackled.

I shot them both a look.

Bova pointed to them. "They started it. They hung that poster without my permission. If they can do that, I can do what I want too." She crossed her arms again. "So there."

I half expected her to stick her tongue out at them. This was not going well.

Kitty coughed and everyone looked at her. "I think it would be appropriate to remind us all of the Father's sermon yesterday." She swallowed, and, to my surprise, quoted me exactly. "'When people around you treat you badly, when they simply ask too much of you, demand more than any polite person would ever dream of demanding, try to meet them with a generous heart. Even when your resources are at their lowest, meeting people with a generous heart opens the doorway to miracles.'" She licked her lips. "I feel a little generosity of heart, from all of us, would be appropriate now."

Maybe. But I'd been pretty damned generous already. A quick

117

glance around the room revealed that all the others felt the same way. Great. Stalemate.

The pocket door rattled as someone knocked and slid it to the side. Ashleigh shrugged as Cousin Donna Hancock floated in. "Hello, hello, hello!" she sang. Her bright red lipstick matched the tie around her hair, the check in her blouse and, I noticed as she circled the table, her dainty flats. She placed two plastic cake containers in the middle of the table and lifted the tops off with a flourish, holding them in front of her like enormous plastic breasts. "Still warm!"

Inside each steamed two different loaves of fresh bread.

"Taste! Eat!" Donna pulled a knife and a small crock of butter from her bag. "I'm just so thrilled to have a church actually considering using my bread for holy communion!" She patted Eddie Zaloumi on the arm. "I don't believe in all that bread-becomes-flesh stuff myself, but if you folks do, that's just keen!" She winked at him.

I had no clue what was going on but didn't know quite how to say so. Another second and I didn't have to.

Bova leaned forward, all smiles. "What do you think? If people want variety in the communion, why not serve several different kinds of bread instead of that same old boring whole wheat stuff we get from The Grind every week?" She pointed to an orangish loaf. "Is that pumpkin?"

"Indeed," cooed Donna. "And cranberry walnut." She pointed to each loaf. "And oatmeal molasses batter bread. And cheddar herb." She pushed the knife toward Bova. "Sample, please."

I grabbed the knife first. "Hold on." I smiled at Donna who I could tell was loving plopping herself in the middle of my crisis. "Thanks so much for all your wonderful effort and contribution. We look forward to tasting it all. But we're in the middle of a committee meeting, so I'm afraid I have to ask you to leave."

She looked stunned. "But how will I get my cake carriers? My knife?"

"Bova will bring them to you this afternoon." I stood. "Again, on behalf of the church, thank you."

It killed her. She moved slower than cold molasses and shot Bova more than one peeved look, but, eventually, I slid the pocket door shut behind her. The minute I did, the Zaloumis twins dove forward to pull chunks of bread from the loaves. I hardly blamed them. It smelled divine.

I tossed the knife down on the table and Eddie grabbed it for the butter. "There is absolutely nothing wrong with the bread we get from The Grind."

Bova shrugged, but didn't look at me. "I just thought if people wanted variety—"

"People want wafers. To dip in the wine because it doesn't break apart. Because it's traditional," I said.

"Bread is what Jesus served," Bova said.

"Not cranberry walnut," I said.

"But everyone would have liked it if he had," mumbled Leon around a huge mouthful of the same.

"Here's the deal," I said. "Next Sunday, I want wafers. I want bread from The Grind. And I want everyone to behave before, during and after the service. If anything goes wrong, I'm disbanding the committee. You'll have no voice in the structure of worship around here. Do you understand?"

I hated the way that all sounded coming out of my mouth, but I'd had it.

They all nodded and I left.

"That reporter called again," Ashleigh said as I tore up the steps behind her.

"Just keep taking messages," I said. "Maybe he'll leave me alone."

Upstairs I plopped into my chair and rubbed the sleeping Linus with the side of my foot. That had gone badly. Badly. Some coach I was, threatening to disband my team. Maybe the good Lord was sabotaging my soccer team to spare them from having such a loser teammate.

Within a few minutes, Kitty appeared at my door, her knobby blue-veined hands folded in front of her. "It was a good sermon. Remember it."

I nodded. "Thanks."

Her crisp dark eyes didn't waver. "I know that the unfortunate rumors around town about your role in what Guy Rittenga did are unfounded. And I know that the events at the cooking show, Deputy Loomis's illness—none of these are your doing."

"Thanks." Kitty's support would mean a lot in the parish.

"That said, some members of the church have expressed their concern, both in person and on the telephone, about your attempts to revive the Well's Belles." She tugged a cotton hanky from the cuff of her blouse and dabbed her nose.

"What concerns?"

"While everyone agrees your determination to re-form the team is admirable, they fear your efforts have become, well, garish."

My stomach felt heavy. "Garish?"

Kitty nodded. "There is a point, after all, when continuing to invite and cajole people to participate in something becomes—well, unbecoming."

"Impolite?"

"The whole town knows your valiant efforts for the team, but it has become a bit embarrassing to watch you practically beg people to play. We are trying to save you from even greater social errors." She inclined her head. "Given your existing image problems."

"I'm trying to convince people to move past those problems."

Kitty offered a thin smile. "Things move slowly in Middelburg. And in the meantime, what you are doing is disturbing sensibilities inside the church and out. I'm here to formally ask you to stop attempting to recruit a church-sponsored soccer team."

What with Bova and Donna Hancock, I was in no mood for this crap. "What if I don't stop?"

"We cannot stop you, of course. But we can withdraw our support for the team. You may recruit players, Father Squires, but you won't have a team for them to play on."

Chapter Sixteen

After Kitty left, I unsnapped my collar from its brass studs, threw it onto my desk, and slammed down the stairs.

"Another reporter—" Ashleigh started.

"Later." I pounded across the street into Central Park.

How the hell could they just cancel my soccer future like that? Just because they hadn't had a team when Peter McGavin had been rector, they'd forgotten how wonderful it could be. We'd won a championship!

And the Belles had saved my life, I was sure of it. Angry and rebellious as I'd been with my parents' marriage falling apart and getting shipped to spend summers with great aunt Katherine, I don't know what I would have done if these women hadn't taken me under their wings. They pulled me into a place where love was unconditional, taught me to channel rage to the field. My college scholarship, the Olympic tryouts, seminary, the very fact that I was marching down this sidewalk in this heat and humidity in a totally inappropriate black outfit was due to the Belles. I'd worked hard to get this team together. I'd wound up in this mess with Guy and the salmon dip because of it. How could they just cancel it?

I wished desperately I had a ball to kick. And kick. And kick. But it was too hot even for kids to be out with a ball.

"Urgh!" I punched the air and spun, then flopped down on the grass. I pulled a strand and began to shred it when my phone rang. It was my mom.

Crap. I'd forgotten to call her back.

"My To Do list sucks," I said when I answered. "Sorry."

"Oh, Lonnie, really, we're all so used to you." I heard a rhythmic clacking that could only be a chef's knife whacking a cutting board.

"What are you making?"

"Greek lemon chicken soup, to celebrate your father's victory. That's why I called. He made the Hot Wheels trivia team. He's the popular culture specialist. You're his phone friend for television. He wants to use Annie for music, but we can't get her to return our calls."

My younger sister Annie dropped on and off the family grid pretty regularly. "You even know where she's staying?"

"I haven't spoken to her in five weeks and four days," Mom said. "Cassie said she called Drew to wish him a happy tenth birthday last week."

I froze. Had I missed my nephew's birthday?

"Of course," Mom breezed, "it wasn't his birthday at all. And he's going to turn eleven. But at least we know she's alive. And evidently somewhere near Bozeman."

I heard my father hollering something from the background.

"Your father says don't forget to brush up on theme songs and cast lists. The tournament goes by decade and the Seventies are first. You'll be free Saturday, right? Eight o'clock our time."

"Sure, but call and remind me, okay? Leave a message on

my home machine." Somehow, compared to everything I'd been dealing with, re-memorizing the words to the theme from *One Day At A Time* sounded like heaven.

Suddenly, I sang it right there in the park, out loud, not missing a word. Why that theme song had rushed to my head of all the Seventies possibilities, I didn't know. Maybe it was because it encouraged me to keep on doing my thing and enjoy it. I yanked a few more blades of grass and threw them one at a time. Maybe because it promised I'd eventually muddle through.

"How did I get into this mess?" I asked the grass, not expecting or needing an answer. I knew full well. What mattered now was how to get out.

I yanked and shredded more grass. *Okay. Think.* If the church took away my team because my image wasn't up to snuff, then the thing to do was power up the image. How to do that?

"Help," I prayed out loud.

Kiss up to Star Hannes, said the voice in my head. My skin prickled and I could feel energy spinning in my gut, the way it does when I know I should listen up.

"No way," I said out loud again. "You can't want me to sell my soul to the devil."

Win Brady's goodwill.

"Ugh. Please. A better idea."

Save Don Loomis.

"I already blew the spread thing." I felt like crying. "Don't rub it in."

Silence.

"What?" I said. "That's the best you got?" I looked around and suddenly saw the image of myself sitting cross-legged in the sun in nearly one hundred-degree heat, dressed in black, talking to myself. A hell of a lot of good this was going to do my image.

"Kiss up to Star, get Brady on my side and save Don. My only options?"

Silence.

I tore up one especially rough and wide blade of grass and stretched it between my thumbs, brought it to my mouth and blew. It screeched like nails on a chalkboard before it popped out of my hands.

"If I did want to do one of those three impossible things, how would I?"

Silence.

"Not fully helpful." I shredded more grass. Maybe I should go for a big run with Linus. The heat would wear us both out and maybe then, my body stretched and exhausted, I could think more clearly about Sunny Spirit Salmon Spread, Tasty Toast Points, Loaves and Fishes, wafers and bread, my dad's trivia team, the now-defunct soccer team.

Or I could go to Marion's and watch *The Simpsons* with the boys and laugh my butt off at Bart and Lisa singing karaoke to the theme from *Shaft*. A dreadful song. As close to pornography as I got before the age of ten. Dicks and sex machines. Sung by Isaac Hayes.

Yeah, maybe some Simpsons would help me think straight about Cousin Donna and her tasty dish.

Tasty fish, I thought. Only it wasn't with my own voice that I heard it. It was a man's with an Asian accent. I was quoting again, only I couldn't quite remember what.

"Tasty fish," I said out loud with a mangled accent. Mentally I flipped through my internal television reference files. "Poison, poison, poison, tasty fish," I said to the grass in my hand, still not sure where the words came from. I pulled a blade. "Poison." Tossed it, pulled another. "Poison." Did it again. "Poison." Grabbed the last blade. "Tasty fish."

Karaoke. An Asian accent. Bart and Lisa. Blades. Tasty fish.

I remembered. The episode I'd dozed through at Marion's house. Bart and Lisa were singing karaoke in a sushi restaurant while the apprentice chef fixed a poisonous fish for Homer. He's trying to identify the parts of the fish and says, "Poison, poison, poison, tasty fish." Only later he learns that instead of serving Homer the tasty part, he served him poison. And Homer thinks he has twenty-four hours to live.

Okay, maybe that will be a trivia question during Eighties week.

Or Nineties. The Simpsons *has been on a long time.* I stood. Well, at least I'd done something to help my dad. Today wasn't a total loss.

I looked back at the church, then in the opposite direction toward town. I could wander over to The Grind, tell Marion my woes. I dusted off my pants. Why the heck not? At least at her place I'd stay out of trouble.

I took a few steps and my left leg started to tingle sending pins and needles up my thigh. I stopped and banged on it to get the blood flowing again.

Kiss up to Star, get on Brady's good side, save Don.

Tingling, paralysis, death.

It all came together so fast in my head that I spun again where I stood and wound up staring at the church.

"Oh my God." *Of course.* I knew what might have killed Guy. Could be killing Don. If I was right, Star and Brady would love me for solving their problems and it might save Don Loomis's life.

Poison, poison, poison, tasty fish.

Chapter Seventeen

By Tuesday afternoon tests had confirmed I was right about the poison fish. Out of the blue, Red called and said she needed to talk to me and Marion, *now*. Something bad was up, I just knew it.

We met at The Grind at two and the place was jammed. Red and I sat at the counter while Marion ran around her place like a border collie herding sheep.

"I don't have a lot of time," Red said as Marion blew by carrying four plates of apelbeignets topped with vanilla bean ice cream.

"Then you talk without me," Marion said over her shoulder as she presented the dessert with a flourish to four blue-haired ladies who oohed and aahed. Mare curtsied, then stuck her head inside the swinging door to the kitchen. "Kaylee! Gentlemen in booth four waiting to order."

She slid behind the counter and grabbed the empty water pitchers to refill. "Okay, talk."

"This information Lonnie helped bring forward," Red said, "about the poison, is going to create some problems in town."

"You sure someone put it in the spread on purpose?" Marion asked over the whoosh of running water. She thrust her wrists under the faucet. "Did it get hot all of a sudden? You guys hot?"

"Tetrodotoxin," Red said "comes from pufferfish or fugu. A Japanese delicacy, but served wrong can kill you."

Marion wiped her cold wrists against her face then grabbed a pitcher. "That's a relief, then. It didn't come from Berend's home-smoked salmon. I recommended they use it." She waggled her eyebrows at me. "That'd be bad for me, wouldn't it?"

I glanced across the diner at Berend Berkoop, sitting at the end table alone with his boiled ham and sauerkraut with caraway mayo on rye sandwich. He ate it here every day. Berend was nearly a hundred years old and nothing seemed to faze him, but knowing he'd accidentally poisoned a man—two men—might.

Especially this kind of poison. I'd looked up tetrodotoxin last night, after I'd called Red and told her what I thought. TTX killed unkindly, by blocking receptors in your nervous system. You get tingly, then paralyzed, starting with your head and hands and feet. The paralysis moves inward, toward the center of your body. You salivate, lose motor control and become violently ill. Just like Guy. Soon your diaphragm is paralyzed too and you can't breathe. Your heart slows. Organs shut down. Sometimes people die within minutes. Sometimes within hours. Sometimes, people who ate only a little and who, like Don, got medical help immediately, survived with the help of a respirator. But that wasn't the worst of it.

"How is Don?" Marion asked, slapping the second pitcher down and filling the third.

"Now that they know what it is," Red said, "the docs feel upbeat."

"I read that if you survive the first twenty-four hours, recovery rates are excellent," I said.

Red nodded. "Did you also read that the poison paralyzes the body but doesn't affect the brain at all?"

Marion turned.

"Even as your body shuts down," Red said, "you remain completely conscious but you can't move. Can't communicate."

I shuddered. That was the worst of it. Trapped in your own body. Alert. Dying.

"Holy Mother Earth," said Marion.

"Because TTX paralyzes even your eye muscles," Red said, "your pupils are nonresponsive. This usually means a brain injury, so docs assume you're unconscious. Everyone goes about their business. You hear everything. Feel everything. But they don't bother to sedate you. Or treat for pain. Because they think you're unconscious."

I thought about Guy's last moments. What had we said? How had we acted? Had we been kind? I couldn't remember.

Red pulled at her forehead. "Some bastard did that to my partner."

I touched her arm. "You'll find out who."

Marion switched off the water. "Be right back." She whirled out again, two full pitchers in each hand, off to refill water glasses.

"I hate this," Red said as we watched her.

"At least business is good," I said.

"For now."

I didn't have time to ask what she meant. Marion came back with a stack of napkins, a tray of cutlery and sticky bands. "Roll." She pulled a knife, fork and spoon, rolled them in a napkin, bound it with the paper band, and put it on an empty tray.

"Here's the thing," Red said, fingering a napkin. "Are you sure we can't talk somewhere else?"

"Not unless you want to help me carry all this stuff to your office," Marion said. "Just let it flow, Deputy. You've got Lon here all tied up in knots."

True. I could just feel that something bad was coming.

"Okay." Red squeezed the napkin. "There were only four

128

people who had unsupervised access to the prep kitchen on Friday. Cousin Donna, Mandy Tibbetts, Lonnie and you."

I dropped the knife and fork I'd been about to wrap. "Hold on. Are we suspects?"

Marion grabbed cutlery and wrapped. "Right. Like we keep cans of poison fish in our kitchens. Order it off the Internet."

"This doesn't upset you?" It upset me. "Why would any of us want to poison the spread?"

"That's why I'm here. To help you think about that. How it looks. Before—"

"Jesus, Red." This was all I needed, getting questioned by the police. "You know better than this."

"Shhh." Red glanced around and I could tell I'd drawn attention. "Look, I'm trying to help. It isn't just me anymore."

Suddenly I knew just being a suspect wasn't the worst of her news. "What do you mean not just you?"

"Wrap," Marion said, pushing cutlery toward me.

"TTX," Red began. "It's one of the most poisonous substances in the world. A tiny amount can contaminate a whole lot of food. Turns out it's one of those items the government keeps an eye on." She paused.

"What do you mean?"

"Regulations," Marion said. "You have to have a license to serve it. To even buy it."

"It only comes into the country via one airport," Red said.

"Legally," Marion said.

"But stuff comes in illegally all the time," I said. "Thanks to real criminals." *Not us.*

"Or by accident." Marion dropped another cutlery wrap on the tray. "That monkfish in Chicago a few years ago that made people sick. Turned out it was really mislabeled pufferfish, with most of the poison cut out."

"But it isn't just regulations." Red leaned forward, lowered her voice. "Because it is so deadly, it's watched as a weapon of terrorism."

I glanced around the restaurant. A few heads tilted our way

but no one looked newly shocked. I didn't think anyone had heard the T-word.

"In Middelburg?" Marion asked. "You've got to be kidding me. Why?"

"The random nature of it all," Red said. "It was put in a spread that could have been served to many people. The targets were random."

"Because no one knew who would win the raffle," I said.

Red nodded. "So it's being looked at as a potential act of— you know. Not my doing. The lab had to report it, by law. The powers that be didn't like the random parts. So."

We waited until I couldn't stand it. "So what?"

"So the Department of Homeland Security has a special unit for this sort of thing. The Domestic Integrity Dine-In Operation."

Marion and I looked at each other. She clutched another knife, fork and spoon. "The what?"

"Domestic Integrity Dine-In Operation. Safety in foodstuffs within the nation's borders."

"Hold on." I tried not to crack up. "Would that be D. I. D. I. O.?" I said each letter separately.

"Yes," said Red. "And if either of you sings 'Old MacDonald,' I'm turning you over to the wolves. To one wolf specifically. Agent Eli Borden."

I wrapped a band around my cutlery. "You're serious, aren't you? About this agent? And us being suspects?"

Red nodded. "I'm here to help you think this through, before Borden questions you."

I didn't like the idea of getting questioned by Homeland Security, even its tiniest branch. Visions of fences and cells and other horrors floated by.

"So, Marion," Red said, "tell me about you and Char setting up that kitchen Friday morning."

Marion wrapped another napkin. "Char and I went over Donna's kitchen specs, made sure the pots and spatulas were the right kind and in the right place and clean." Wrap, drop.

She grabbed more cutlery. "Checked that the appliances were working right both onstage and backstage. Reviewed the stocked ingredients. Everything was perfect."

"So when were you alone?"

Marion dropped her next bundle, started a new one. "Char had a lot to deal with and I certainly know how to check off a supply list, so I told her to go. Maybe fifteen minutes and I was done."

"And you knew there'd be fish on the menu." Red dropped the napkin she'd wadded into a ball and grabbed another.

"Wrap that around some cutlery." Marion pushed the tray toward her. "And yes, I knew there'd be fish."

"It's called Loaves and Fishes Culinary Ministries, for God's sake," I said. "Everyone knew there'd be fish."

"Not that it would be smoked, which would hide the taste of additional raw fish. And not that it would be pureed in a spread, which would allow the poison to go a long way."

Marion dropped a knife and spoon. They clattered onto the tray in the wrong slots. "Wait a moment." She closed her eyes, took a long slow breath, then opened them. "Are you saying I'm the only one who had a chance to poison the spread who actually knew there would be a spread?"

"Unless you told Lonnie."

"Cousin Donna knew," I said. "Mandy Tibbetts knew!"

Red ran her fingers through her curls. "I know. But they just don't seem the most likely suspects here."

"But Marion?" I waved a fork in her direction. "Come on. It might as well be me. I left the fish alone when I tried to stop Star from stealing seats."

"True," Marion said, "but you didn't know you'd have access to the fish in advance. And I doubt you—or anyone else—was carrying pureed pufferfish in your purse Friday. Just in case."

I stared at her. "Come on, there has to be something else!" I couldn't believe that my figuring out what had killed Guy and nearly killed Don had somehow put my best friend under suspicion. Serious suspicion. Federal government kind of suspicion.

"Frankly, I know it's ridiculous. But right now, there's no line pointing to anyone else and until there is, Borden's going to follow this one." She winced at Marion. "Sorry. Thought I should warn you."

"What if Cousin Donna or Mandy did it for the publicity?" They didn't quite believe me, but I was remembering Star's little plan from last spring. "I mean, look at how Donna loved hearing that thieves tried to steal her food. Any publicity is good publicity, right?"

"If you're desperate maybe," Marion said. "But she sells out." She picked up her dropped cutlery, wrapped it slowly. "I don't know what to say."

"Say nothing, especially to this Agent Borden," I said. "No one thinks you did this."

"Borden arrives later today," Red said. "You're tops on the list for interviews. I wanted you both to know."

Marion fingered her smiling sun pendant. "This sucks."

"Yeah, it does," I said.

"I'm trying to help."

I spun on my stool. "Then tell them it's crazy to think Marion did it!"

"It'll give me a new nickname on the soccer team. Terrorist. What do you think? Strike fear into our opponents' hearts?" Marion forced a smile.

"Stop trying to be brave," I said. "Be angry."

"Cooperate," Red said.

"What I probably should do is go home and clean my house." She studied the bustle of the crowded restaurant. "I hate to leave, but maybe I should hang a flag. Put away a few other things." Her house was full of drums, masks, holy texts from world religions, prayer rugs and newsletters from all kinds of activist organizations. I understood her worry—how would that look to an already suspicious federal agent?

"I've got a meeting to get to." Red rose.

I grabbed her arm. "Someone must know something else.

Something!" Thoughts flashed around my head like popcorn. "Maybe Don really was the target!"

"How do you figure?" Red didn't look like she bought it.

"Well, think about it." I hunched forward, driving for the goal. "You want to poison Don Loomis, but don't want it to look like you were after him because for some reason that would identify you as the murderer. But you know that if you poison something at the show it'll get eaten. Someone will get sick or die and the cops will get called. That means Red and Don show up. And just maybe you're lingering around and you suggest to Don that since that lovely salmon spread is just going to go to waste, he might as well take it home and enjoy it!" I took a deep breath. "See? There are other possibilities."

Marion grabbed a knife. "Even I think that's crazy. Maybe, Lonnie, maybe you ought to keep your crazy theories to yourself."

She might has well have driven the knife right through my ribs. "Hey, I was right about the fugu."

"And you might be right about someone trying to kill Don. But it won't take too long for someone to come up with a reason for me to have wanted him dead." She rolled her eyes at Red. "Which I didn't. But you can make up anything if you want to, if all the facts aren't in and people are running around half-cocked."

"This isn't my fault."

Marion dropped the knife. "Lon, you're like a loaded gun without the safety, firing willy-nilly. Your bullet might hit a wall. But it also might hit someone in the heart." She grabbed the tray of wrapped cutlery, surged to her feet and banged through the swinging door into the kitchen.

"The cutlery doesn't go in the kitchen." I pointed to the shelf where Marion kept the wraps ready for setting each empty table. She'd wanted to escape me.

Red squeezed my shoulder. "Don't sweat it. You did the right thing."

"Totally screwed my best friend. Or set it up so others could."

Was I like a loaded gun? A dangerous weapon? Bova Poster had practically accused me of the same thing. "Shit. I gotta do something." I looked at Red. "I have to find out something—anything—to prove Marion isn't the only suspect."

"Don't do it. This is the feds, not just me and Don."

"It's Marion."

Red chewed her cheek. "Well if the feds don't scare you, remember this. Whoever poisoned the spread didn't seem to care too much about whom they killed. You don't want to get in their way."

Chapter Eighteen

I thought about Red's warning as I drove out of town to the Silver Skates Motel. Mandy Tibbetts knew more about Cousin Donna and the whole Loaves and Fishes Culinary Ministries enterprise than anyone. If anyone had any ideas about who might have poisoned that spread, why or how, it was Mandy. And since, as Marion had pointed out, my crazy ideas had gotten her into this mess, I wasn't going to just leave her there alone. *No way*.

I'd get something from Mandy that would open this up, something to hand to this Agent Borden.

Thank God Mandy had been willing to talk. Invited me right over for a chat.

"Thanks for coming," she said as she invited me into the pale pink and blue room. "I really don't want to go out. The press keeps managing to find me." She closed the door and threw the bolt and chain. "You see any reporters in the lobby?"

"No." The thought hadn't even occurred to me. I hoped I wouldn't have to dodge more than phone calls, especially once the feds showed up.

"You mind if I keep ironing?" She directed me to the guest chair in the corner and placed herself between the ironing board and a pile of clothes on the bed.

I told her about the terrorism aspects of the case, about federal agents coming to town.

"Christ." She looked at me wide-eyed. "Sorry. But federal agents? I—we can't afford bad publicity." She pulled a blouse from the tangled pile. "How are we going to straighten this out?"

"That's what I came to talk about. Maybe we can come up with something to help the case along."

"You figured out that weird Japanese fish poison." She zipped the hot iron back and forth, then repositioned the blouse. "Everyone says you're a miraculous amateur detective." Her arm pumped back and forth. "I'm just a business manager. Not sure how I can help."

I looked around the room. Faded print of a watercolor windmill on the wall. Magazines piled on the bedside table. "Have you got any ideas about why someone would want to cause Cousin Donna such bad publicity?"

"Because ruining Donna's life sounded like a good idea?" She walked past me, absently neatened a pile of stuffed manila envelopes on the desk as she passed them, then pulled a wooden hanger from the closet and neatly hung the blouse.

"She have a lot of enemies?"

Mandy crossed back to the ironing board and pulled jeans from the pile. "When you get a certain amount of fame, you have enemies. Stalkers. People who want to be you. People who think you shouldn't be you. It's why so many people change their names to write books, act, direct, whatever. Especially these days."

"And people have threatened Donna?"

Mandy pressed the button for steam and set to work on her denims. She was actually ironing jeans.

"Some. Our security system usually works."

"It was a disaster this time. Not only the poison but people breaking in, assaulting a security guard, attempting to steal prizes."

Mandy lifted the iron, staring as if she had no idea what I meant.

"The women who broke in?" I reminded.

"Oh, right." She adjusted the jeans.

"And Char mentioned that a lot of people got pretty irate about the two-ticket limit. Any threats from that?"

Mandy smiled. "Not serious." She flipped the jeans.

"So, does Donna have any exes? A former husband? Boyfriend? Girlfriend? Anything?"

"No!" Mandy shook her head hard enough to rattle her brain. "No. We're on the road two hundred nights a year. Who has time?"

"You too?"

"Me too."

"No boyfriends or—"

"I don't see how my life matters," she said, lifting the jeans and inspecting them.

Interesting. "Must be hard to stand on the side, or backstage, and watch her get all the glory." I looked around the room again. What was her life, this young attractive woman locked in a hotel room, fleeing the press in order to support a performer who, from what I'd seen, treated her like dirt? No fast-food wrappers, teddy bears or trashy novels anywhere. Just a tangle of laundry on the bed, an empty laptop case on the desk chair and stacks of papers, envelopes and CDs next to the closed laptop on the desk.

"I mean," I continued, "you make it all happen. Running for kosher salt, keeping Donna under control for the public, guarding the preshow kitchen, and organizing security. Seems sort of thankless."

"Yes, well. I'm sure the same could be said about the priesthood. We chose our careers, didn't we?" She walked the jeans over to the closet and clipped them to a pants hanger. This was a woman who liked things smooth, that's for sure. This situation must really be killing her.

"Actually, I've only been in this parish three months. You've done this a long time."

Mandy stared into the closet's shadows. "I was fresh out of college and looking to get into entertainment media. Her show had started to take off with books and tours. It looked like a great way to break into the business."

I sensed the vibration of the unsaid. "But?"

"But nothing." She pulled a white blouse from the pile. "I do what needs to be done."

I wondered what that cost her. "So, what do you think needs to be done now?"

She flapped the blouse and with arm movements of military precision spread it on the ironing board. "Minimize the damage to Cousin Donna and to Loaves and Fishes Culinary Ministries as quickly as possible."

"What about you?"

"What's good for Loaves and Fishes is good for me." Her jaw tightened.

"Donna doesn't treat you too nicely. She that way with everyone?"

Mandy looked at me with newly bleary eyes and half-smiled. "Donna is not the easiest person to be with."

"Why not quit? You're young, seem able to handle a lot. Why not get something else?"

Her eyes shifted to the desk. "Oh, I don't know."

She did know, I could tell from the way she said it. She just didn't want to tell me. Fine. I stood, stretched and moseyed past the desk toward the window. I recognized the pattern of writing even upside down. *Résumés*. She wanted out.

Would bad publicity for Loaves and Fishes somehow help her escape her job? She'd had access to the kitchen, after all.

I watched an eighteen-wheeler blow by on the highway and thought of Red's warning. Was I standing here with Guy's murderer armed with a scalding iron?

"Then why do you stay?" I crossed the room, glancing again

at the résumés—there must have been a half dozen—and leaned against the wall near the door.

"Great experience." Mandy's arm pumped the iron. "Everyone's heard about Cousin Donna Hancock."

Didn't seem wise to tell her that until Loaves and Fishes had come to town, I'd never heard of her. But I had to ask about the résumés. "Just between you and me, are you worried about what would happen if Cousin Donna found out you were job-hunting?"

Mandy glanced at the desk, then at me, then sighed. "I knew I should have hidden it all. It just seemed like so much effort." She tipped the iron up and sat. "I'm tired of hiding it all the time, I guess."

"It is hard work hiding something so important to you."

"Donna has a lot of…" She paused. "Personal peculiarities. Best not to antagonize her." She flipped a finger toward the desk. "That would antagonize her. For sure."

"Would she fire you?"

Mandy smiled. "Fire me? No, good Lord, never fire me." She stood and started ironing again. "She couldn't bear to be alone, even the week or two it would take her to hire someone else. No." She exhaled heavily. "She'd do everything she could, though, to sabotage my efforts. Tell stories about my incompetence. Who knows?" She tipped the iron up. "I don't worry about getting kicked out of Loaves and Fishes. I worry about escaping."

She didn't seem like a murderer. "So all this negative publicity?" I settled back into the guest chair.

"I wanted to be gone months ago. But one thing after another fell through. 'Send us another head shot, Mandy. Sorry, you're not our type, Mandy. Can you get us a longer audition tape, Mandy?'" She sighed. "Now, I'll probably go down with the ship."

"Sorry." I looked at the faded windmill above the headboard. "Are you sure you can't think of anyone who'd benefit from discrediting Donna?"

"No. But, do you think—" Her eyes darted around the room.

"Do you think the family of that man who died, the professor—"

"Guy Rittenga."

"Yes. Do you think they'll sue Loaves and Fishes? Maybe even sue me because I'm in charge of the production?" She pushed to her feet. "I've got this package in with WCJD, a public television station in Tennessee and they're thinking about me this week. A suit would ruin my chances."

"I haven't talked to them," I said.

"Everyone says you got him fired," Mandy said as much to herself as to me. "They didn't sue you, did they?" Fear sparkled in her wide eyes.

"No."

"Maybe it'll be okay then." She picked up a blouse and examined it for wrinkles. "Maybe I should go to the visitation?"

I stood. "I'm going there now."

She looked frightened. "Maybe not. Draw more attention."

"We should keep in touch. Help each other out, okay?"

Mandy nodded. "Anything you can say, you know, to keep them from suing. Don't put any ideas in their heads, but you know. To help me. And I'll help you. Anything I know that's relevant. It's yours." Her eyes shone blue on blue. I didn't get a bad vibe from her, just a trapped one.

But then I wondered about the poisoning and whether it would really harm her chances of getting out of Loaves and Fishes. Would the bad publicity so harm Cousin Donna's revenue that the cooking school guru would have to let Mandy go? Would she be willing to poison someone else just to gamble on that chance?

Chapter Nineteen

The first time I'd visited Van Dykema's Funeral Home, I'd overseen Great Aunt Katherine's send-off into the great beyond. She'd made me swear that I'd keep that casket closed, no matter what my father, her nearest relative, wanted. She predicted I'd have a battle on my hands and she'd been right, as usual. But I was more scared of her than I was of my dad and sisters combined. I knew she'd haunt me forever if she didn't get her way.

The downtown parking lot and streets around the funeral home were packed and as I walked the two blocks from the car, Aunt Kate popped into my head again.

Darned good thing you spent those summers with me, young lady.

I heard her voice so clearly I had to resist turning to look behind me. "Go away," I whispered.

You were a spineless, frightened troublemaker. Hardly blame you, though, the way your parents dropped the ball.

I couldn't argue with her there. They'd dropped the ball on all three of us girls, bickering for years, sending me away, descending into a divorce they didn't really mean.

You needed tough love.

Tomato, tomahto. Her tough love had felt like plain old meanness to me. Unnecessary torture, since Mom and Dad got back together as soon as Annie got sick.

"Gotta focus now, old woman," I whispered to my aunt. "Go away."

Don't be a wimp. Aunt Kate always did have to have the last word.

Everything in the visitation room sounded muffled, as if someone had cupped their hands over my ears. The thick rose carpet, the velveteen wallpaper of carnations and dahlias, the rotund velvet chairs and sofas—all of it deadened sound, an attempt to deaden our abilities to feel anything at all.

People stood in black clusters. Star, Elyse, Mimi and a few other perfectly coiffed women of a certain age stood nearest the coffin, murmuring intently about the Lord only knew what. The perfect location for Star to be sure everyone saw her.

The gaggle of folks from the college milled about in the center of the room. Provost Brenninkmeyer's suit draped his large body with exact tailoring, falling from perfect seams and creases to a precise length over well-polished shoes. He stood out among the others in ill-pressed coats, unmatched trousers and comfortable well-worn shoes. Pia Hakksen wore a smart blazer and trousers with modest gold at her ears and neck. Professional, sure, but she didn't seem to fit.

Maris Rittenga stood among them, her head tilted toward the Provost who gripped her arm as he spoke. Her eyes bore the empty look of the recently traumatized. She needed rescuing.

"—in any way we can," the Provost finished as I stepped up beside Maris. Everyone's eyes shifted to me.

"Hello." I nodded at the group. "Maris." I tried to find her eyes with mine, to send her the nonverbal message that I would extricate her if she wanted me to. I couldn't imagine that today, as she stood in a room with her husband in a coffin, she wanted to talk to the bastards who had forced him to retire. "How are you holding up?"

"Fine." She reentered her eyes a little.

"Such support from the community," the provost said. "It's really wonderful."

Where the hell were you all when he was alive? I wanted to ask. I looked at Pia, who dropped her very blue eyes.

"Well, Reverend Squires," the provost said, then waited.

I stood through a few seconds of silence.

"It was nice to see you," he said, his thin smile saying otherwise.

He was dismissing me! Like I was the one who shouldn't be talking to Maris. I felt energy surge through my limbs. I took a deep breath and planted, like I was defending an open goal in a one-on-one.

Everyone else shifted and Pia's eyes shot back and forth between us.

Brenninkmeyer smiled as if to apologize for my cluelessness. "I—uh—understand you are the one who figured out the true cause of—uh—" He glanced at Maris. "Professor Rittenga's passing."

"Yes." I didn't shift or smile.

"So it's you we have to thank for the great brouhaha we'll have to endure in our science building tomorrow morning." The professors' eyes all lifted to the skies, a chorus of sympathetic murmuring.

"The science building?" asked Maris. "Guy didn't work there."

"No, no," Brenninkmeyer explained. "But, for a school our size, our laboratories are some of the finest in the nation. We conduct high-level research, especially in the summers. Naturally our labs have, among the many chemicals used for research, some of this chemical. The chemical that the police now believe is involved."

"Tetrodotoxin," Pia said.

"Yes, that," said the provost. "Thank heavens Ms. Hakksen keeps such excellent records in her role as our Governor of Laboratories. I have every confidence that she can prove quickly and without a doubt that absolutely none of our—uh—chemical was missing."

"Tetrodotoxin," I said just to be a pain.

"TTX for short," Pia said.

"Of course, we will cooperate fully with officers of the federal government." Brenninkmeyer puffed up his already cumbersome chest.

So, the Homeland Security people had arrived. Well, at least they were looking at something besides Marion. That was the best news I'd had all day.

"Our processes ensure maximum safety," he continued. "Essential to quality organizational functioning. Prevent trouble before it starts. Or if it starts, cut it off in the bud."

That explains why they dismissed Guy. He'd started trouble of the liberal and loving kind.

"In education," he went on, spreading his hands expansively as he lectured, "this is a constant challenge. Helping to keep students on the narrow path toward the Christian life."

Normally, this is the point at which I'd flee from a conversation, but I wasn't abandoning Maris. Her vacant look had returned.

"You lead us well in that," said a young sandy-haired man who looked about thirty. Probably wasn't tenured yet and saw a good opportunity to kiss up. "I really appreciate the support you gave to me with those plagiarism cases last spring."

Murmurs of agreement from the others.

"Such a shame," the provost said to me, "the way young people these days are beleaguered by Satan. Cheat, copy, steal. I'm sure you ran into that in your former line of work," he said to me.

"Pre-schoolers rarely cheat. It hasn't occurred to them yet."

"Mmmm," the provost said. "Moral confusion does come with age, I'm afraid. Even good people," and here he glanced at Maris, "can be misled. By someone." He stared at me.

144

"You know," Pia said, "someone told me once that in all the years he taught at Five Points, Guy Rittenga never had a single student plagiarize in his class. Is that true?"

Everyone nodded.

"Legendary," said a man with a frosted beard. "Put the fear of God into them, I guess."

"Or the fear of the provost," said the sandy-haired man.

They all snickered politely.

"I think he just spoke to them honestly about the temptations and the consequences," said the provost with a solemn head shake. "He had such a long and thoughtful career."

Maris gripped me and when I looked, her eyes were full of herself again and she was angry. "Reverend, can you take me to the lounge? I need a moment's rest."

The cluster of academics parted for us and I walked with Maris out of the room into a small sitting room. From the corner of my eye I caught Star and her flock watching us.

Maris folded into a chair. "Is it so very wrong to hate them for what they did to my husband?"

"No." I sat opposite her. "Not today."

She blinked at me, eyes clear and tearless. "Good. You'd think I'd hate the person who poisoned Guy, not the people who shut him out after thirty years of service, but I don't. Not yet." Maris reached to the end table and straightened a vase of silk carnations. "My husband trusted you. When he wanted to give that talk, he talked to you." Pause. "Not even me."

"I didn't tell him to make that speech—"

"I know that. No one could tell him anything. Anyone who thinks you put that idea into his head didn't know my husband very well." She smiled. "You know, he had terminal cancer. He was diagnosed last fall, after it had already metastasized. Refused treatments. Never told me a thing. In a way I figure whoever poisoned him helped him die without suffering. Maybe that's why I can't hate them. But these people—"

I waited.

"He never said so, but I knew they'd forced him out." She

145

clasped and unclasped her hands. "And now, there's something else and you—" She pointed toward me. "You can help me."

I smiled. "I'm not sure I'm the best person to help anyone with anything. Not many people in town are too happy with me right now."

"Oh, I've heard about the soccer team failure," said Maris with a sad smile.

With Marion on the chopping block, that was the least of my worries. "Yes."

"You know, Reverend, everyone repeats the gossip, but not many actually believe it. They just act on it because they think everyone else believes it. It's how this town works. Things might not be as bad as they seem. So, will you help me?"

I sighed. *As if I don't have enough on my plate already, Lord.* "If I can," I said.

"I think the college is doing something dirty with Guy's salary. Normally, he runs the household accounts, but I had a look the other night. To be sure about the cash situation." She swallowed. "Anyhow, Guy's last few paychecks don't match his earlier ones."

"What do you mean?"

"Each one is short. I know the college was supposed to pay him a full salary for a year. But the last three paychecks, the ones Guy hadn't put into the household account yet, were a thousand less. Each." She gripped her hands. "I don't want them to cheat Guy any more, even if he's gone. It's a matter of principle."

Her anger crackled in the air. The provost had boasted of such excellent record-keeping at Five Points, I doubted they had made such a mistake.

Why would they short someone's paycheck on purpose? Was Five Points under budget pressure? Had someone regretted the deal they'd made with Guy? Had someone even gone as far as to eliminate the extra expense?

I felt the creeps as I glanced through the lounge door toward the provost holding court with the faculty. His gray hair gleamed. He projected power and security. What if his position

146

had somehow been threatened? He had TTX on campus. Would he have used it to protect life as he knew it?

"I'm not much of a financial person," I said, "but I'll have a look at it."

We agreed to meet for dinner the next night.

But before we do, I thought, *I need to find out a bit more about what's going on over at that college.* I hoped Pia would be up for a little chat.

Chapter Twenty

After the visitation and several hours making pastoral calls, I went home and walked Linus through the purple evening haze, up and down the long rows of laden blueberry bushes. The thick fruit bowed the branches out and down into wide arcs, but still the plants towered over my head. I could see only leaves and fruit on either side, a long row in front and behind, and the deepening sky overhead. Since the workers had gone for the day, I let Linus run and he headed straight for the neighboring field where a water cannon thuk-thukked. Watching him, I checked my cell. Nothing—not even from Marion. I called her house, but when no one picked up, I let it go. Maybe if she slept on it a night, she'd see none of this was my fault. When Linus returned, glittering silver drops clinging to his coat, I realized the shadows had grown longer than the light. I had to get home.

As we approached the pines in front of the house, my fears

spun out like nunchucks battering my heart.

"Stop it," I said aloud to myself.

Chickenshit, said Aunt Kate's voice, her favorite phrase when I'd balked as a kid.

"Butt out," I said.

Get some guts. You'll never be anything in this world without some guts.

"Drop dead."

She cackled.

After the day I'd had, I didn't need my ninja anxieties or my nasty great aunt taunting me. "You never have anything constructive to offer, so back off."

Lorraine, you need—started my aunt.

"Not you. I never needed you."

But then I took a look around me. I was standing on my porch. I'd walked through the pines without holding my breath, without trying to hear an approaching footstep over the thunking of my swollen heart. Without looking for spots of my own blood on the ground.

Aunt Kate's ghost cackled in the distance as she returned to whatever corner of heaven she now called home, probably to tell her fellow spirits that she'd kicked her great-niece's chickenshit ass once again. I refused to thank her for it.

The whole thing lightened my spirits, though, and I had a great evening on the Internet boning up for my dad's trivia competition—singing hits from the Seventies, remembering the toys and games and candy and television I'd loved as a kid.

Perhaps I did a little too much singing that night because the next morning, as I was trying to put together a list of hymns for the Committee on Music to consider, all I could hear in my head was hits by The Partridge Family. Pieces like "Come, Thou Font of Every Blessing" morphed suddenly into "I'm on My Way Back Home Again." By noon I badly needed a break.

I thought about swinging over to The Grind for lunch, but Marion hadn't called me yet. We almost never went this long without checking in, so I guessed she was still angry. No way was I setting myself up to get scolded again in front of a crowd of Middelburgers. So I wandered downstairs to raid the parish house kitchen.

Ashleigh stood behind the desk, digging her keys out of her purse. "Oh, like hey. You need anything? 'Cause, I'm about to go to lunch, you know, with Tom."

"Not Josh?"

She rolled her eyes. "No. He's nice and all, but still such a boy." She fingered her car fob. "Tom's twenty-six."

I nodded. "Enjoy."

She picked up a stack of envelopes. "Here's your mail. Plus this week's *Middelburg Review*." She pouted. "Not so sure you're gonna like what's in there."

I smiled so she wouldn't see how that worried me. "It'll be fine."

She placed a pink message sheet on top of the stack. "Channel Eight wants an interview for tonight's news. I told them you were visiting a convent."

I laughed and carried the stack with me into the kitchen. Armed with a glass of milk, an apple, a cheese stick and a Three Musketeers bar, I sat down to sort it through. An Almy's catalog full of clergy shirts, robes, communion silver and the like. Umpteen appeals for money. New issue of *Christian Century*. Book catalogs. DVDs marketing Sunday school programs. And on the cover of today's local weekly, Star Hannes smiling bravely out from the color shot in the center of the front page, one hand placed protectively around poor, maligned culinary evangelist Cousin Donna Hancock.

The article cost me my appetite, so I skipped the apple and went straight for the candy bar. It reviewed the case against Marion in an even darker light than what Red had told us yesterday. DIDIO. Agent Elizabeth Borden—a woman it turned out—didn't deny that Marion was under investigation. And Star's quotes, of course, mentioned her concern with safety in local restaurants, slamming Marion indirectly like a soccer ball slamming off someone else's header and breaking your nose.

And, of course, Star mentioned me in connection with Guy four separate times. All of it was true, but it all pointed to untruths. But in this day and age, I didn't think anyone would bother to stop and think that through.

Maybe Ashleigh's idea about the convent wasn't so crazy after all.

After lunch I finished up the hymn work, instructing Ashleigh to take messages from two newspaper reporters, Channel Eight again and Agent Borden of the Domestic Integrity Dine-In Operation branch of Homeland Security. I wasn't talking to anyone until I had more information to give, to spin Star's story in a different direction and get the spotlight off Marion.

When I called Pia and begged, she agreed to talk to me, but only if I could come that afternoon. "Everyone has gone out to celebrate getting cleared by DIDIO. They won't be back until four at least." So just before two o'clock, I drove up the dunes to the virtually empty campus.

I had no trouble finding the science building—large blue signs marked every building on campus. The sprawling two-story stone structure blended beautifully into the surrounding woods. Solar panels lining the walls reflected the trees and sky. A sign on the front door announced the building was LEED certified.

"What's LEED?"

Pia stood in the lobby, looking ready to serve in running shoes, jeans and a baby blue polo shirt embroidered with a Five Points logo. "Leadership in Energy and Environmental Design. It's a national benchmark for green construction." She led me down the main hall, our shoes squeaking on the dull textured floors. "The floors are recycled vinyl," Pia explained. "Wears like iron but squeaks when wet. The guys just mopped in here."

Along the hall, large windows opened into vast rooms lined with aquariums and books. "We have a lot of wonderful things going on up here that people don't know about. These are our freshwater labs," she said. "We receive a great deal of support from associations around the Great Lakes to work on freshwater ecology. Troubles with invasive species like the zebra mussels and gobies. Stewardship of the environment is an important value at Five Points."

I spotted an aquarium that held a white frog the size of a loaf of bread, its eyes golden marbles. I wanted to ask about it, but I had to trot to keep up with my guide as hallways branched to the left and right leading to door after door.

"So, why are you using TTX to study lake water?"

"Great Lakes ecology isn't all we do." We turned a corner, passed a few more doors, then paused while Pia inserted a key card into a slot. "I'm going to show you why the TTX that killed Professor Rittenga could not possibly have come from this campus."

We entered a supply room cramped with cabinets of bottles, envelopes and boxes, all behind locked glass. The door clicked shut behind us. "You need a key card to get in, or out," she said.

I reached back and tried the door. Sure enough, I was locked in.

"There's twenty-four seven video surveillance." She pointed to a camera in the corner near the ceiling. "Each cabinet has its own key." She pointed to a metal box hanging at the end of the row. "And each row has a key box that contains those cabinet keys. The key boxes have different codes that have to be typed in to open them. Plus," she said with a dramatic wave, "the chemicals are measured. So if you take two grams, it's recorded. It's impossible for someone to sneak off with a little extra—it would be caught within a day."

"So, to access a chemical, you need a key card, a box code, and the right key from inside the box?"

Pia nodded. "Only me, the dean and the head of campus security can even access this room. Only the secretary and I have the box codes. And only the department chair knows which key is which because they're not marked."

"Isn't that inconvenient?"

"And anal retentive as hell." Pia used her card to get us back into the hall. "Obsessive. Like wearing pants with a belt and suspenders. It's a huge pain on the days when someone calls in sick. But that's our provost. And when that federal agent walked in here asking about the TTX, everyone was darned glad that the provost has that particular pickle up his butt." She glanced at me. "So to speak."

She started off down the hall and again I had to stretch my legs to keep up. "You sure you don't want to play soccer?" She shook her head.

"So, about the TTX. If you're so big into the environment here—"

"Five Points is very committed. LEED certified buildings like this don't come cheap."

"Really? More than regular buildings?"

"Much more expensive up front. But it pays off in the long run. And good publicity."

"So, the college has lots of money?"

"Donations paid for this."

I didn't even try to track our progress as she showed me through a maze of halls and labs filled with machines I couldn't begin to identify.

"So the college *doesn't* have lots of money?"

Pia paused outside the lab, next to a colorful floor-to-ceiling bulletin board at least ten feet long. "The sciences have plenty of money. We all get grants. It funds our work, our supplies, some of our salaries. I don't pay much attention outside of this division." She rested a hand on the bulletin board. "You asked why we have the TTX on campus. It's for cancer research."

"Seriously? A strong poison like that?"

She showed me how the bulletin board outlined the history of the chemistry department's research on alternative treatments for cancer patients. It had a section on new chemotherapy drugs, new drugs to boost immune systems, new drugs for combating pain.

"Here." Pia tapped a small purple card, just a tiny piece of the huge presentation. "Tetrodotoxin," she read. "Most commonly found naturally in tetraodontiformes, including pufferfish. Also found in some newts, starfish and octopi. Source: a strain of bacteria living in these animals. If ingested, shuts down the nerves by disrupting the sodium-ion channels." She paused. "Well, the gist of it is, it makes nerves not work but doesn't disrupt the brain."

"So I've heard."

"Nerves transmit pain, of course," she said, then read again. "Used in specific ways, TTX is a thousand times more potent than morphine as a pain controller. On TTX people stay alert and don't need ever-increasing doses, unlike morphine. Labs around the world are testing pharmaceutical grade research TTX as a non-addictive, non-consciousness altering painkiller."

"You're doing that kind of work at a college?"

Pia glowed. "Sure. In conjunction with people at other labs, of course. We do some really cool stuff, even if the politics are a little totalitarian."

"But aren't there other places you could work where you, you know, wouldn't be afraid to play on a soccer team? Where life would be easier?"

Pia raised her eyebrows. "Aren't there other Episcopal churches in the world?"

Good question. I'd landed here when I'd been with Jamie who refused to leave the area. But now that she'd left me, I could go anywhere in the country. There were plenty of jobs. So why wasn't I looking?

"I have a feeling," I said, thinking as I talked, "that I'm just supposed to be here. That there's something this place and I have to offer each other."

Pia leaned against the wall. "Me too. Plus, I can do good work here."

"Yeah." We stood like that for a few quiet seconds, until a new idea swirled into my head like clouds on a horizon. "So what if someone's good works included killing Guy?"

We studied each other for a few seconds. Then, I explained what I needed her to do.

Chapter Twenty-One

"Pia Hakksen said she'd find out about any spills." I'd finally gotten Red on the phone as I drove south along the lakeshore to Maris Rittenga's house for dinner. "Or if any of the clinical trials had aberrant results."

"Which might explain how someone smuggled TTX off campus? You think DIDIO didn't think of that?" Red's stress voice—thin and tight. "Plus, now you think someone might have done it out of the goodness of their heart? To help Guy Rittenga?"

"It's possible." It was just after five o'clock, so the sun still hung fairly high in the sky. The beach was still packed, the lines at the hot dog and ice cream carts snaking across the crisp sand. "He was facing a painful terminal illness. The college had booted him after thirty years of strong service. He was legendary among faculty for inspiring students to high moral and intellectual achievement. Maybe someone involved in those pain trials liked him enough to snatch some TTX to help him kill the pain while keeping his mind active."

Red exhaled a long breath. "And what? Guy used it to kill himself? At a cooking show?"

"Accidentally. It's possible."

"Lon, I appreciate your devotion to Marion. I want her cleared too. But Borden is going to want evidence, not theory."

But I wasn't done yet. "Did you know there are several companies that make pharmaceutical grade TTX? Maybe you should contact those companies, track their shipments. Maybe someone around here got some they shouldn't have."

"You think a company would keep track of illegal shipments?"

"Maybe. Didn't some doctor in Florida give research grade botox to his patients, make them all sick? I remember my sister freaking out about it at the time." Cassie had started botoxing her eye wrinkles after she'd had her second kid.

"Okay, I'll pass it on."

"And, hey, have you talked with Mandy Tibbetts yet?" I explained how trapped Mandy felt by Cousin Donna and her search for another job. "Maybe this is her ticket out."

"Jesus, preacher, I can't keep up with you! *Now* you think Mandy might have put TTX in the spread to get a new job?"

I swallowed my frustration. "It makes more sense than Marion doing it."

"Just so you know," Red said, "Borden is doing a decent job. Reinterviewed everyone about the cleanliness of Frontline Church. Talked to every tech guy who helped set up the kitchen, to everyone involved in Donna's trip, to folks up at the college. Looking at the big picture, not just Marion."

"Is Marion clear yet?" Silence. "Then it isn't good enough."

"Well, you tell her that. She tells me you haven't returned her calls."

"I'm busy doing her job. Someone has to after that newspaper this morning."

"Borden couldn't deny Marion is under investigation. She even said they were looking at lots of other things, but you know how it is."

"There has to be something we don't know yet. Some reason someone would want to ruin Cousin Donna's franchise." I swerved to avoid a black squirrel, which darted from among some dune grass into the road.

"We're looking, Lonnie."

"Not hard enough."

"Borden's twenty-four seven. The woman never sleeps." Red sighed again. "She's running me ragged."

"Good investment of our tax dollars, then." I hung up as I pulled onto Plover Way, part of Five Points' faculty ghetto full of Frank Lloyd Wright-style houses. Maris waved at me from her front window and stood on the porch before I got out of my car. Chattering welcomes, she led me into a hall lined with antique photos. A refinished dry sink held a vase of lavender and small sunflowers. The fragrance of cooking triggered my hunger.

"I hope you like stuffed peppers, twice baked potatoes and homemade whole wheat dinner rolls." Maris and I entered a formal dining room, neat as a pin. "Would you like a glass of wine with dinner?"

The food steamed from platters just like my grandmother used to serve, far more than we could eat. Delicate hand-painted buttercups glistened on the china and Irish crystal held our water. The bread pudding with caramel sauce for dessert threatened to put me into a coma, but stout coffee perked me right back up, so I was alert, happy and grateful when Maris spread her financial records on the cleared table.

She scooted a chair next to me and opened her checkbook. "There is probably a simple solution to this," she said. "Once you explain it, I'll feel better." She pointed to several lines in the register, all made in bright blue ink and in the same tight handwriting. "Guy wrote his paycheck amounts in every two weeks. Twenty-seven hundred and forty-nine dollars and seventy-two cents. Except for occasional medical reimbursements." She reached across the table and fingered two envelopes from Five Points College and Seminary. "These are the last two paychecks— one from last Friday, the day he passed, and one from two weeks ago. He didn't keep stubs, but I found this one in his desk from the pay period before that." She handed them to me. "Each is for exactly one thousand dollars less."

"You're sure about the earlier ones?"

She flipped the check register pages. "I've gone back through the last three months—all the same amount since he was, well, since he retired. It was lower before that, but I figured this must be part of the settlement they reached."

"And that was?"

"Two years at full pay and benefits until he reached sixty-five. They weren't happy, but it was the only way he'd agree to their confidentiality agreement. Made him promise never to talk about the school to any media or writers."

"His pay doesn't drop in the summer?"

"No." She tapped the checkbook. "I don't like to accuse people of unethical behavior, even though the college already behaved so badly to Guy." Sadness welled in her eyes. "But Guy had terminal cancer and didn't tell me. You grow old with someone, you know death will come. You hope it's later, but it's coming." Large tears hovered on the edge of her lids. "But a deception like that. Even if the person thought maybe he was sparing you worry, that doesn't justify the deception. It breaks my heart to call my husband deceitful."

"Then don't." I was the last person to judge anyone for keeping personal secrets. In general, I avoided deception because I wasn't good at keeping lies straight. On the other hand, I survived by keeping quiet about my sexuality, by letting people assume things were one way and never telling them otherwise. Though some parts of the Episcopal church were quite open, others were not. And this town! Survival looked better with that little tidbit kept firmly in the closet.

"Maybe he was afraid of telling you that something bad would happen?"

She wiped her eyes quickly. "He did protect me. That's why he kept the accounts." Her voice drifted away.

I looked around. The house and things were nice, but not expensive or up-to-date. "Why'd he keep such a tight watch on money?"

"He was afraid." Her eyes focused somewhere else, someplace else.

"Of?"

"Losing me." Maris tilted her head. "Not that I require money, you understand." She twisted her wedding ring. "But when we were younger, Guy was still in graduate school and there was—I had—a miscarriage."

I realized I'd seen no pictures of young people in the house. "I'm sorry."

"I don't remember all the details but it was complicated. I nearly died. There was a long hospital stay. The bills were insurmountable."

I waited.

"I cared less about the bills, of course, than about learning I'd never have children. But Guy assured me we would be enough, together." A smile wavered. "And he set out to make good on everything we owed. He's watched every penny since."

I glanced over the financial papers. "Is there still a debt?"

"Oh, no." She patted the checkbook. "But old habits die hard, my dear. And I think my husband believed that by controlling money, he controlled my happiness." She paused. "I want you to look at something else, please." She rose. "Follow me."

We wove through the kitchen and a leather-appointed television room to a dark study near the back of the house. It smelled like old books and old tobacco. Papers and files towered precariously in every corner and a light glowed in the corner of a dark computer screen.

"Guy's study," she said, clicking on the silver halogen desk lamp. "I've barely begun to figure out what's in here. But I did find this." She opened a wooden box, exposing a stack of cards and notes. She opened the first one. "Professor Rittenga, so good to hear from you. Thanks for your support and understanding all these years. I'm working now as a surgical nurse and owe it all to you." She read another half dozen or so, all basically the same, from people in various careers. "More secrets," she said. "What did he do for these people? I don't recognize any of the names."

I shrugged. "He had a lot of students from different majors, right?"

"Yes, he taught the required New Testament class. Every student took it junior year."

"Well, over thirty years, he had hundreds of students. These are just a small percentage. It makes sense."

She nodded. "And then, this one." She handed me a business envelope. Inside a slip of paper wrapped around a check, made out to Guy, for twenty dollars. "It arrived Monday. I don't know that person either. Why would he send Guy money?"

I sat in the desk chair and looked at it all. "I have no idea."

She sat on the edge of the desk. "You live with someone all of your adult life and even though you know that you can never fully know anyone, you allow yourself to think you know the core. You believe there are things a person simply isn't capable of. I certainly thought that about Guy. Now, I'm not so sure."

"Maybe," I said, "maybe as some time passes more will become clear. You could contact some of these people."

"Guy only saved the cards. No envelopes. I don't know who they are. Except for the address on that check. And this one."

She pulled another envelope from a file. "It came Friday morning. Open it."

Inside I found a check for seven hundred dollars with *THANKS!!!* scrawled in bold script across the memo line.

Wow. "You know this Bryce Archer? It says he's in Saugatuck." This was an artist's colony tourist town about forty miles south of Middelburg.

"No. But I found this." She pulled a drawer open and fingered through the files, pulling one. "This whole section of the drawer—it's his favorite students. He's here."

I flipped through the file. Papers and worksheets from 1989.

All with excellent grades.

"What do you suppose this money means?"

"I think this is way too much to guess about right now." I put everything back where we found it. "Maris, you've been through a lot in the last few days. In the last few months. I don't think you should let your imagination run away with you just yet." *Mine will do plenty of that for both of us.* I closed the box. "Maybe Guy contacted these favorite students with final encouragements because he knew he was sick. Maybe that's why these cards all showed up."

Maris's face brightened. "That would make sense. Would you call this man who wrote the check? See what he says?"

I promised I would the next day. When I left after eight, I had foil-wrapped leftovers and a grateful widow to warm my heart. I felt good about helping here, but I wished I could do something more for Marion. I tried her cell. She didn't pick up.

Help, help, help, I prayed. And waited. Nothing. Just wind in my open windows.

And then the phone rang. "This is Star Hannes."

I rolled my eyes heavenward. *Not funny.*

"You and I need to speak," she said. "About the case. And Reverend Squires, no one can know."

Chapter Twenty-Two

The next morning, after a night tossing over what Star Hannes could possibly want to tell me, I drove along the lake south of town to Hannes', just four mansions past where my great aunt's old cottage had stood. It was a funny looking stretch of shoreline road. The right side felt stiff with huddled million-dollar mansions and clean-cut landscaping. The left side relaxed with tiny 1930s cottages built in the heyday of the South Shore railroad from Chicago, their lawns blotchy, the bushes and flowers needing a trim. Every mile or so a corner held a tiny market, flower shop or hamburger joint.

I hadn't driven out here more than twice since I'd moved back to town—both times to drop something off for Red at Carson's Garage, a flat-topped whitewashed building with bright red garage doors and an ice cream parlor next door. When I was a kid, I'd bike here from Aunt Kate's for the homemade

Toasted Coconut Tulip Pops—vanilla dipped in dark chocolate and rolled in toasted coconut. No resemblance to a tulip at all, but the tourists liked the name. Carson's always had lines of cars in front, from old Jaguar roadsters to newer station wagons and minivans. Since Red's father had died, her brother, Baxter, had run the place, with Red helping out on weekends.

Another half mile and I passed Aunt Kate's old property. The cottage with its crankcase windows and expansive wraparound deck had been bulldozed years ago. The dune grass and the bank of eight-foot rhododendrons I'd planted and the brick walk I'd laid—all of it scooped away and replaced by a manicured lawn of unaltered green and a meringue yellow three-story house. I didn't know who lived here or, if like most of their neighbors, they only visited occasional weekends in the summer. No one considered these new property owners part of Middelburg, including them. When they did visit, they drove south to Holland or north to Grand Haven for shopping and dining. Marion's Windmill Grind didn't suit the summer folks' taste.

I turned between two flagstone pillars topped with concrete lions into Hannes' turn-around drive. Pink and white impatiens stood in orderly rows like willing soldiers and bushy fuchsias spilled from chair-sized concrete planters.

My old Honda looked bedraggled next to all this intricate perfection, so I patted its roof and left it in a shady spot underneath a tulip tree. The doorbell bonged like Big Ben and I took a few deep breaths to ready myself for Star's secret huddle.

The heavy door opened and Star glared down at me, her orange fingernails glowing against the dark wood. Behind her, shadow yawned.

"Reverend Squires?" she asked, much too loudly. "What are you doing here?"

"I—"

"Shut up," she whispered, then stepped onto the porch and slammed the door. Her Clementine-colored suit clashed so badly with the pink and white floral palette of the yard, I blinked. "No one can know I called you." She fiddled with the ever-present string of pearls that lay on the top of her breastbone. "I pray I won't regret this." She swallowed. "I have information about Cousin Donna that might be pertinent to the investigation into the poisoning."

"Then why not take it to DIDIO?" Getting publicity as the one who helped solve the case would be more Star's style.

She twisted her pearls again. I'd never seen her this nervous. "They are capable, of course, but lack discretion."

I began to understand—she needed me for something. *Well, hot damn.*

"Does this information implicate Marion?" If it did, I didn't want to hear about it.

"In fact, no." She looked almost disappointed.

"And what do you want me to do?"

"Handle it. Keep me out of it. *Unless*, of course, there is positive publicity to be gained. In which case, you'll step back and I'll take full credit."

A breeze ruffled my hair. "And why would I do that? In fact, why wouldn't I just go to the police right now and tell them you have something you're hiding?"

Star curled her thin-lipped attempt at a smile. "To help your friend, Marion. To get your soccer team up and running. To help things go more smoothly in town for your congregation."

These were some big carrots she was dangling and she knew it. Whatever she had, it must be big.

I took a deep breath. "I want you to praise my church publicly for wrestling with important and controversial issues." I stepped back up onto the porch. "For having the courage to engage such matters, instead of closing them off."

Star's jaw tightened until her lips disappeared. "Agreed."

"Okay, then, I'm in." I narrowed my eyes at her. "But so help me, if you miss the ball on this, I will tell everyone everything about who you are and how you operate."

Star licked her lips and pulled a folded three-by-five card from her blazer pocket. "To be clear, I remain convinced that Donna is innocent of any wrongdoing. That is why I continue to offer her hospitality in my home. I would, of course, never welcome her if I suspected her of—"

"Murder?"

"Anything untoward." She thrust the card at me. "I found it in Donna's apron while doing her laundry. And yes," she said when I raised my eyebrows, "I do laundry for my guests as need arises."

I opened the card and immediately recognized the fluid blue pen and tight writing.

Friday—I will meet you thirty minutes after the show. Guy Rittenga.

I kept my face still. "And why don't you just turn this over to the police?"

She rolled her eyes, unable to contain her disdain for my stupidity. "If you'd think for even a few seconds, the delicacy of the situation would become obvious." She touched index finger to index finger. "The woman is a guest in my house. The rules of hospitality forbid betraying a guest in one's house." She touched the next finger. "I could ask Donna about it, but she claims not have known Guy. This proves she's a liar, so why would I bother asking her?" She touched another finger. "And there's poor Elyse." Star's eyes softened, the picture of dramatic compassion. "Imagine how the town would feel to learn she'd invited her old friend here and the friend turned out to be—how can I put this— inappropriately involved with a member of the community? Not to mention the further strain this would put on poor Maris."

I saw through that. "More importantly, by implicating Elyse Orion's high school BFF in an affair, you'd wind up on the bad side of Middelburg's billionaire family."

"I could have simply thrown it away," Star said, her tone strained. "But of course, I didn't. I mean, a death has occurred."

"I'd have thought you'd just plant it somewhere for someone else to find and deal with." The light that passed through her eyes told me she *had* thought of it. "Ah, but then, if something important came of it, you wouldn't get any credit." I nodded slowly as I realized how completely she'd thought this through.

You couldn't fault Star for lack of planning. "I'm your only hope."

"It's a mutually beneficial agreement."

I considered the note. "I want to talk to Donna about this. Now. Before I go to the police. Because, as you said, this is the last thing Maris needs to have hitting the gossip chain."

Star gripped the brass doorknob. "Tell her you found it somewhere. That's why you're here. I've done my best to keep you out, but you've convinced me it's urgent."

"You want me to lie."

"I want you to work toward a bigger truth. With the least collateral damage. Surely you understand that."

The shock as I realized Star and I had more in common than I liked to admit didn't please me. But I had my church, my soccer team and Marion on my mind. I nodded.

Star pushed open the door. "Welcome to my home."

Chapter Twenty-Three

I stepped through the massive doorway straight into a Michigan version of *Gone With The Wind*. Sprawling central staircase. Thick, dark oil paintings of flowers, fruits and vegetables hung in heavy gold frames. Dark wood floors topped with thick ornate rugs. It felt like what someone thought an important lawyer's house ought to look like.

The vast kitchen felt entirely different. Two of its walls were glass, coming to a point like the bow of a boat pointed directly toward the cloudless sky floating above Lake Michigan. A dining deck led to a set of stairs, which followed the grassy bluff down nearly a hundred feet to an empty white beach. Sunlight glittered off the black-and-gold-flecked granite counters and hanging copper pots. Water boiled in two vast Dutch ovens on the stove. A wire basket hung in the window over the sink with onions and garlic and other assorted twisted roots.

Double, double toil and trouble.

On the deck, Cousin Donna sunned herself in cuffed khaki shorts and a white blouse tied at her belly button. Her enormous white plastic sunglasses and floppy grass hat tipped toward the latest issue of *Oprah*. For a second I thought Aunt Kate had returned from the dead, but then I remembered her floppy hats had always been purple. And she never wore a blouse with the cleavage open to her belly button. The thought made me shudder.

"Reverend Squires insists on seeing you," Star told her.

Annoyance flared across Donna's face as she set the magazine aside, but her voice was all homey welcome. "Well, then, let's set her to work. Time to pit those cherries for the jam I need for Friday's show. Three pairs of hands will do better than two!"

Soon we all sat at the patio table with pitters and bowls of cherries. "Life is a bowl of cherries," Donna said, holding a blood red bulb between her fingers, "and this is a sure sign of God's grace." Then she put it in the pitter and stabbed its stone from the middle.

I shivered and looked at my own pitter. I'd never used one before.

"Pits here," Donna said tapping one bowl. "Fruit there. Sort of like separating the sheep from the goats." She laughed. "Speaking of sorting. I hope you've come to tell me the situation with my Sunny Spirit Salmon Spread and Tasty Toast Points is getting sorted out. Those recipes are pillars of Loaves and Fishes Culinary Ministries."

"Almost no one blames you for Guy's death," I said, slipping a cherry into the pitter, "since I figured out the spread was poisoned." Couldn't hurt to remind her she owed me.

Donna's cool façade crumbled. "Almost no one? Who then?"

"No one of any importance," Star said.

Donna's pitter hit the glass table with a clatter. "Will the world never stop persecuting innocent Christians?"

That seemed like a fine cue. I pulled the three-by-five card from my khakis' pocket and laid it face up in front of her. "Can you tell me why Guy Rittenga wanted to see you after Friday night's show?"

"I told you I didn't know him." Donna's faced twisted until she saw the card. Then something else filled her eyes. Fear? She bit her lip then picked up her pitter and settled back to work. "I choose not to discuss it." Red cherry juice ran down her fingers.

"If you don't discuss it with me," I said. "I'll turn it over to the federal agents."

Donna kept pitting, tight-lipped.

"Agent Borden will wonder why you didn't mention it." I shook my head and dropped a pit into the appropriate bowl. "Won't look good."

Donna pinged another pit into the bowl. "I did nothing wrong. I certainly didn't kill that man! Why is everyone being so mean to me?"

"Tell me how you knew Guy Rittenga."

Ping. Ping. Ping.

Finally, Donna sighed. "He was my professor at Rock of the Ages Bible College in Texas. A long time ago. We'd kept in touch. I was one of his favorite students."

The ping I heard then wasn't a cherry pit hitting the bowl but an *aha!* going off in my head. Was Donna Hancock in the file of "favorite students" Maris had found?

Star picked up a cherry and held it toward the light like a diamond. "I was never anyone's favorite student." She put the cherry into the pitter and plunged the handle, pushing pit and sprays of juice out the other end.

No wonder.

"Did he have a lot of female favorite students over the years?" I asked.

Donna's nose tilted upward. "I am a good Christian woman!" she huffed. "He's a married man! I would never!" Red patches blotted her neck. "Loaves and Fishes Culinary Ministries spread the good word of great food for families nourished by Christ. I would not destroy marriages!"

I repressed the urge to roll my eyes up into my head. "That doesn't answer my question."

"I have no idea about how many females he interacted with. But the man was my professor, at least fifteen years my senior." She screwed up her face as if she'd eaten a wormy cherry. "He was *old*!"

"Then why did he want to see you?" I asked. When Donna glanced back to her work, I tried again. "If you tell the truth and it has nothing to do with Guy's death, no one will mention it beyond this table. Right, Star?"

Thank heavens the woman nodded and didn't give me any trouble.

"Were you having an affair with him?" I asked again.

Donna glared at me for a second. "How desperate do you think I am?"

"You spend a lot of nights on the road, alone," I said gently.

Donna dropped her pitter and shoved back from the table. "Good gracious, Reverend. Look at me." She stood, posed with hand on hip. "Do you think that some dry old professor is the best this body can do?" She leaned forward on straight arms, her lips curled upward at the corners. "I can get much better. Can and do. Right here in your righteous little no stoplight town."

She must've heard Star's intake of breath as clearly as I did because she cocked an eyebrow. "Young men, muscles rippling, sweaty. Eager to learn a few things from a wily cougar." Her eyes glinted. "It's the same in all these conservative towns. The girls tease them with bare bellies and tattoos and giggles, but when it comes right down to it, they wave the virginity flag. Well, healthy young men don't put up with that for long." She licked her lips.

"But you—you said you supported families." Star sounded like she'd swallowed a cherry down the wrong pipe.

"Which is why I would never, ever, sleep with a married man." Donna sat again. "That would be wicked."

Silence pounded around us, the leaves shaking in the breeze. Donna pitted her next three cherries with verve. Star looked like she might vomit.

"Don't look so surprised," Donna said. "Why do you think it is always so easy to find beefy boys to work security for a weekend cooking show? Not to mention two weekends."

The faces of the six boys who'd worked Donna's shows bubbled into my mind's eye. Char would die if she knew.

"You mean, since you got here last Friday?" Star said. "Our own boys?"

"I've slept with several lovely young men, yes." Donna smiled. "My reputation precedes me, thanks to the Internet. They even have contests, like young gladiators. And being with them helps calm my nerves before and after a show. The pressure is terrific, having so many people expect so much of you." She shot me a sour scowl. "None of them is a dried up old professor. So there!"

Ping!

"Where did you—" Star had gone green around the gills.

Donna giggled. "My trailer, of course. You know, when I first heard about that poor boy with the broken nose, I thought there'd been a fight about me. It *has* happened."

"His name is Paul," I said.

"He was the sweet one," Donna said. "He—"

"How many?" Star asked.

"How young?" I asked.

"I am not a deviant," Donna said. "Always over eighteen. And really, not that many. Since that cop got sick and the police and reporters have been everywhere, it's been difficult to—"

"How many!" Star roared.

"Counting Paul, just four."

Ping!

"Four." I'd never seen Star Hannes as completely hornswoggled as now. I wished I had a camera.

"So you see," Donna continued, "there is absolutely no reason for me to have ever engaged in sexual relations with some old professor."

"Okay. So what did he want?" I asked.

She shrugged. "Now that he's dead, we'll never know. Maybe an autograph?" She batted her eyes just a little too demurely for me. She knew something else.

I set my pitter down. "I think maybe the police should decide how to handle this."

Donna shrugged again. "Fine. Only, of course, I'll have to tell them about my lovers, just like I did you, in order to prove there was nothing between the professor and me. Names and all."

Star kicked me under the table then shot me a look that said *no way*. I thought about the photo of her with Donna on the front page of the *Middelburg Review*. If this came out, she'd be in the spotlight all right, for housing and defending a sex addict. The thought appealed to me.

"In fact, if you'd rather find the poisoner than persecute me, go talk to Mandy Tibbetts. She's been acting odd. Forgetful. Never where she says she'll be. Maybe she's having an affair with Guy? She'd be the desperate kind."

Mandy's behavior sounded like her secret job-hunting. Still, I did want to talk to her again. Why hadn't she told me about Donna's sexual behaviors?

"Or," Donna continued, "you ask that woman who owns that unfortunate Grind place."

Ping.

"Her name is Marion Freeley," I said.

"I hear she'd been threatening me for weeks before I arrived. Jealous." She smiled. "Happens all the time."

Ping.

Donna looked as satisfied as I'd seen her. And Star? Star looked like a fish on the bottom of a boat, wide-eyed and gulping for air.

Chapter Twenty-Four

As I sped away from Star's house, I dialed Mandy Tibbetts. She must've guessed what I found out because she didn't balk at my demand that we talk, only requesting that we meet somewhere away from any and all reporters. We agreed to meet at the Hickory Trailhead in twenty. I hated the vision of those four goofy college boys having sex with Cousin Donna, but it proved that lots of people had reason to ruin her.

On my way, I kept praying *Thank you!* over and over. If she had sexual trysts in every town, then there could be dozens of mothers, sisters, girlfriends or rivals who wanted revenge. Or maybe a former partner had gotten too attached.

This would surely divert attention from Marion and I couldn't wait to tell her, but when I called The Grind, Kaylee told me she wasn't there. "After the newspaper, you know, she figured she'd better stay away so people will eat here. It's still slow though." I called the Freeley house but the machine picked up. "Marion, I'm onto something but I can't do it alone. I need my Stopper. We can seal this thing if you help me."

Nothing. She must really hate me.

Help.

Next, I called Maris Rittenga and asked her to check the favorite students file for Donna Hancock. She didn't think her husband knew the cook. "But then, it would be one more important thing he never bothered to mention."

When I pulled into the park's gravel lot, dust billowed around the broad white blooms of Queen Anne's lace and the blue chicory flowers. I wished for Marion. I'd feel a lot better with a second brain watching and thinking.

Mandy's eyes darted behind her hair fluttering in the breeze. "I'm almost afraid to ask."

"Let's walk." As we entered the cool shade of the oak and beech woods, I recapped what Donna had told Star and me. I expected some sort of surprise or denial, but Mandy just sighed.

"How many people has she told?" Mandy asked.

"As far as I know, just me and Star."

"Is the councilwoman likely to go public with it?"

"She's not likely to associate herself with someone who's been sleeping around with Christian college boys. Assuming it's true that Donna only sleeps with young single men?"

"Yes." Mandy ducked to avoid a low sassafras branch. "She says it's just like teaching young women to cook. The skills they learn now will help them make a successful marriage in the future."

I hopped over a fallen tree that had come down in the early June storms. "People can always find ways to justify an addiction."

"My job is to keep her performing," said Mandy. "And since there is nothing illegal about her affairs, I haven't tried to reform her. I just recruit the security teams."

Here was a twist: Mandy procured Cousin Donna's men and knew it.

"Everyone must've gotten a surprise when Char showed up with a women's soccer team," I said.

Mandy smiled. "That had never happened before. I tell local organizers they need plenty of able-bodied young men. You all were the first to bring a bunch of pumped-up women."

My former soccer team strikes again.

We crested a hill and paused. Mandy puffed beside me. Below us the forest spread in each direction, the dark browns and grays of trunks and roots and dirt dappled with golden sunlight.

"So, with men in all these places," I said, "you ever run into any trouble?"

"Trouble?" She pulled strands of hair from her eyes.

"Like with the young men's girlfriends?" I asked. "Or their mothers? Maybe a guy who wants more of a relationship?" We headed down the hill, circling around toward the trailhead.

"Why would there be trouble?" Mandy asked.

My inner smart-ass came roaring out. "Oh, I don't know." I shrugged. "Christian cooking guru sleeping with young men all over the country. Their families and girlfriends high on jealousy? Betrayal? Outrage? A lot of people with emotional ammunition to try to ruin Donna's reputation?"

"No," Mandy said. "No trouble."

"What about those women who broke in Friday night? We assumed they were wacky fans, but maybe they came to poison something. Found the salmon spread. Then pretended to be fans stealing food." The idea fired me up. "The cops must still have their names. They could question them."

"Wait." Mandy stopped and rubbed her face. "They didn't do it."

Crap. I felt an important revelation coming. "You know this because?" I asked.

"I hired them. To pretend to steal food." She closed her eyes. "They're actresses from Chicago."

The breeze picked up, causing the trees above us to crackle and weave. Light and shadow danced across our faces.

"Why?" I asked.

"Donna can't know," Mandy said. "She's been so depressed lately. Demanding more of me and my time. And with me trying to get out. I thought I could soothe her ego this way. If fans actually broke in to steal food, she'd have a high that would last for weeks."

"Wow."

"You saw her in the security briefing," Mandy said. "She was ecstatic. And she's been off my case since."

"You're going to have to tell the federal agent," I said.

Mandy nodded. "You think they'll tell Donna?"

"Well, it does show how much you try to help her."

"Well, if I'm going to talk to the feds, there's something else." Mandy looked back and forth between the treetops and me. "Tell me what to do. I don't want to hurt anybody, especially the kid. But I'm afraid of how it will come out."

For a minute I thought she'd slept with one of them too.

Mandy tipped her head back and stared at the canopy of leaves. "I had to Fed Ex a package. It couldn't wait."

One of her résumés. "Did you leave the kitchen unattended?" If she had, it changed everything.

"Of course not. I grabbed that boy, Paul. He told me where to go in Holland for a Fed Ex drop. And then he said he'd take my place in the prep kitchen until I got back."

So someone else had been left alone in the kitchen, someone other than me and Marion.

Mandy looked at me. "Should I tell? They're coming down so hard on anyone who spent time alone with the prep food."

"Mostly Marion," I said.

"No one knows he was there except him and me. I asked him to keep it secret because I didn't want Donna asking questions about where I went."

"And now he probably doesn't want any more attention, especially after the broken nose," I said.

"Don't tell," said Mandy. "What are the odds the kid had anything to do with it? I mean, he didn't even know he'd have time alone with the food, so unless he just carries poison on him all the time, it makes no sense. No need to involve an innocent kid."

Or maybe not so innocent. Paul was the one boy Donna had named, said she'd "entertained" before the show. Maybe he'd left the kitchen unguarded to hook up with her.

Time for another talk with that kid.

Unfortunately, I had to spend some solid time at church finalizing things for the parish program year. I had committee meetings all afternoon and evening and a zillion details to clear up with Ashleigh. I'd never get out there tonight.

But I did manage one last thing. Between returning messages from possible Sunday school teachers and helping service men puzzle out the ancient air-conditioning system, I called Bryce Archer, the Saugatuck man who had sent a seven hundred dollar check to Guy Rittenga on the day he died. He answered the phone at Archer's Arts cheerfully, but as soon as I explained who I was and why I'd called he went all monosyllabic on me. Only a grunt when I asked if he'd heard about Guy's death. Another grunt when I said Maris had found the check and didn't know what to make of it.

"Would you share with me why you sent a check for seven hundred dollars to Guy Rittenga?" I asked.

"No."

"Does it have to do with outstanding debt? Something that Maris needs to be aware of?"

"No."

I wondered if the threat of the federal agents would make Bryce Archer open up the way it had practically everyone else. "Mr. Archer, I know it's none of my business, but with Professor Rittenga's death ruled a homicide, everything strange is being investigated by a federal agency."

"You're a priest, not a cop."

Multiple syllables! Progress!

"We haven't told anyone about this yet. We want to find out more before we do."

I could hear his breath fold across the phone. Finally, "Can't an alum give money to his alma mater?"

"Good try, but it won't fly. It was a personal check to an old professor."

"Look, that's all I have to say. Tell the wife to cash the check. She can have it. Or tear it up. Whatever. I don't care! Just leave me alone!" And Bryce Archer hung up on me.

Definitely something more to discover there.

But not tonight. I needed to focus on my real job, not getting a soccer team together or clearing Marion, or even trying to make my Committee on Liturgy behave. Just the nuts and bolts of running a great parish. The evening reminded me why I'd become a priest in the first place. The members of the other new parish committees—but not my bickering Committee on Liturgy—came together like champions. We finalized speakers for adult education, drafted program summaries, designed flyers, assigned Sunday school teachers, ordered supplies, worked out a schedule for choir rehearsals. I ordered pizzas and answered questions and delighted in something I hadn't seen much of since I became rector at Woman at the Well—folks pulling together to work hard and challenge themselves. I even asked a few of the women if they'd reconsider joining my soccer team, but the upsurge of good feeling didn't go that far. Yet.

By seven thirty everyone had gone except Ashleigh and the bulletins for Sunday still weren't done. "You mind if I leave?" she asked. "I promise to come back Saturday afternoon and finish up, but I've got this date." She grinned.

"With Tom?"

She blushed. "Third date in two weeks!" She straightened the stringy straps on her top. "I think he likes me."

Watching her bounce out made me feel more middle-aged than my almost thirty-five as I trudged back upstairs to work on my sermon. Linus snored in the corner and I curled into the beat-up chair I usually kept piled with books. The old parish house creaked around me in the wind, but it felt cozy. Safe. I opened the lectionary to find out what biblical texts I had to deal with this Sunday, read them, and promptly fell asleep.

I don't know if it was the reading, preparing for trivia with my dad, thinking about *The Simpsons* or simply not sleeping enough lately, but I had a heck of a dream. In it, the disciples were huddled in a boat, tossed and terrified by a storm. They holler for help and look to the skies for an answer, but see only dark clouds swirling and lightning cracking. Then Jesus, wearing baggy khaki climber shorts, Birkenstocks and a Road Runner T-shirt, his hair pulled back in a ponytail, walks across the choppy waters toward them. The guys are a little unsure if this really is the guy, so Jesus agrees to prove it by having Peter walk on water along with him. So Peter, eyes popping with fear, leaps from the boat and tries running across the water toward Jesus. His legs go so fast they blur. And he doesn't sink. He's just skimming along, hair flapping, running like mad across the water.

In the dream, I was watching all this, wondering, *why don't they cheer? This is amazing!* But instead everyone watches in silence and Peter looks down. Then he looks at me, does a cartoon double-take and looks down again. Then he stops and looks at me in a panic. He holds up a sign that reads *Uh oh!* And slowly starts to sink. I hear a whistling from above and look up to see a cartoon anvil falling from the sky, surely going to hit the poor fellow on the head.

I snapped awake as Linus stood and shook, jangling his tags. No water here, just wind and a creaky house. As Linus settled, I let the crazy dream replay in my head. What a wacky mixture of this week's gospel story and a Loony Tunes cartoon!

It had never occurred to me before how much Peter in this story acts like Wile E. Coyote. He chases the Road Runner right off a cliff, but keeps running full tilt across the open air, no problem. Until he looks down and realizes that he shouldn't be doing what he's doing. Then he falls. Miracles in both cases overshadowed by doubt. Peter and the coyote both get what they believe, that walking on water or air simply isn't possible, even when they are doing it at the very moment they believe it can't be done.

There was a good idea there somewhere, I thought, as I

snuggled deeper into the chair. Something about doing the impossible. Having faith. Not letting common wisdom drag you down. Maybe if I napped on it a little more my dreams would make it all clearer.

Maybe. Except I didn't nap this time. I fell deeply asleep. Next thing I knew it was two in the morning, Linus had to pee, and I had a whomping crick in my neck. I decided not to go home though and after a quick trip outside, settled us both into the lounge for the night.

I spent Friday morning—my day off—getting us back to the cottage, exercising at the beach and cleaning up the house a bit. I emptied the box of Cap'n Crunch in my second bowl and realized I hadn't grocery shopped in over a week. I jotted a quick list, crated Linus and headed into town. First on my list of errands, another chat with Paul Geiger.

Chapter Twenty-Five

Evidently college boys sleep very late. Jeff opened the door clad only in holey sweatpants, his red hair like windblown dune grass, even though it was after eleven.

"Hey, Reverend." He pushed his glasses up his nose and scratched his head in an attempt to smooth his hair.

"Paul around?"

He rubbed his fiery cheek stubble. "Maybe." He pushed the screen door half open, then stopped. "Uh, nothing personal, Rev, but maybe stay on the porch, huh? I don't know who's dressed yet."

I backed up. "I'll be right here, thanks." I sat on the old couch and the smells of wet dog and mold curled around me. Paul hadn't been too happy when I'd talked to him here before and I'd been sure he was hiding something. Maybe this thing with Donna was it. Especially if three other guys who lived in this house had also slept with her.

"You wanted me?" Paul padded barefoot onto the porch, his long tan legs coated in blond fuzz descending from baggy athletic shorts, and wearing a too-tight T-shirt advertising Christ the Lord's Own Sainted Elect Reformed Seventh Church's Walk Against AIDS in Africa. His biceps strained the sleeves and his choker twisted in the shirt's collar. He hadn't been awake or dressed for long.

I didn't stand. "Sorry to bug you. It's important."

"Told you I didn't take that fish spread."

I nodded. "Yes, you've been very honest answering my questions."

"Rev Lon!" Josh banged the door open. His blond hair jabbed every which way from underneath his ever-present ball hat. "Jeff said you were here." He offered his hand and I shook it. "You seen Mrs. Freeley lately?"

"No, Josh. We've been swamped."

"Well, it totally sucks at The Grind. All the churches in town cancelled their communion bread orders." He heaved himself up to balance on the porch railing, big feet dangling.

"Not all the churches," I said.

"Oh, yes." He tilted his head like a professor. "Yours too. Got a call yesterday late. Whoever it was said she'd make the bread herself."

It took every bit of self-control I had, and lately it wasn't much, not to leave right then, hunt down Bova Poster, and punch her in the nose.

"Tell you what. Just ignore that," I said. "I will look forward to seeing you Sunday morning as usual. If it's worth it to deliver loaves to just one church?"

Josh shrugged. "Mrs. Freeley will bake it. And I can use every hour. It's been slow. Thank God Mrs. Maarten's paying us to work security this weekend."

"Dude, you work more than any of us," Paul said, then turned to me. "Don't know what he spends it on. Hasn't got a girl. Mom sends him food."

182

"Saving for business school," Josh said. "You want to earn the big bucks, you got to lay it out for business school. And that isn't cheap."

We looked at each other for a beat before I said, "Josh, would you excuse us? I need to speak with Paul privately."

"I got nothing to say," Paul said. "I already told that Borden lady everything."

"All of us did," Josh added.

Evidently, I was the only person in town who had successfully avoided Agent Borden. "Well," I said, still playing it casual, "I'd bet you didn't tell her about this. Because she doesn't know about it. Yet."

I hoped I'd said enough so that Paul would tell his housemate to disappear. Instead, the two guys looked at each other and Josh shrugged. Paul turned to me. "That Mandy person told you she left for nearly an hour and put me in charge of the kitchen, didn't she?"

"That's part of it."

"So what?" Paul had that checked-out stare on again, looking past me into the depths of the couch's nubby upholstery.

"Cousin Donna also mentioned some other details." I paused, gave him a last chance to stop me. *If you don't help me, kid, I can't help you.* He didn't. "She says she asked you to do something with her. I want to review the timing of that."

Paul kept staring into the couch. "I don't understand."

The hell he didn't. "If Agent Borden gets a hold of what Cousin Donna told me about you, she'll take a much closer look at you, your house, your housemates."

Paul's eyes flicked to me and away. "I didn't do anything illegal."

"Geiger," Josh said. "Maybe you'd better—"

Paul shot him a look that clearly said *Shut up!*

"Dude," said Josh. "I don't want them nosing around here more. It'd get all over campus when school started. I'm just getting Ashleigh to pay attention to me. Plus, if this got out, you know." He paused. "Chrissie?"

Paul banged his head against the porch pillar. "This is so fucked up." And he immediately bit his lip and looked at me. "Sorry about the f-bomb."

We were talking about weird sexual antics and he was apologizing for using a swear word. *Give me a break!* "So, guys, what's up?"

"The girls around here are so nice," Josh started. "Nice girlfriends, you know."

"They'll be good mothers and wives and stuff," Paul added.

"But a guy worries about—well, later—and being, you know…" He trailed off.

"Worth some great girl," Paul finished. "Entertaining and all."

I held up my hand. "I don't need you to tell me *why* you did what you did. I just need to know what happened, what time and whether or not that backstage food ever got left unattended."

"No!" they said in unison.

"I lost the toss," Josh said. "So I got stuck with the food."

"The toss?"

They looked at each other. Paul banged his head on the pillar again, then rubbed the end of his still-purple nose with a fist. "Cousin Donna called my cell. She didn't know I was backstage, that Mandy had left, you know? She asked me to come to her RV to help her lift something."

"We knew what she really wanted," Josh said. "We all wondered who she'd call next."

"Well, Maarten didn't really know," Paul said. "He was helping his ma."

"Maybe. But Will and Jeff had already—"

"Stop, stop," I said. "Are you telling me you knew what each other was doing?"

"Sure," said Josh.

"Duh," said Paul. "We'd all talked about it."

"We're friends and want to stay that way," Josh said. "So no harm done."

"We all agreed," Paul said, "a great chance to learn—"

"No one got hurt," said Josh to me.

I realized after a few seconds that I'd been staring at them in complete incomprehension. I swallowed. "So, after Donna called you, you called Josh?"

Paul nodded, rubbed his nose again. "I wasn't going to leave the kitchen unguarded. I'm not a jerk."

"So when I got there," Josh said, "we tossed a coin to see if I could go instead. We didn't think she'd mind. But I lost. So he went and I sat in the backstage kitchen. I figured if Mrs. Maarten found me I'd say he was in the john and I didn't know where Mandy was."

"Did you leave? Even for a few seconds?"

"No, ma'am," Josh said. "If someone had found the place empty there'd have been all sorts of questions and that wouldn't have helped me get my private time with Cousin Donna."

I turned back to Paul "How long were you, uh, gone?"

Paul shrugged. "Half an hour?"

"So let me get this straight," I said. "We had the security briefing, then I watched the kitchen. Then Mandy took over for me, but then she asked you to do it. What time was that?"

Both guys shrugged and I realized for the first time neither wore a watch. God, I wished I'd paid better attention to the time!

"Okay," I continued. "Then Josh took over for you for a half hour, but you came back and took over the kitchen again before Mandy got back, right?" She'd told me she'd run to Fed Ex just after five o'clock for forty-five minutes.

Paul shrugged.

"Since then," I asked, "has Cousin Donna contacted you? Threatened to tell on you?" Both shook their heads. "Have you gotten any inkling of other guys hanging around? Angry girlfriends or anything?"

More shrugs. "Guys wouldn't hang around," Josh said. "It's not like this is about a relationship. It's more like—well, like tutoring."

"You think Ashleigh would agree?" I asked.

"Girls say they don't like a guy who fools around, but they like having a guy who has a little experience," Josh said.

"Can make 'em real happy," Paul said.

As much as I wanted to do a little tutoring of my own on sexual ethics, I decided this wasn't the time. The boys didn't have any information that showed a new opportunity for the salmon to get poisoned. I decided to try another subject.

"You guys both knew Professor Rittenga, right?"

"Everyone has to have him for New Testament, to graduate," Paul said.

"Did you see him at Frontline Church before the show?"

"No," said Paul.

"I didn't even know he was there," Josh added.

The back of my skull buzzed. Something wasn't fitting.

"You gonna tell the cops this stuff?" Paul asked. "We told you the truth."

"If it turns out not to have anything to do with the case, I won't tell."

"What about that Mandy woman?" Paul asked. "She gonna tell?"

"I don't think she'll say anything unless it affects the case." I stood. "Thanks for your honesty. But fair warning. None of that crap tonight at the show, got it? And I'm coming back and we're all having a talk about sexual integrity."

Now neither one of them would look at me. But I'm a priest. I had to say *something*!

I tried not to think too much about the boys and Cousin Donna as I drove back through town toward home. Instead I considered Wile E. Coyote and Peter, and wished I could have a miracle work out this case. And that I'd be wise enough to see it.

Just as I turned away from the lake into town, I noticed a navy Ford sedan behind me. A couple blocks later it was still there. Weird enough as I went through town, but when I turned north toward my cottage and started to drive through nothing but farms and fields, the car followed. It stayed back maybe half a mile, but on these straight flat roads, I could see it clearly.

My knuckles began to turn white and I forced my hands to relax on the wheel. I didn't know the car, so it was probably just a reporter. That made my heart jump—I didn't want anyone paying attention to me or to my life. I checked my watch.

11:23.

I thought about Red's warnings. A reporter might be the best-case scenario. What if the driver was someone who didn't like me asking questions? Who maybe still had a little fugu poison stashed away somewhere?

A mile or so passed and the car didn't turn off. I slowed down and so did it.

Chapter Twenty-Six

I dialed Red but she didn't answer and I threw my phone down with a curse. One thing for sure, I did not want to lead whomever straight to my house in the middle of nowhere. I scanned my mental map of the area. Between where I was now and my cottage lay nothing but the occasional house and field after field of blueberries, separated by oak and red pine windbreaks. The roads ran in a grid, each about a half mile from the other. I could make a few left turns and head back into town—but to where? The church was empty on a Friday. Almost no one was at The Grind. I could go to Colleen's Cuttery, but seriously, what sort of protection were a bunch of hair and nail stylists, even armed with shears? Plus, Linus was home alone and needed me.

Am I being a paranoid idiot?

No, I decided when I looked in my rearview mirror. The car still hovered there.

Let's test it. I turned right and drove past my house. The car followed. Two miles and I turned right. Still there. Another mile, another right. Still following. I made the third turn, heading back the way I'd come and sure enough, the car hung tight.

I loosened my hands again, tried to swallow. Definitely following me. So, where to go?

I debated driving back to the boys' house. They were big and there were a lot of them, after all. But suddenly my dry throat and nervous pulse shifted into something else. A surge of electricity from my gut zapped its way down my arms and legs. *Enough of this crap*, my body said. *You want to take me on?* "Let's go!" I shouted. I was going to find out who this idiot was and what they wanted. Head on! I hit the gas and looked at the sky. "Help, please."

Just ahead, the familiar blue pickup truck stacked with bright yellow plastic cases crossed the road ahead of me, bumping down a dirt ramp and disappearing into the blueberry field. The harvesting crew! Plenty of witnesses to whatever might happen between me and my harassing shadow.

I pulled hard to the right, down the dirt ramp into the field, following the two ruts between the bushes sagging with purple-gray fruit. Branches screed along the car like nails on a chalkboard. I couldn't see anything except straight ahead and the truck had disappeared! It must have turned off somewhere.

I glanced behind. Only empty two-track. Whoever it was hadn't followed me into the field.

My teeth clacked as I hit a hole and the car sunk then rose again with a whine. "Sorry," I told the Honda. I slowed a bit, trying to see to either side for a sign of the truck. Nothing. I checked the mirror again and *damn*!

The sedan had begun to creep down the dirt ramp.

I pressed on the gas and my butt left the seat as I hit another hole. Where in God's name was the truck? Glance behind—car still there. And gaining.

Faster!

Suddenly, an opening in the bushes flashed to my left. I slammed on the brakes and slid in the dirt. I shoved the car into

189

reverse and backed up, spinning more dirt. Ahead stood the truck, men with wide-brimmed hats handing empty plastic pallets down from the truck to the others.

I turned toward them and they froze, no doubt stunned to see my old Civic wagon speeding across the field toward them. They dropped the pallets and stepped back into the bushes. Even I wasn't sure if—at this speed—I could stop before I hit the truck. But the skid stopped a few feet clear and I leapt from the car.

"Hi, uh, hello!" I scanned the faces for one I recognized. There were a lot of crews who worked these fields. "I'm Lonnie. I usually walk with my dog, Linus?" I held a hand out about knee-high. "He's big? And black?"

"You lose your dog?" A young man with a thick Mexican accent stepped forward.

I recognized his soft brown eyes as they crinkled toward his blue hat. "No. I need help."

Just then the blue sedan turned down the row. We watched it pull up, trapping my car between it and the blueberry truck. The man turned and said something to the others. I cursed my laziness in my college Spanish class—I didn't understand anything he said. Still, I felt better as the sedan door opened.

The young man stepped closer to me and I smelled the sun's heat and earth on his clothes and was comforted.

Two enormous high-heeled boots appeared on the ground below the car door, black, topped with flared black slacks. The guys behind me murmured as the driver stood, rising above the door until a tall, broad-shouldered woman of at least my height stood beside the car. She slammed the door and stood facing us. She wore a tailored black suit, fitted to what can only be called voluptuous curves, and owl-like sunglasses. Brilliant blond hair flipped under at the shoulder. Her white blouse flashed against her blazer all the way down her devastatingly deep cleavage, revealing firm curves and a simple gold chain with an aquamarine pendant.

The guys behind me shifted, whispered, but, God love 'em, didn't move.

She took a deep breath that strained her blazer in all the right places, then sighed, running a tongue along her teeth until it ended in a quiet *tsk-tsk-tsk*.

She reached into her jacket pocket and pulled out a stick of gum and started fumbling with the paper wrapper. "You Lorraine Squires?"

The guy in the do rag looked at me and I answered, "Yes."

She folded the gum into her mouth, chewed a second, looking at everyone looking at her. "Here's the thing." She folded up the gum wrapper neatly and tucked it back into her blazer pocket. "In addition to gum, the other thing I've got in this pocket is a badge that says I'm a federal agent."

"You're Borden?" I asked.

She nodded. "I could flash that badge here," she said, pausing to chew, "but if there's anyone in this crew whose papers are maybe not up to snuff, or who knows anyone without papers, or who simply doesn't much trust federal agents, well, then they're going to have a scare that, really, they don't deserve."

I sensed new tension in my friends.

"I have absolutely no interest in harassing anyone," Agent Borden said loudly enough for all to hear. She sucked her front teeth again. "No interest at all. But if you make this an incident, Reverend Squires, something I have to go and file a report on, then I'll need witnesses and, of course, I'll have to take down everyone's information."

Many pairs of deep eyes turned toward me.

"As it is," Borden said, looking at her car, "I'm going to have a hell of a time explaining the scratches on this car."

I stepped up close to her. "Just show me your badge." After all this, I wasn't going to assume she was telling the truth without some sort of proof. But she was, in fact, Elizabeth Borden, agent of Domestic Integrity Dine-In Operations, as the leather covered ID papers proved.

I wasn't thrilled to see her, but at least she wasn't a murderer.

"Understand you live out here," she said. "How about

inviting me over for a glass of lemonade? Maybe some fresh blueberries?"

It took some maneuvering of truck, Honda and blue sedan to get us out of the field, but as I led Agent Borden toward my house, I promised myself I'd bring a picnic for all of the guys as soon as I got the chance.

Linus bounded out of his crate and right up to Agent Borden who stood on the porch waiting to be invited in. She gripped a neat black bag in one hand and patted his head with the fingertips of the other. "Good dog. Go away."

He looked at her with tilted head, then decided to find a place in the yard to pee.

"Do you routinely drive your car into the center of blueberry fields?" Borden asked.

"Only when some stranger is tailing me. You scared me to death!"

She cracked her gum.

I called Linus into the house and invited her to squeeze past me. She really was tall—taller than me by an inch or two. I could look straight into her eyes.

"You live here alone?" Borden's sharp eyes took it all in. They looked green, but it was hard to tell after all that bright sunlight.

"With Linus," I said.

"Is that a yes or a no?" She set her bag down on an end table and opened it.

"Depends whether or not you count dogs." I remembered her perfunctory pat and thought she might not.

She pulled a black leather-cased reporter's notebook and pen from her bag, flipped it open, made a few notes.

"Have you been avoiding me?" she asked, stepping into the kitchen after me.

I stuck my head in the refrigerator and let the cold air brush my face before I emerged with a jug of cold water. "Yes."

She watched me make her a single serving of powdered lemonade. As I stirred, she sat at the kitchen table, crossing her long legs into the middle of the kitchen—they wouldn't fit under the table. She was a classic Amazon, no doubt about it, huge, broad, round, with high cheekbones and a wide forehead and full lips doused with deep red color. She was the sort of woman who walked through a room and left every man—and lesbian—with tongue hanging.

I replaced the jug and grabbed a few fresh blueberries from a bowl and dropped them into her lemonade, along with some ice, and handed her the glass.

Linus slurped enthusiastically from his bowl, soaking his muzzle. The clock on the wall ticked.

"So you're the amateur detective priest who magically came up with the idea that a southeast Asian food delicacy, highly controlled in the United States because, improperly prepared, it contains one of the most lethal toxins known in nature, had somehow miraculously found its way into a spread made of salmon caught locally in Lake Michigan and smoked by an octogenarian and mixed up by an evangelical Christian chef, resulting in the death of a retired religion professor in a miniscule town no one has ever heard of settled by Dutch people and surrounded by hundreds of acres of blueberry fields." She folded her hands primly across her knee.

"I guess so."

"That's a yes," she said. "I didn't think people like you actually existed."

I spread my hands wide. "Ta Da!"

She just cracked her gum.

No sense of humor.

"I could arrest you for refusal to cooperate with my investigation. Making me chase you all over town. Through fields. Forcing a confrontation in which I was outnumbered twenty to one in a remote location."

"Will I get shipped to Guantanamo?"

More cracking as she made a note on her pad.

"I haven't called you," I said, "because—"

"I don't care why," she said. "I only care that you didn't and now my car is scratched. So." She flipped to a new page. "I'd like to know precisely how you claim to have come up with this theory of yours about fugu poisoning. It's a rather spectacular set of coincidences, and I'm not sure I buy it."

Chapter Twenty-Seven

I knew Agent Borden had certainly heard this from Red, but as I talked she wrote down each detail as if it were brand-new to her.

"And this episode of *The Simpsons*," she said, "you'd seen it before?"

"Sure." I shrugged. "On TV. In reruns. That's how I knew the whole thing, even though I only saw part of it at the Freeleys'." I had a bright thought. "So you see, practically anyone could have seen it, gotten the idea to put fugu into the salmon spread. You certainly don't have to be a cook to have thought of that!"

Borden scribbled, then looked at me as she took her first sip of lemonade. She ran her tongue across her teeth and *tsk*ed again. "The fact is that the episode was on in the Freeleys' house the week before the crime."

Oh, for the sake of the Good Lord. "Why not try to hang it on

Mitchell, then? Or maybe Cameron? They watched the video over and over."

She watched me, cracked her gum, made a note.

"Come on! That DVD in their house means nothing."

Borden tipped her head. "It inspired you to correctly theorize what the criminal had done. It certainly could have inspired the criminal's initial plan as well."

"But everyone watches *The Simpsons*," I said.

"Evidently not in Middelburg." Borden took a sip. "In fact, other than the Freeleys, you're the first person I've talked to who admitted to it."

Linus trotted back into the kitchen with squeaky Toad, shiny with wet from his still-dripping muzzle. I could tell he was headed for Borden and I didn't stop him.

The agent watched him approach but didn't draw back or squeal. She just stuck out one short-nailed unadorned finger, placed it on the end of his nose and pushed.

Linus's eyes slid sideways, hardly believing it as she held him there. Eventually, he gave up and brought Toad to me. I threw it into the living room.

"You know they actually have bottles full of TTX up at the college," I said.

"Yes."

Linus walked back in, eyeing Borden sideways but making no move toward her.

I tossed Toad again. "And you know that Rittenga was actually fired by the college, not retired like they stated publicly. Anyone tell you that during your interviews?"

She made a note. "Do you have reason to believe that anyone specific affiliated with the college might have wanted Professor Rittenga dead?"

"He embarrassed the college! Jeopardized their relationship with their donors." I took Toad from Linus. "Agreed to retire and stay quiet only if they paid him out with a two-year package. Have you checked the financial status of the college? Because his recent pay stubs don't match earlier ones and his widow thinks

196

they might have been shorting him."

She sipped again, licked her teeth.

"And what about Donna Hancock?" I asked. "Have you checked for any connection with Guy Rittenga?" If it weren't for my promise to Star I would have told her everything, just to show her up. But then I thought, *Screw it. She should have to work as hard for her information as I have for mine.*

"You didn't answer my question."

I'd lost track of her question, to tell the truth. "Your questions are too narrow!" I pushed away from the counter as I hurled Toad into the living room, where it smacked the wall. "Everything isn't that simple in the world of human beings."

"Isn't it?" She looked at me the way Linus does when I talk long sentences at him, trying to understand, but not getting it. "When it comes down to the bottom line, isn't it exactly that simple? Someone did this. The rest did not. That's what I'm interested in."

I yanked out another chair and smiled as I sat. "Bull crap. You're a game player. That's why you followed me into the field. Otherwise, why not just knock on my door?"

The tiniest tickle of a smile pulled at her lips. "I wanted to see what you'd do."

Okay, maybe she's not so simple after all.

She put her pen down. "I've heard a lot about you from folks I've interviewed. Depending on who I talk to, you're either Satan incarnate come to destroy this God-fearing community with your smoking wings, or you are the only person who can find the true source of evil in this community and root it out so that justice may prevail. I'm leaning toward Satan, personally, since you're the only one who wouldn't return my calls. That's why you caught my interest. I wanted to see what I could learn."

"Well, you scared me so badly I wasn't acting normally."

"I still learned a great deal. You are resourceful. Unconventional. You see the big picture. You're willing to take a step without having to have the whole journey mapped out for you. You believe in the goodness of others."

Pretty impressive, I had to admit.

"I also learned that you're afraid of someone. Afraid enough to risk ruining your car, which, I reason, is not something you can easily replace." When I didn't say anything, she went on. "It wasn't me you ran from. In fact, you stopped running when you knew it was me. So, who was it?"

She shifted, crossed her long legs the other way.

"I don't know," I said.

"Really?"

I nodded. "I've had a bad year."

She ran the tip of her index finger around the rim of the glass, smoothing the beads of condensation that had gathered there. "Because of the attack in the spring? Or something else?"

"Spring," I said, but for some reason, Aunt Kate sprang into my head. "It doesn't make sense, I know. I'll shake it."

"It makes a great deal of sense. Someone tried to kill you right here, in your home, where you should be most safe. If you aren't safe here, where are you safe?"

"Yes!" My hand hit the table. "I am not safe. No one is. But I don't want to go through life afraid."

"Bottom line: can you find peace without the illusion of safety?"

I thought about Peter and Wile E. walking on water and air as long as they had the illusion.

Borden wiped the wet tip of her finger against a coaster. "You may be right about the conclusions you've drawn, but do they do you any good? Do they move you toward your goals? Or do they just make you miserable?"

"But it's true."

"Maybe not. Maybe the truth is that you're completely safe every other day of your life but that one. How can you know?"

I considered her again. "Now you sound like Marion."

"Mrs. Freeley and I are not without our philosophical similarities." She pushed the glass toward me. "Which is why I think we both like you."

Surprise.

She folded her hands on the table. "I know full well you're investigating this situation because your friend is in terrible trouble and it's your fault."

Tears pricked at my eyes and I shifted my gaze to the window.

"But frankly, you're no dummy," Borden continued. "It's impressive to come up with fugu poisoning though there's no known fugu within three hundred miles. Under pressure in the car just now you were resourceful." She licked her teeth. "Driven, smart and resourceful. I'd be kidding myself if I thought there were a chance in hell you were gonna simply walk away from all this just because I've arrived. That's why you haven't returned my calls, right?"

I shrugged.

"So, rather than fight you, I'm going to use you. Blatantly. I've got enough on my hands without battling a priest with a guilty conscience. Plus, this is a closed community. Conservative. Religious. Iconoclastic. Not likely to share the truth with an outsider, period."

"I'm an outsider too," I reminded her.

She laughed. "Not next to me. So here's the deal: I'll let you in on some of what I know—"

"And I'll let you in on some of what I know," I finished.

"I'd prefer it if you'd tell me *all* you know," she said.

"Sorry," I said. "Clergy confidences."

She narrowed her eyes at me. "Don't forget, I could just throw you in jail for obstructing justice."

"Then you'd have even more trouble on your hands." I tossed off a challenging grin.

She thought a second then leaned forward, shadows dropping into her cleavage. "For now, agreed. But don't screw with me, Reverend."

I held up my hands to prove my innocence.

She leaned back. "To prove my good faith, I'll go first. The TTX in the salmon spread was not research grade chemical but directly from fish tissue."

"So it didn't come from the college." *Damn.* I'd liked that possibility.

"Of course, we've inquired into the shipment of fugu into the upper Midwest. So far, nothing except well-tracked shipments to approved restaurants. No hard evidence on Mrs. Freely. Or anyone. And Reverend, here's what concerns me. What if this salmon spread and toast points tainting was our poisoner's test run? What if next he or she slips the TTX into something more people ingest? Hundreds? Maybe thousands?"

I remembered the details of Guy's horrible death and thought suddenly of my sisters. Then, I started talking.

Chapter Twenty-Eight

Relief flooded me as I spilled much of what I knew about the Loaves and Fishes Culinary Ministries and the scene at Frontline Church last week. I hadn't realized until just then what a burden it had been to carry all this on my own. It made me miss Marion more.

Right in the middle of my description of Guy's death, Maris Rittenga called. Turned out Donna Hancock did have a place in Guy's file of favorite students.

"There are thirty-seven," Maris said. "From his whole career."

"All women?" I asked. I hadn't completely given up on the notion that Guy had conducted multiple affairs with students, despite what Donna had said.

"No, men too," Maris said. "More men, I think. I didn't count."

I considered that the presence of two genders didn't mean it wasn't a list of potential extramarital partners. "What would you think if I contacted a few, found out more?"

"Yes, please! They should know about Guy," Maris said. "I can't bear to call everyone." She agreed to e-mail the names to me, then asked what I'd learned about the pay discrepancies. "Nothing yet. I don't know if I can get anyone at Five Points to talk to me about personnel records." But as I said it, Borden grinned and pointed to herself, fluffed full of her federal clout. "But I think I know someone who can."

With Maris's permission, I explained to Borden—who told me to call her Eli—the situation with Guy's pay deposits, the list of students, the checks. But no names. "I don't see how it relates," I started, "but—"

"Loose ends should be tied up." Eli made a note. "I'll have the details on his compensation by tomorrow morning." She studied me. "Then you can think about telling me something you've withheld today."

I ignored that. "Tomorrow's Saturday."

"Won't matter. Trust me."

Maybe working with the feds wouldn't be so bad after all.

I told Eli everything Mandy Tibbetts had told me about Donna's sexual addiction, leaving out what Donna herself had said or what the boys told me. I also told her about Mandy's desire to escape, the hiring of the actresses to pretend to steal food. She kept *tsk-tsking* and taking notes.

"You stationed around here normally?" I asked.

She kept writing. "Why?"

"Don't suppose you want to play on a women's soccer team?"

"It would be fun to play with someone who nearly made the Olympic team." She looked up. "You bet I checked your background. Still, I have to say no. Thankfully, I live nowhere near here."

"It isn't so bad," I said, startling myself with my own defense of Middelburg.

"And you think you're an outsider!" Her laugh showed off perfect white teeth.

Then I had a great idea. "So, you want to learn more about what's really going on around here? Send me in to talk to Star Hannes. I could wear a wire. Ask her anything you liked."

Eli laughed again. "No, no. Reverend Squires. I just want you to continue being who you are. People talk to you. You talk to me." She stood, took her empty glass to the sink. "Eventually, you'll trust me and tell me what you're still hiding."

Like the boys' involvement with Cousin Donna. But I couldn't go there. Not without a better reason.

As soon as she left, I dialed Star's office. A cheery campaign staffer informed me that, sadly, Councilwoman Hannes had gone out to meet her public. I couldn't wrangle a cell number from her, so I hung up and called the house and tried to leave a cryptic message. "Just calling about those soccer players we discussed. Please call me."

Shortly after five o'clock, I ordered fifteen pepperoni pizzas and several two-liter bottles of cola, which I took over to the guys in the blueberry field. They'd brought in the wagon with the big floodlights, so they'd be out there for hours yet, working until well after dark and it was a little way to repay them for not ditching me when I brought a federal agent into their field.

That left me some time to myself, to watch Linus sniff for a spot and to review where things stood. What amazed me about nearly everything in my life right now was how little of it I'd actually started myself.

Guy came to me for feedback on a chapel talk he'd prepared.

Colleen begged me to sub for her on Char's security team.

Star and Elyse hired me to find a missing salmon spread.

Maris asked me to figure out why her husband's finances had suddenly gone wonky.

Star turned over the note from Guy to Donna to me.

And now, Agent Eli Borden, who I wasn't sure I liked, wanted me to help her investigation.

Not to mention that my parents had sucked me into being Dad's phone friend at this weekend's bar trivia tournament.

Really, the only part of this whole mess I'd started myself was the resurrection of the Well's Belles.

Which made me think of Marion. Part of the reason this investigation was such a mess was because I was going it alone. I could no more figure this thing out using just my own sorry brain than I could play forward, midfield, and cover the defense all at the same time. It was time for me to find her and make her talk.

When I called the house, Marion's husband Denny told me he'd come to the same conclusion. "I told her to go to The Grind or get a divorce," he said. "I couldn't take another night of smoking white sage and aura clearing."

"Do you think I should go over there?"

"As she would say, Great Goddess Gaia, yes! When she's not talking to you, her chi gets all twisted or some dang thing. I never know exactly what's going on, but it hasn't been pleasant." He paused. "She misses you, Lonnie."

Not much later, I wandered in to her restaurant. Friday night. Just after six p.m and plenty of seats to be had in The Windmill Grind Kaffe Klatsch and All Dutch All The Time Café. Possibly a sign of the apocalypse. Just an older couple from out of town sitting in the booth in the window, the Zaloumi twins eating pieces of apelbeignets and ice cream across from each other, Kaylee dusting the top shelves of knickknacks behind the bar, and Marion sitting at a back table with a mug of coffee and a giant plate of some flaky something, studying a catalog. I'd never seen Marion in The Grind *sitting*.

Definitely a sign of the end of the world.

When she looked at me, her lids sagged and the exuberance that was Marion didn't shine in her eyes. "I don't really want to talk."

I sat down anyway. "I'm so sorry about all of this."

"Shut up!"

I nearly tipped off my stool. Zen-loving, goddess-worshipping, peace-in-the-moment Marion never spoke like that. So I shut up.

"Goddess help me," Marion said after a silence. "I am completely losing my center. I've tried walking meditation, chanting. I've smudged the whole house three times."

"Denny mentioned that."

"I even took a djembe to the beach to drum. Nothing works. I'm a karmic mess. My aura probably looks like a kid's fingerpainting." She rubbed her face, which had no makeup. I realized she wore no earrings either. I'd never seen her like this in public before, though given the scant crowd, this was hardly public.

"You need to do something to shake that stuff loose. And frankly, I need your help."

Marion leaned in close to me. "Before you say anything else, I just want to say one thing."

My stomach lurched but I told myself to hang tough. If she wanted to let me have it for getting her into this mess, I would take it.

"Fuck!" she whispered.

Her eyes shimmered.

"Goddess knows how I hate that word, but that is just how angry and sad and scared and messed up I am right now. Like everything is just one big f-word!"

She laid her hands flat on the table in front of us. "Okay." She drew and exhaled a big breath. "Okay. I'm back to 'f-word.' I've got control over something." She blinked and exhaled again. "Lon, I gotta tell you, I'm not sure helping you is in my best interests."

That still hurt.

"I mean," she said, "my place is empty. Are they scared I'm a poisoner? Or all at Cousin Donna's show tonight? Which is worse?" She wiped her forehead.

I could tell she still needed time to settle, so I poked at her catalog's display of neti pots, aromatherapy inhalers, hemp handcreams. "Find anything fun?"

She closed the catalog slowly. "I'm just making sure I have a place to look when people walk in here and won't look at me." She gazed toward the front window. "Or worse, walk on by. Here." She pushed her pastry toward me. "Have some apelbeignet. Kaylee'll bring you a clean fork."

Which Kaylee, more on her toes than usual, did.

"Josh told me this morning that everyone's dropped their communion bread orders," I said. "He tell you that I had nothing to do with my church's call? I still want the bread."

"It's okay, Lon. I know you can't control what your vestry decides."

"Bullshit," I whispered. "I'm the rector and I want your bread. And your priest hosts. If you're willing to get up early and bake."

She studied the food on her fork. "Nothing else to do. But won't that just make your life worse over there?"

"They can just grow up. What do they think? That the bread is going to be poisoned?"

Kaylee dropped a fork by my elbow and I took a bite of the dessert. The apples inside the crunchy batter melted in my mouth. "My God, this is good."

"Beer batter makes it perk the apples up and I make vanilla sugar." Marion leaned closer. "So, what ever happened with your Wafer Wars?"

"Don't ask," I mumbled around my mouthful. I swallowed and told her about Bova's sabotaging of last Sunday's Eucharist.

"Can she go to hell for that?" Marion asked.

"Not as an Episcopalian, no." I wiped my mouth. "But she's a big part of making my current life hell." I told her about how the church had decided to drop sponsorship of the Belles. Suddenly weary, I rested my head in my hands. "It's all so darned hard. Maybe God doesn't want me to have a soccer team in town."

Marion put her hand on my shoulder. "If I weren't so out of touch with my own spirit guides, I'd have something wise to say. Sorry. But I do know this. The universe doesn't usually conspire to keep us from the things we love."

I thought about my life and all the time I'd spent not doing things I loved. "I'm not sure I believe you," I said.

"It's usually us," Marion said. "Us and our fears. That's what keeps us from soaring."

I thought of Wile E. Coyote and Peter. "You're sounding pretty wise, for someone whose karma got run over by local dogma."

She shrugged, flipped open the catalog. "So, what're you doing about the team?"

"What do you mean? I'm still short two players and a sponsor. There is no team."

Marion looked up. "Sounds like your karma's roadkill too. I've never known Lonnie Squires to quit when it came to soccer."

"I've been busy. And like I said, I need your help."

She flipped a page.

"Please?"

She sighed and closed the catalog. "I'll listen. But if your half-cocked shenanigans start to fry what's left of my good energy, I'm kicking you out of here."

I swore her to the super-best-friend level of secrecy and told her everything. About Elyse hiring me to find the spread. About Mandy's secret attempts to escape Donna, about Maris's worries and Guy's paycheck changes and the file of favorite students, about Star's manipulation of the evidence she'd found, about Donna's sexual exploits across the country.

Marion gasped. "Great Goddess, does Char know? She'd die!"

I told her no one knew except Star and the two of us. "Oh, and Eli Borden." And I told her about the blueberry field car chase and my information exchange deal with Borden. "I kept Star's secret as promised. But I did tell her what Mandy told me about the trysts." I grinned, feeling damned proud of myself for handling all that all alone, but Marion just stared at me.

"You're working with Borden?" She dropped her forkful of baked apple onto her plate. "The woman hanging me out to dry for all this, just to make herself look good?"

"No, Mare," I said, pumped with positivity for the first time in a week. "It's all good. She wants me to help find proof that someone else did it. To open doors for her to investigate."

Marion's face stayed blank. "You're joking."

"No, no." I grabbed her mug and sipped her coffee. "She says they do this all the time, hire locals to help get information that folks just won't tell to government agents."

"Did she send you here tonight? To grill me and report back on what you heard?"

I froze, mouth full of the last bite. "What?"

Marion pushed back from the table. "Great Goddess Gaia, Lonnie Squires, how can you be so incredibly stupid?"

I tossed my fork down. "Exactly what is so stupid?"

"You believed this federal agent? Your new buddy, Eli?" She whined the name. "You really think a federal agent would be so awed by your powers as an amateur detective that she'd want you to help her with her investigation?"

"She said people don't talk to—"

"So you're going to spy on your neighbors?" Marion looked at me like I was a ghost. Or worse. "And tell their secrets to the government?"

"I'm trying to save you."

"Really, Lonnie? Or are you trying to save yourself? Things are out of control at church and in your personal life, so you're partnered up with the likes of Star Hannes in some desperate attempt to live up to your superstar sleuth image."

"Wait a minute!"

"Has it occurred to you that Borden's using you, with no concern at all about how it's going to affect your life around here after she leaves?"

That hadn't occurred to me. I slid my plate away. "How stupid do you think I am?"

"Not stupid. Desperate to make something in your life work out."

Heat and energy twisted through me. "Who's calling who desperate? You're always claiming to be so balanced, so in tune with the universe and spirit guides and the great goddess. But what happens when one little thing in your life goes awry? You collapse into a whiny, depressed, selfish martyr! Poor me! No one loves me." Power galloped through my veins. "Driving your family crazy and ignoring friends. Some faith you have."

Tears welled up in her eyes. "Thanks for all the help. Some priest you are."

I practically leapt from the stool. "I've been doing nothing but helping." *Trying, anyhow.* "And I am not your priest."

She wadded up her damp napkin. "You aren't wearing a wire, are you?"

My face burned. "Of course not."

Marion closed the catalog. "I don't know if I believe you."

After I'd busted my ass for her! "Just because I can't figure out who the hell really did this, you think I've turned on you?" I stood, noticed Kaylee watching us with big eyes, then I bent over. "Don't you worry, I won't darken your doorway again. And you had better find another soccer team to play on. Because when I do get this team up and running, I'll need a stopper I can trust."

"You don't have a team, Lonnie Squires. And acting like this, you won't get one, no matter what Elyse Orion promised you."

The venom in her voice stung, but I maintained my dignity. I thanked Kaylee and waved to the Zaloumis as I left, then drove home to be alone. *Screw Marion.* I needed to study for my father's trivia tournament tomorrow night anyway and I definitely did not want to see or think about anyone who had anything to do with Middelburg, Michigan. Not tonight.

Chapter Twenty-Nine

Well, Lon, I thought as I dug into my second bowl of Cap'n Crunch before eight on Saturday morning. *You're a hell of a whiz at conflict resolution.*

I hadn't been able to sleep. I hated fighting with anyone, especially Marion. I wanted to pick up the phone about a dozen times, but I couldn't do it. I couldn't get over how she'd insulted me for doing everything to help her, including working with a federal agent who scared me half to death.

Plus no I was back to needing three players for my team.

When the phone rang I jumped so fast to answer it I knocked the last of my sugary milk out of the bowl and onto the floor. I hopped to avoid stepping in it and grabbed my phone.

"Lonnie," said a voice not Marion's, "this is the most curious list of people. Thirty-seven names, all the way back to Texas. And I don't believe I've met one of them."

It took me a minute to jiggle my mind out of disappointment that Marion hadn't called and reconnect to Maris Rittenga. "You mean the people in the favorite students file?" I shoved Linus's nose away from the milk with my toe and grabbed some paper towel. Cranking my shoulder to my ear to hold the phone, I wiped up the spill with one hand while holding the pup at bay with the other.

"Lonnie, Donna Hancock has a file there."

I sat back on my haunches. "What's in the file?"

"Same as all the others. Copies of papers, all of them A's. Glowing comments."

I watched Linus lap up the rest of the milk, as I considered. What were the odds that Donna Hancock had ever written an A paper on the New Testament? On the other hand, it was her favorite subject and I shouldn't be such a nasty judge.

"Seems strange, though," Maris continued, "that Guy never told me he knew her. What with her coming to town and him getting a ticket and all."

Not to mention arranging to meet her privately after the show.

"Pretty soon I'm going to start losing sleep over more than his death," she said. "I'm beginning to wonder where our relationship went wrong."

I could relate.

Something hummed at the back of my brain. It had to do with Guy getting a ticket. Or meeting Donna. Or something. I tried to hold my brain still for a few seconds, to let the thought break through, but it didn't.

"There's other names," Maris said. "I've never met them, but I know them. People from town."

"Really?" I patted Linus's head and tossed the towel into the wastebasket.

"Would you like to come over and look at the files? I started cinnamon buns just after five this morning, so they'll be hot and gooey around ten."

Exciting as the files were, nothing called to me louder than fresh baked goods, especially those with pronounceable names.

So after taking care of Linus, cleaning myself up and driving south of town, I found myself sitting on the floor of Guy's study, surrounded by files, a steaming bun with sugary orange glaze melting down its sides.

The files had surprised me. Every note to Guy which Maris had found since his death had come from one of these people. Including Bryce Archer. Two others had included checks for two hundred and fifty dollars, no explanation. Neither of them lived in the Midwest. Donna's held only her paper on Galatians, no notes. But most surprising of all, both Paul Geiger and Josh Hogewoning had files as well. Neither of them had said much about the professor, yet both had wound up in the favorite students file.

As I chewed my first bite of thick spicy bread, I wiped glaze from the corners of my mouth and checked out the papers again. My first look through had revealed the sort of thing you'd expect in undergrad New Testament classes. Explicate this set of Bible verses. Trace the historical context for a particular passage. Watch a secular movie and explain how it does or does not promote a Christian worldview. The papers all had margin notes written in the same cramped professorial hand. "Noteworthy!" "Excellent!" "Brilliant!" "Publishable!" I read a few of the passages Guy loved so much and agreed—they were particularly smart examples of theological thinking. I could see how these writers earned their places as favorites.

Even Donna Hancock's paper contained ideas I'd never have thought her capable of. Nuanced, funny, insightful. "I can't believe she wrote this," I said to myself as I swallowed Maris's strong coffee and took another big bite of bun.

Then the voice in my head chimed in. *Maybe she didn't.* I quickly checked another paper. Then the rest. Not one had a single bad comment on it. Even the ones where the papers had weak writing, grammar errors, none of it had been noted. Only the really smart stuff.

Too smart.

I slid folders around on the floor until I found Paul's and

Josh's. Skimming Josh's paper on whether or not Christ was a feminist revealed a particularly smart section on Jewish code and the treatment of women in Jesus' time.

No way. I knew the passage.

Paul's paper made me certain. He'd focused on Episcopal parishes in Virginia which left the church after a woman, Katharine Jefferts Schori, was elected presiding bishop. They objected to a woman leader and to her support of inclusion of homosexuals in church life. In the paper, Paul called Schori a "green and trendy liberal," a phrase I knew well. Columnist Patrick Buchanan had used it to refer to her and regardless of how he'd meant it, I couldn't think of a much higher compliment. In fact, I'd copied the words onto an index card and taped them over my computer as a reminder of what I wanted to be someday.

There were other echoes in Paul's paper too. And every echo I sensed, Guy Rittenga had marked as "terrific!" Nowhere did he accuse the writer of plagiarism.

I ate more bun. At the memorial service, the other profs had revered Guy's reputation for scaring kids into academic honesty. But he had files of papers, some obviously plagiarized, and I bet if I spent some time with Google, I could prove the rest were too. And the students, thanking him, saying they owed him. Sending money. And checking account deposits that did not match his pay stubs, at least not since he died.

Now I was dying to see what Eli Borden found out when she checked his pay history.

And whether he liked it or not, Bryce Archer was going to talk to me about his check.

I thanked Maris, gleefully accepted two buns to go, and drove south around Holland to Saugatuck, a charming artists' village nestled between the Kalamazoo River and Lake Michigan. The Blue Star highway led me from I-196 toward the lake, past a sports bar, a Sixties-style motel, and a place that offered dune buggy rides through Lake Michigan's giant sand dunes. I'd have sped right past it if I hadn't caught sight of the old-fashioned hand-painted wooden sign shaped like an artist's palette, announcing the turn to town. The roads twisted and turned beneath looming oaks and maples, amid refurbished turn-of-the-century, the twentieth century, cottages, white picket fences and tiny green lawns.

Summertime Saturday found the place jammed with people, singles, elderly couples, young husbands and wives giving kids shoulder rides, same-sex couples holding hands. Boats crammed the docks, piggybacking four and five deep. I cruised looking for a place to park, noting all the Illinois license plates and rainbow stickers. Eventually, I parked up the hill near the local Episcopal church and found my way past wine shops, spice shops, art galleries, shops with knickknacks of every shape and size, including a high-end collection of designer dog toys. I confess to almost stopping to see if they had something Linus would love, but I forced myself to keep walking toward Water Street and to Bryce Archer's gallery, Archer's Arts.

A brass bell tinkled when I walked in and the blast of cool air reminded me of Frontline church. Soothing New Age music wafted through the nearly empty gallery and a copper tub of ice-chilled bottles of Tasmanian Rain water was "For Clients Only."

A heavyset red-bearded man smiled at me. "Welcome to Archer's Arts." He waved an upturned hand toward the water. "Help yourself. We have to stick together to beat this heat."

His smile grew when I asked to speak to Bryce Archer. He rested his fingertips against his heart. "*C'est moi!* What can I do for you?"

I approached a cozy corner with two soft chairs and a table between. The price tag on the sofa-sized oil painting above was thirty-two thousand dollars. "May we sit?"

"Certainly." He bounced into the chair. "Are you furnishing a new home? Looking for a piece for the dining area of your boat? A husband's birthday present?"

"I'm Lonnie Squires."

He remembered me all right.

"It's my personal business who I choose to loan money to, okay?" He sprang up, ramrod straight. "Please. Leave." He wagged a finger toward the door.

214

I didn't move. "Things have changed since we last spoke. I've got a list of Professor Rittenga's favorite students, and all the files to go with it. You, and a paper you wrote for your New Testament class in nineteen eighty-nine, are in it."

He didn't bend. "I got an A on that paper."

I nodded. "I've discovered that several of the papers in that file contained plagiarized material. It's only a matter of time before the rest are investigated." I waited.

He stared at me. Wavering.

"Mr. Archer, when we spoke before, I only knew that you had sent the check. But now I have a list of thirty-seven people, all of whom I'm willing to bet were caught plagiarizing by Guy Rittenga over the last three decades. And Guy Rittenga was poisoned. Right now, an innocent woman, my friend, is getting skewered by the media and small-minded rumors for something she didn't do." I paused. His eyes darted around. "You can bet that if you don't help me figure out who else might have done this, I'm not going to be quiet or careful with the information I've dug up on you or anyone else. Talk to me and I might settle down."

That did it. I saw resignation seep through the cracks in his resolve.

His shoulders loosened. "Look, it doesn't matter now. I have a great business." He swung outstretched arms in a circle. "No one cares what went on twenty years ago. That's one reason why I left law." He flopped down in the chair next to me. "That life was brutal. My cholesterol. My blood pressure. Two mild heart attacks and I thought if I don't get out of this it's gonna kill me! Now I'm surrounded by loveliness all the time." He smiled paternally at the paintings.

"So, you did plagiarize in your paper?"

He flapped a hand toward me. "Lady, I stole the whole thing. Will never forget the partying I did the night before the thing was due. Met the first love of my life when we were both partied out. Don't regret how it all worked out either." He grinned and stroked his beard. "Been with Ty almost twenty years now. And

Rittenga let me pay the fine and be done with it. Copying that paper was the best decision I ever made."

I cared less about his love life than what happened after he got caught. "Fine?"

He rubbed his hands and crossed his legs. "That's how old Rittenga worked. You got caught plagiarizing and instead of turning you in, he just fined you. I imagine he made a cool bit of cash on the side. Deal was, kids tried to get away with crap all the time and he didn't think it should be made public the way Five Points does it. So he'd just fine the student and make us promise never again. Deal was, if he caught us again, he'd turn us in. Two plagiarisms at Five Points meant expulsion."

"But wasn't he afraid that you'd turn him in for blackmailing you if he tried to get you expelled?"

He scrunched up his face. "Like anyone at Five Points was going to believe the word of a two-time plagiarizer over that of the respected New Testament professor! We knew where we stood. Far as I know, no one ever tried twice."

"So, tell me about these fines."

"Two percent of a year's full-time tuition, in cash, and the matter was forgotten. I paid him two hundred and forty, I remember, tuition being about twelve thousand back then."

That probably meant the going fine was closer to six hundred. "And that was it? No further payments?"

Archer shook his head. "Never heard another word about it. Was always grateful though, because I was headed to law school and getting caught could have kept me out. Mattered then. Like life or death." He tugged his beard. "Funny how what matters changes. Occasionally I've wondered, if I'd gotten nailed and couldn't go to law school, would I have found my way to all this sooner?"

"Before the two heart attacks?"

He smiled. "And the forty pounds I put on eating my troubles away."

"So, why the check last week?"

Archer shrugged, looked past me at a steel abstract sculpture.

"When I got the letter about his illness, I wanted to do something. But didn't have the cash, you know, until I sold one of Ty's last week. For more than that." He pointed to the painting above the couch. "So, it seemed like the least I could do. I mean, in a way, he saved my life once. Felt like I could help him. Good karma and all."

"Letter? When?"

He shrugged again. "Maybe early spring. Said he had cancer, was keeping it a secret so he wouldn't be forced to quit. He needed money for an experimental treatment insurance wouldn't cover." His eyes hardened. "Don't I know about those bastards and their niggling policies. Just as soon have you die. Cheaper for them."

"He told you he was sick?" And lied about an experimental treatment in order to get money out of them? Poor Maris. This would hurt.

Archer nodded. "And he said since he'd once kept all our secrets he trusted us to keep his. And he asked us to send money. Said he still had all the files and this one final token of regret from each of us would assure he took our secrets to the grave."

"So, he extorted you?"

Shrug. "I guess. He didn't even specify an amount. Just wanted the help." He tugged his beard. "You know, I won't give to the college, actually. Bunch of bigoted holier-than-thous. My money wouldn't be good enough for them, if they knew about Ty. But this professor, he cut me a break. And then I heard about the talk he gave at graduation, and how they fired him. And I thought, I can help him." Shrug. "So I sent him the money. I'm sorry he didn't get it."

"So you still have the letter? May I see it?"

He shook his head. "Sorry, no. I got too much paper coming through here to keep stuff like that. It's long gone, soon as I wrote the check."

"Do you know how many others got the same letter?"

"No. It was clearly a form letter, not personally addressed or anything." The front bell jangled as a well-tanned couple in

217

matching nautical-striped Windbreakers walked in. He leaned forward to whisper, "You've got the files. Ask the others." Then he jumped up again. "I'm sure that will suit your needs perfectly," he cooed, loudly enough for the others to hear. "So very glad I could help." And with barely time for a deep breath, he was off to gush with the couple over several brightly colored abstract collages.

This explained the notes, the deposits not matching the pay stubs, the cash arriving by mail. If Guy sent some final request for money to everyone in that file, it opened up the possibility that one of them had panicked, fearing their secret would be revealed, and found a way to poison their old professor. Archer seemed unlikely, but others, who had spotless reputations to uphold, might not have been so calm about it all.

Chapter Thirty

I left Archer's Arts and wandered downtown to pick up a box of fudge and a toasted coconut ice cream cone, even though it was barely noon. Assuming what Bryce Archer told me was true, I still didn't know if what Guy Rittenga had written was true. I needed more insider info from Five Points. So I called Pia Hakksen again, told her I knew scandalous stuff about her colleague and the college, promised that if she swore secrecy I'd not only tell her, but I'd buy her an ice cream cone as well.

She bargained for fried lake perch at Wally's and an hour later we were seated on the outdoor patio surrounded by bikers clad in black leather kicking back early afternoon beers, staring at the remains of our fabulous and very unhealthy meals.

"So, tell me your secrets," Pia said. She wore a white cotton tank top and khaki shorts over a lean tan body, her hair pulled back into a ponytail.

"Are you *sure* you don't want to play soccer?" I asked.

She just narrowed her eyes at me. "I'm only talking to you because no respectable person from Five Points would even visit this den of iniquity."

I looked around. I loved it here, but I saw her point. "And if they do, you can rat them out as soon as they do you." I told her what Bryce had told me about Guy's extortion of students, about his letter last spring. I didn't go into the paychecks or Maris's concerns—that was still the private business of the living.

Pia's eyes grew wider the more I talked. When I finished, she burst out laughing and bent over, wheezing, wiping tears from her eyes. "I'd sure like to see that on the front page of the paper," she said. "Or all over the TV news." She sniffed. "Except, of course, it would hurt Maris. So not really. But I'd dearly love to see any and all of Five Points and its holier-than-thou systems exposed for what they really are." She wiped both eyes again. "That was probably a wildly inappropriate reaction."

I lifted my glass in a toast. "People react in funny ways to exposure of the truth. Theirs or other people's." *After all*, I remembered as I sipped my pale local brew, *that's what got Vance killed last spring.* "So, does Archer's story ring true to you?"

"What?" Pia wiped her cheeks with her napkin. "That students would submit to blackmail before they'd want their plagiarism made known? Hell yes. Get into a toxic environment like that, where an inhuman godliness is held up as the norm, and people will pay virtually any price to keep up appearances."

"Like not playing on soccer teams."

Her eyes narrowed. "You want my help, back off."

I held up my hand. "You're right. Sorry." I changed tacks. "What I don't get is why students would plagiarize, knowing the penalties."

She picked up her glass and held it between us. "Same reason they hide alcohol under their beds, break parietals, do drugs. They're kids. Think they'll never get caught or hurt. And they've been kept so sheltered by mom and dad that they don't believe that anything bad can ever really happen." She sipped her wine and replaced the glass. "I know a guy, caught a student plagiarizing right off the Internet. Had him cold. And mommy and daddy showed up one day in his office, unannounced, with the family attorney, ready to sue him for libel because he accused their darling son of such a dishonest and unchristian deed. Took the poor guy weeks to get through it."

"You make me glad to be a priest. Crazy as they are, our politics sound easier to navigate."

She raised her glass to toast me. "You can say that again." And suddenly we were friends.

"So, do you think what Guy said is true? If he had cancer, would his job be in jeopardy? Would his treatments not be covered?"

"That seems unlikely. As much as I might bitch about Five Points, they insure us really well. It's part of us all appearing as one big happy family. I have a colleague whose husband got super sick all of a sudden. Had to be treated in Ohio. She took a leave and spent nearly a whole term there with him. Not only didn't they cut her insurance, they paid her full salary." She drew a french fry through some ketchup on her plate. "So see, they can be pretty decent in some ways."

"Well, if he didn't need the money for treatment, why did he send that letter?" I stared at the patterns of fry crumbs on my plate. "I mean, why reopen all those files. If you think about it, it was quite a risk. Some old alum, like Bryce Archer, maybe doesn't care so much any more and decides to turn him in." Now that I said it, it seemed like a hell of a risk. "He must have needed the money badly. I mean, it would only be another twenty or thirty thousand. That doesn't go far."

We sat in the midst of the bikers' hubbubing and the jukebox thumping, lost in thought.

"He really was sick?" Pia asked.

"Terminal cancer. Refused treatment, his doc says, and only had a few months to live." So why would he need money so badly? Sad as it was, his death should leave Maris well off. She'd get his whole retirement. Life insurance. Anything else they had. Only one of them to support through old age.

"Did the college provide life insurance?"

"Sure. Why would—? Oh." Pia ate the last bite of french fry. "No, his wife would collect the insurance. But!" Suddenly her face broke open like a ray of sun from behind a thundercloud. "How old was he?"

"Early sixties," I said. "Why?"

"Not good enough. Exactly how old was he?"

I thought. I knew this. Someone had said it. "Sixty-three."

She sat back hard in her chair. "His pension. He was worried about his pension."

"What do you mean?"

"Our pensions are run through the CLOSER church. And they have a rule that you have to work until you're sixty-five in order to get your full pension. Or, at least, the college has to pay your portion until you're sixty-five."

"Even if you're ill?"

She nodded. "Church rules."

"What about early retirements?"

"Well, the college still has to pay into the pension fund the same percentage they would have if you'd stayed employed until you were sixty-five. So it saves them some money, if they aren't paying you. But they still pay." She leaned over the table. "Do you think that's it? He asked for money because he knew he was dying and would leave Maris without the full pension?"

Maris had told me Guy worried obsessively about money, about providing for her. That would be important enough for him to risk approaching all those former students and asking for money.

"Do you think?" she asked again.

"Maybe. But wait." I thought back over what Maris had told me. "Part of Guy's early retirement deal—"

"Forced retirement deal," Pia said.

"Right. Forced retirement deal, part of it was that his salary would be paid to him or in the event of his death to his wife. Maris told me that. It was the condition he insisted on before he signed the confidentiality papers. So that would vest him, right?"

Pia wadded the napkin and dropped it on her plate. "I guess, yeah. Damn. I thought we had something."

It tickled me to see her wrapped up in the investigation. At the same time, I felt a twinge of missing Marion. "But you know, that agreement came after the graduation speech, later in May. Archer said the letters were sent late winter. Maybe this was his first idea to do something to make Maris secure."

She nodded. "Maybe we did something useful here after all." She patted her flat belly. "Other than eat wonderful, lovely perch drenched in bread and beer batter and grease." She looked at me quickly. "And no, I don't want to play soccer."

We parted promising to keep in touch in case either of us thought of something.

I followed her out of town and back toward Middelburg, cursing a social system that kept a woman like that off my team. Or out of my life in other ways as well. Just as well. Single life kept things much simpler in my world.

Then I decided that damn it, someone could just make my life a little easier. I called Star Hannes' cell. She didn't pick up but I left a message. "You still owe me two soccer players. And if you think Don Loomis got you out of the spread deal, remember our little deal about the note and think again. Two players. Before the deadline."

Somehow, that made me feel a lot better. Still, as I cruised up I-196 toward home, I thought about Guy, his diagnosis, his panic about providing for Maris as he'd promised her all those years ago. Had he sat in the same room I'd sat in, maybe even smelling her homemade cinnamon buns, knowing that she'd only receive part of his pension when he passed? Had he opened that drawer, fingered those files, weighing the pros and cons of getting more money, anything to make Maris more comfortable when he was gone? Had he been disappointed with the results?

Out of the blue a thought dropped like a sonic boom. "Oh my God!" I yelled, jerking so hard I swerved the car over the edge line and onto the wake-up ridges. I pulled myself back into the lane, heart careening off my ribs.

The money from the favorite students hadn't been enough. He'd needed to do something more.

And that was when Guy Rittenga had decided to give his speech at graduation. It was when he'd gotten me involved in this whole mess.

That speech. An eloquent, Bible-based piece of progressive theology asking all listeners to consider the message of the Gospels as they considered full acceptance and inclusion of gays and lesbians into the CLOSER church. A contentious issue in my church, this was the atom bomb issue in a church as conservative as the CLOSERs. All hell had broken loose. He'd been fired. As he knew he would be.

Even Pia had told me early on that she wondered what he'd been thinking. They all knew their jobs were at risk if they stepped out of line like that.

Sweat stood on my face and neck. He hadn't taken a risk to promote dignity and respect for all people. He'd done the thing that he knew would so piss off his employers he could bargain for a forced retirement deal.

That son of a bitch.

He'd used me. He'd used the terrible marginalization of homosexuals. Used us for his convenience, to get what he wanted from life.

I fumed the whole way around Holland and north on US 31 toward Middelburg. Even the acres of laden blueberry bushes didn't cheer me. But about the time I turned toward home, I had to admit he'd also used his church's narrow-mindedness against them. And he'd done it to ensure his pension. Take care of his wife. I kind of admired him for that.

Question was what was I going to do with this information now? Five Points College would probably love it. They could go crazy with the story of their wacky professor who, alleluia, hadn't gone over to the dark side in support of gay rights, but in fact had just pretended to in order to provide for his wife after his death. Who could blame him? He was dying after all. And how would it affect Maris?

I stewed on all this as I arrived home, changed, and took Linus for a jog. After the first mile, I turned to head for home and made my decision. I wasn't telling anyone what I'd just figured out. Guy's decisions and motives didn't pertain to this case and I wasn't going to give Five Points the satisfaction. Guy could go to his grave a martyr for the cause. And then I stopped and turned back around. I was going to go another mile, maybe another two. Soccer team or not, I was getting back into shape. I needed to be stronger to deal with the world.

Chapter Thirty-One

Got home and my legs and stomach hurt like hell, but in that way that says you've cleaned your pores, stretched your muscles, and started to get your body back. Tomorrow, no fried perch. I thought about heading back into town to talk to the boys about their papers but decided I could catch Josh tomorrow before church or Monday. I checked messages, finding only two.

First, Red reported that Don was off his vent and regaining some motor control. "He's pretty embarrassed," she said. "Call me when you can."

Second, my mother called on behalf of my dad to make sure I was studying up.

Did you see the Longstreet *fan site?*

Can you name all the Walton children? The actors who played them?

How many times did Roddy McDowall appear on The Carol

Burnett Show?

Can you name the chimp who played Bear in B.J. *and the Bear?*

Can you sing the theme song from The Banana Splits?

This last I wondered about, since it went off the air in 1970, but if Dad thought it might come up, I'd review it. Right now it was after three and I needed to eat and shower before I engaged with Sid and Marty Kroft's man-sized puppets.

I'd been out of the shower long enough to have stepped into shorts and a tee and was still toweling my hair when Linus jumped up. A car pulled into my driveway. Borden's sedan. I wished I'd put on something other than my old soccer shorts, but it was too late now. I invited her in.

Linus wagged his whole body and she reached out to touch his forehead with her fingertips. "Good boy. Now go away."

He collapsed on his bed with a sigh.

"I need a drink." I led her into the kitchen and held out a cold beer. "You'll want one too after we talk."

"Water is fine." She set her purse on the table and pulled out her pad and pen. "I'd like to start with what you observed at the Windmill Grind last night."

I put two glasses of water on the table and sat. "I observed my best friend in a mostly empty restaurant in a hell of a mess. I observed enough that today I got out there and found out something that the rest of you have overlooked."

Borden held up a hand. "One thing at a time. What exactly do you mean by 'mess?'"

I told her how empty The Grind had been, what it usually looked like on a Friday. I reminded her that she was a big part of why folks thought Marion was a poisoner. I dumped all my frustration right into her lap.

After a second, she spoke. "I'm sorry about your friend." Her eyes were hazel, direct and crackling with energy.

Suddenly I wondered what it would be like to kiss Agent Eli Borden. The urge came on so quickly I gasped. Then I had to pretend to choke and sip water. I started getting tingly in places that hadn't tingled in a long time. Marion had blown up at me just for helping with the investigation. She'd never speak to me again if I had a fling with a federal agent.

Eli tilted her head exposing her long neck. "You know, in some places, people would flock to eat at the restaurant of a suspect poisoner, so later they can say, 'I ate her blue plate special.'"

"Delft plate specials. Monday through Friday, four to six p.m." I smiled as she wrote it down. I wanted to pluck the pen from her hand and touch her palm.

Outside, a low growl of thunder rolled, louder and louder, until the windows rattled in the panes. I hadn't even noticed the clouds gathering.

"People are punishing her," I said.

"For poisoning the spread?"

"No. For getting tangled up in it at all. For becoming their scapegoat. Around here, bad opinion means you aren't right with the Lord. And if you aren't right with the Lord, no one wants to be around you, because they don't want it to rub off on them."

"What, the Lord's anger?" She cracked her gum.

"No. Other people's bad opinion."

She dropped the pen and lowered her hand until it rested against her long thigh. "Seriously?"

I nodded. My mouth felt dry and I licked my lips.

Another rumble of thunder rose and fell, rattling things around us again.

"You said mostly empty." She picked up the pen. "Who was there?" When I told her, she asked why the Zaloumi twins weren't shunning Marion like everyone else.

"The Zaloumis love Marion's apelbeignets and ice cream more than life itself. Plus they're nearly ninety. They don't care much what anyone else thinks, including God. I've heard them say so. In church, no less. Heck, if they knew for *certain* Marion had poisoned Guy, they'd be in there eating her apelbeignets."

She nodded and my body felt as if it were coated in warm molasses. "This helps me understand things around here much better. Invaluable, really." She pulled an envelope from her purse. "Here's my information for you."

Our fingers touched as I took it from her and heat surged through me. I hoped I didn't blush as I unfolded the paper.

I expected Guy's pay history, which I knew wouldn't match his deposits. But it wasn't that at all.

It was a letter written by Star Hannes, on behalf of the Town Council, to Agent Borden (and copied to her superiors at DIDIO headquarters) requesting that The Windmill Grind Kaffe Klatsch and All Dutch All The Time Kafe be shut down immediately as a public health hazard.

Heat of a different kind surged through me now. My legs bounced as I tossed the letter back at Borden. "That bitch."

"Why would she want this?" Borden carefully folded the letter. "She seems to want to avoid negative publicity."

I knew instantly what Star was up to. "To cement Marion as the town scapegoat so that no matter who else gets implicated in all this, poor Marion will stick in people's minds as always guilty."

"And why would she feel the need to do that?"

I stood and paced into the living room and back as I talked. "Because she's afraid something is going to come out that will taint her." *Her welcoming, even protecting, a sex addict.* "This way, if anything comes out, she can just point back at Marion's unproven innocence, redirecting negative attention away from her."

I felt my legs burning to run. Like all the way into town so I could find Star Hannes and kick her in the shins. Studs up.

"You can't close The Grind." I stood in the doorway, intent on keeping Borden here as long as it took to convince her of this.

She shrugged. "Legally, I can."

"I meant, don't. There's no reason. In fact—"

"I agree." She cracked her gum. "Though it crossed my mind to do it, just to see what Mrs. Hannes would do next."

I slid back into my chair, leaned forward. "You can't do that to Marion."

"No, not without compensating her for lost business." Eli pulled a folder from her bag. "I haven't got the budget for it."

I heaved a sigh of relief and slumped back in my chair. Disaster averted. "She'll try someone else. Something else."

"Yes. Why? What is she so desperate to hide?"

I stared at my hands.

"Well, it will come to light eventually." Borden slid the folder across the table to me. "This is what I promised you. I think you'll find it equally interesting, and perhaps just as aggravating."

I opened it to find a printout of Guy Rittenga's pay history for the last eighteen months, but I barely glanced at it. "It doesn't match."

She ran her tongue over her teeth. "No changes. Evidently the widow doesn't understand finances."

"What she didn't understand was her husband." And getting myself a glass of water, I told Eli Borden everything I'd learned from Bryce Archer and Pia Hakksen. "So you see," I concluded, "there are at least thirty-seven new suspects who had more motive than Marion to see to it that Guy Rittenga didn't live long enough to reveal any secrets."

Borden had written it all down, those hazel eyes locked on the paper instead of me. I'd probably just cracked her investigation for her, but she barely gave me a glance. She folded her notebook. "Tomorrow night we should meet again. I want to hear about your day." She stood.

I followed her to the door. "It's just church."

Now she paused, smiled at me. "People talk a lot at church, Reverend. To each other. To God. Probably to you as well."

I felt that heat warming me all over. "Okay, then. Would you like to come for dinner? Maybe drinks?"

She pulled her keys from her purse. "A quick visit would be more efficient."

"I wasn't thinking about the investigation just now." I stood about four inches too close for casual conversation.

She looked at me, puzzled. "What else?"

Argh! I felt doused by the cliché bucket of ice water. She had absolutely no interest in *me* at all. I was just a cog in her investigative machinery.

I stepped back, embarrassed, hoping she was too preoccupied to realize I'd been throwing myself at her and said goodbye. Pure business.

"Well, Linus," I said as we watched Borden drive away. "Mommy is evidently feeling a little desperate. I'm acting like a complete idiot." He wagged.

Dear Lord, I prayed as I took Linus out to pee, *please send me enough soccer players. And a sponsor. I need to start playing again so I quit making up other games wherever I can. Next I'll be throwing myself at Bova Poster.*

I looked at the churning thunderheads and low white curlicues, but heard nothing.

It took a couple of hours and some stern self-talk, but by six o'clock, I had my head back on straight for Dad's trivia tournament. Theme songs, cast lists, commercial jingles and '70s appearances in advertisements of future stars. It wasn't soccer, but I was going to play like it was. To prove it, I dressed in my fuchsia soccer shorts and a Women's World Cup T-shirt. I thought about putting on cleats just to really feel the rush, but decided on my lime green spangly flip-flops instead.

About six thirty, just as I was fighting the urge for another bowl of Cap'n Crunch, the thunder burst into splatter buckets of rain. As much as we needed it, the rain was bad news for the tournament. This killed my cell reception way out here in the boonies where it was always weak.

I looked at Linus. "Team Squires won't go down without a fight!" He cocked his head. "We need a computer, munchies and strong reception, huh boy?" So we jumped into the car. "It's off to church we go," I sang.

The rain pelted drops that sounded like rocks on my car. Water flooded the roads and a spray flanked us. The parking lot at Frontline was jammed for the last night of Cousin Donna's benefit. In town the streetlights had come on even though sunset was almost three hours away.

I parked in front of the parish house right behind Ashleigh's car and we ran through the rain, stopping on the porch to shake ourselves off. Ashleigh sat in her spot surrounded by stacks of unfolded bulletins. Josh sat on her desk.

"You're too big to be drowned rats!" Josh grinned at Ashleigh, clearly encouraging her to appreciate his joke.

She must not have told him about Tom yet.

"Ignore me," I said. "Gotta get some sermon work done."

Ashleigh brought me up-to-date on the last of her work for tomorrow's services. "Just a little more to go here. I'll bring up a copy of the bulletin when they're done."

Upstairs, I tossed my dripping flip-flops into the bathroom sink and pulled out the old towels I kept in the cupboard to dry off Linus and me. The old computer was warming up and I thought I'd raid my stash of chips and diet cola. No better companion when playing with my dad—or writing a sermon for that matter.

As I barefooted it down the hall, Josh's voice came up the stairwell. "A note from your boyfriend?" He sounded dramatic, teasing. "Let me see!"

"Josh!" Ashleigh's voice was high, not really angry. "Give that back."

As I descended, I could see her chasing him around the front office. "Give it back!" Ashleigh repeated, laughing.

Well, at least he got her to go after him.

I decided the snacks could wait and turned to retreat when Ashleigh's voice soured.

"Don't!"

I stopped to see what had changed.

Chapter Thirty-Two

Ashleigh stood in the doorway looking out. Josh must've been on the porch. "I'm serious, Josh. Give it to me."

He laughed. "Ashleigh and her boyfriend sitting in a tree. Isn't that what you girls sing?"

"Like, in second grade." She stuck her hands on her hips. "Give it."

"Let's have a look first."

"Josh!" She shifted from one leg to another.

"So, his name is Tom," came Josh's voice. He moved and I could see him on the porch through the front window, reading the note.

"And *he* would never read my mail!" Ashleigh said, girly pouting in her voice. I couldn't figure why girls got whiny when boys acted like asses. I'd have kicked his butt if I were her.

"Then maybe he doesn't really care." Josh crumpled the

note. "Ash, you don't need this loser."

Her posture deflated. "What do you mean?" Teasing all gone.

Josh took a few steps and reappeared in the doorway. "Good thing I was here." He held up the crumpled ball. "He's done, Ash. Not interested." He held it up. "Here. But seriously, don't read it. It's pretty cold."

I felt Ashleigh's self-esteem dissolve and plummet like the heavy drops outside.

"You don't deserve this kind of crap," Josh said, his voice soft.

"You're right. I don't." Ashleigh sounded caught between tears and fury.

I retreated up the stairs, but not before hearing the metallic ping I knew well: someone banking a wad of paper off the trashcan.

Back in the safety of my office, I opened several screens on the Internet, the faster to access information if I needed it. Next I opened my word processor of sermon notes and was skimming them when Ashleigh came in, bright-eyed and smiley. "Here's a bulletin. The rest are below. Anything else?"

"You okay?" I tried to sound as if I knew nothing. *Nothing.* And I thought of Sergeant Schultz on *Hogan's Heroes.* Played by John Banner.

"Nope," Ashleigh said, perky and peachy-keen. "I'm going to a movie with Josh." She spun so fast her hair flew out around her. "See you Monday."

"Okay," I said. Young people. I definitely could not keep up with them. Seventies TV was more my speed. That and sermon writing. Which I needed to do before my dad called. I jotted notes on a yellow pad, circling words, drawing lines and finally jotting notes.

Wile E. Coyote runs on air. Peter walks on water. But both fall the minute they—what? Look down. Why is it that—instead of becoming afraid and falling—they don't shout out, "Holy Cow! Looky what I can do!"? Isn't it interesting that even in the very moment that they do the

234

impossible they do not believe, and so, their unbelief is manifested.

They don't even see the miracle they are smack in the middle of!

In those crucial moments when we realize we are in the midst of a miracle, instead of thinking, "Oh my gosh, I can't do this," we should think, "Alleluia! Looky what I can do!"

Why is that so hard? I think it's because in order to accept the miracle, we have to admit that something we believed our entire lives was wrong.

And we won't do that. In our desire to be right, we divorce ourselves from the holy.

We'd rather be right than receive a miracle. How sad is that?

And there my pen ran out of ink.

Sadness pooled in my chest. *Guilty as charged.*

I have to be right to help Dad in a trivia contest. And I sure want Eli Borden to be right when she arrests someone for Guy's murder. Right wasn't all bad.

But I wanted Marion to see things my way.

I wanted Eli Borden to see the potential between us the same way I did.

I wanted Star Hannes to quit running town the way she did and to do things the way I thought she should.

I wanted everyone to value women's soccer like I did.

I wanted my Committee on Liturgy to act like compassionate adults, not whiny preschoolers.

I wanted . . . I wanted.

Yikes. I smiled a bit and looked at the ceiling. *Message received.*

Maybe I should let the soccer team go. I didn't have a sponsor anyhow, and what fun was it with two players who'd been strong-armed into the game by Star? I could drive into Holland or Grand Haven to play.

The thought didn't help the sadness in my tummy, but chips would. I checked my watch. 6:54. Just enough time before Dad's tourney started.

I ran downstairs and grabbed dog biscuits, a Diet Coke and some pretzels then headed to the supply drawer in Ashleigh's desk for new pens. My hands were full but of course I didn't put anything down and sure enough, I dropped the loose biscuits into the trashcan with a series of bangs.

Linus leapt into the can after his treats, tipping the thing over and digging its contents out as he searched.

A wad of blue paper caught my eye. I saw the words *Love, Tom* in black ink.

Hmm.

I couldn't resist. I leaned up against the desk, pushed Linus's insistent nose out of the way, and read the note. Tom hadn't dumped Ashleigh. He'd said he'd loved her. That little jerk Josh had read the note and then lied to Ashleigh. Lied damned well, too. I'd believed him.

It irritated the hell out of me. When Mr. Josh delivered the bread tomorrow morning he was in for a little chat about more than plagiarizing papers!

We'd rather be right than receive a miracle, said the voice in my head.

"What?" I said out loud to God. "He doesn't deserve to get his butt kicked for this?" Silence. Okay, I guessed we all did stupid stuff when infatuated—look at me and Eli Borden. And he was a smart, hard-working kid. Maybe I'd tell him he didn't deserve to degrade himself like that.

I worked on my sermon until almost nine o'clock, occasionally breaking to check my cell reception and make sure my Seventies Web sites were still up and running. Looked like Dad hadn't needed me after all. It was like getting all pumped up and spending the game on the bench.

Figures. All that work for nothing. Just to impress my dad. By being right.

And then the cell rang.

"It's crunch time, Lon," Dad said. I could hear crowd noises in the background.

"You having fun?"

"No time for chitchat. If we answer this right, my team wins. Five hundred bucks, Lon. I hope you're ready."

"Ready, Captain." I saluted in Linus's general direction.

The phone bumped and rumbled as he handed it off and I heard a click and more roaring.

"You're on speaker, Lonnie!" Dad shouted. "The whole place can hear you!"

"And I can hear them," I said, which brought a huge cheer. I thought I heard my mother shout, "Hi, Lorraine," in the middle of it all.

"There's a sixty-second clock," said another man's voice, "and it begins with the question. In that time your father has to supply an answer, with you as his advisor. Do you understand?"

"I do."

"Your father's team is behind by ten points. If he answers this correctly, his team will win. If not, losers."

"LOOOOO-SERRSSSSSS!" hissed the crowd.

"You can do it, Lonnie!" Dad yelled.

"Ready." I poised my finger on the mouse.

"Here we go," said the other voice. "In a nineteen seventy-eight episode of *Columbo*, a restaurant critic kills a man with poison from the toxic pufferfish. How is the poison administered? The clock begins now."

The hair stood up on the back of my neck. Pufferfish? What sort of cosmic joke was this?

"Did you say pufferfish?" I asked. *No way.* "Tetrodotoxin?"

"Lonnie! That's not the question. Focus!"

I didn't know a thing about this episode of *Columbo*, so I scanned the open sites. One focused on Seventies television, but a quick search didn't bring up anything on "Columbo" and "pufferfish or fugu."

I clicked on Google.

"What do you think, Dad?" Half of my head was still spinning. One restaurant person, a critic of the other, had killed a cook? God, if Borden got hold of this she'd say it sounded just like Marion and Donna.

"I remember something about a filling. Or a crown? You know? A tooth?"

I Googled that and found an episode that involved poisoning through dental work.

I scanned fast. Where had the pufferfish come from in the *Columbo* episode? Had my killer seen this show, modeled it to poison the spread?

No mention of pufferfish in this synopsis. "It's something else," I said. "What about food? In a fish spread or something like that?"

"I don't remember anything like that," Dad said.

"Forty seconds," said announcer's voice.

Back to Google, I tried "Columbo" and "pufferfish" again. Lots of sites, but none looked good.

I added "episode" to the search and skimmed a few results—all no good. Either too long and scientific or too short, mentioning the episode but no plot details.

"I remember the dentist episode," Dad said.

"The computer says that was made in nineteen ninety. Too late."

"But the show ran in the Seventies," he said.

"From 'sixty-eight to recently," I said.

"Twenty-five seconds," said the announcer.

"Lonnie!"

I needed a different search. What else? What would bring different results entirely? A completely different starting place. I needed "Columbo," but what about splitting the other term? I typed "puffer fish" and hit return. I scanned the results and there it was! I clicked on the site.

"Twenty seconds."

I scanned. The murderer injected puffer fish poison into the Corkmaster. Then the unsuspecting restaurant owner sealed his own doom when he used it to open wine which he then drank.

"A Corkmaster bottle opener!" I shouted.

"I don't remember that," my dad said.

"But it was! IT WAS!" I shrieked. "A Corkmaster!"

"I remember the dentist. The crown."

"Dad! I'm right!"

Silence.

"Fifteen seconds," said the announcer.

"I'm looking at it online!" I leapt up, pointing crazily at the computer screen.

"You can't always trust that Internet," Dad said. "Damn. Lonnie, do you have a coin?"

"Dad, say 'Corkmaster bottle opener!'"

"Flip the coin, Lonnie."

"Ten seconds."

"Flip it," Dad said. "Tails, I say tooth crown."

I grabbed a quarter out of my desk drawer and flipped it. It came up tails. I thought about it for one second.

"Five seconds," said the announcer.

"It's heads," I lied. He'd never know.

"A Corkmaster bottle opener," my dad shouted.

Silence. Tick. Tick.

"You're right!" shouted the announcer. The crowd roared.

"We did it, honey!" he shouted. "We won! Mom'll call you later!" He clicked off.

I dropped into my chair and pumped my fist. "Yeah," I whispered and held my hands up to acknowledge the accolades from the invisible crowds. "Squires scores! Victory goes to the Belles!" My little fake-play had paid off.

Linus lifted his head and wagged at me, then closed his eyes again.

We'd rather be right than receive a miracle.

"Yeah, yeah," I said to the voice in my head. "But not in a trivia contest." I clicked into my e-mail. "Not in a trivia contest, thank you very much."

I felt smug but also just a little concerned that maybe my dad and I had proven that my sermon was a bunch of sanctimonious bullshit. But I'd think about that tomorrow morning. Before heading home, I scanned through the twenty-some e-mails that had arrived in the last few hours. Better not to be taken by surprise on a Sunday morning if I could help it.

Parishioners apologizing that they wouldn't be in church

the next day. A bawdy joke about priests and parachutes from Leon Zaloumi. Three from Bova Poster worrying that the patens wouldn't be large enough to hold bread and wafers, would I please respond to her? A fourth expressing her deep disappointment that I'd gone ahead and ordered bread from The Windmill Grind bakery—did I not feel concern for the safety of the congregation? She would bring her own loaves, just in case.

It promised to be an interesting Sunday.

Chapter Thirty-Three

As I drove into the office at six thirty, the early light dappled the blueberry bushes with silvery yellow. I finished my sermon over the first pot of coffee and then sat quietly watching the clock tick. I hadn't realized how much I needed some brain downtime.

At seven fifteen I did my preservice walk-though of the church. First, I went to check the patens set by altar guild, assuring myself they were indeed big enough to hold both bread and wafers.

I stood at the front edge of the altar, tapping the sanctus bell lightly with my foot. I didn't want Bova Poster getting the best of us all again. I wished I had someone to babysit the setup and keep Bova from sabotaging it again. Or that I could think of some way to rope her in, turn her energy and concern to the positive. If only I could get Bova out on the soccer field for a little one-on-one. Fair and square. Clear winner. But life, certainly church, didn't work that way. And it wasn't a very smart strategy for reconciliation.

In a flash a nice little game plan came to me. Call it a sabotage insurance policy—there if I needed it and if I didn't, well, fine. No one would have to know. It only took a few minutes to set up, and I'd just finished running around when Josh came in holding two zip bags high.

"Good morning, Rev Lon. Bread. And a priest host." He looked so cheery this morning even his stubble glistened.

I stepped down from the altar and met him in the center of the aisle. "You got a minute?"

"Mrs. Freeley wants me to get back and help her clean out the storage stuff. Said we might as well, since there aren't customers." He shrugged. "It keeps me getting a paycheck."

"Follow me a sec." We walked back behind the altar to the credence table, where the communion stack sat waiting for the morning's service. "How was your date last night?" I lifted the top half of the stack off, down to the square pall that covered the paten.

"Great, thanks."

I put the fresh priest host in the stack paten, and then looked up at him. "You know, I heard what you said to Ashleigh last night about that note from Tom."

He nodded. "Yeah, poor Ash. She deserves better."

I leaned against the table, trying not to look too threatening. I wished I weren't wearing my clergy blacks and that we weren't standing beneath the crucified Christ. "I found the note, Josh."

It took him a few seconds to fully understand and when he did, his grin melted off his face. "You went through her trash?"

"You lied to her."

"You eavesdropped on our private conversation?"

"You know, sometimes when we really want attention from someone else, we do stupid things. We all do it." I took the baggie of bread and set it on the altar where the guild members would find it when they came in.

"I can't believe you're a snoop." Josh sneered. "What people say about you must be true."

My plastic clergy collar stuck to my neck. I wanted to go carefully, not make this boy my enemy. Just make him hear. "You did something that didn't just get Ashleigh to go out with you. You lied to her about another person and potentially ruined two people's happiness."

He shoved his hands in his cargo shorts. "You gonna tell her?"

I sighed. "I'd rather you did."

"Yeah." His flip-flops scraped the red carpet. "Okay, I'll make it right." He took a step away.

"Hang on," I said. "There's something else."

I thought I saw him roll his eyes, but decided to let that go.

"I just found out that you and Paul were some of Professor Rittenga's favorite students."

He smiled, but not as steadily as before. "Maybe Geiger, but not me."

"I've seen his files. You're there." Plagiarizing and now lying. "That's twice, Josh."

For the first time he looked genuinely afraid, glancing out toward the empty church. "Who else knows?"

I left Maris out of it. "No one. I know the professor threatened to tell."

He nodded slowly, staring at the large print Bible on the pulpit. His whole body sagged. "It sucks."

Voices rose from outside the church and I heard the dry cackle of the Zaloumi twins and their heavy steps on the stairs. I stepped to him, put my hand on Josh's shoulder. "Let's talk more," I said. "After the service. I promise not to talk to Ashleigh or the police or anyone until after we talk, okay?"

He shrugged my hand off and stood back. "Yeah, I guess. I gotta go." His sandals smacked down the aisle and at the rear he grunted greetings to the Zaloumis.

"That boy's up early," said Eddie to me as they approached the altar.

"As are you two gentlemen." They weren't part of the altar guild, so I didn't expect them, or the rest of the congregation for another forty-five minutes. Even the guild wouldn't be here for another half hour. "What's up, fellas?"

The old men looked at each other, waggling bushy brows.

"We didn't exactly expect to see you here," said Leon.

I realized he'd been holding his hands behind his back. Uh-oh. Frog? Snake? Patch of skunk weed? They'd never messed with a service before but since Bova had wrecked things last week, maybe they thought it was fair game.

"What are you two up to?" I asked, reminding myself to smile.

They shrugged in unison then Leon revealed a plastic bag full of communion wafers.

"Just in case," said Eddie.

"We thought we'd stash 'em up behind the altar somewhere," said Leon. "Eddie's LEMing today, and that way, if Bova snatches the wafers like last week, we have refills."

That was exactly what I had planned! I'd already hidden my extra wafers behind the altar, under the draped frontal cloth. I bit my tongue so I wouldn't laugh.

"Don't trust her," Eddie said.

We looked at each other, then Leon handed me the bag.

"You have 'em, Reverend. You decide. We trust you to handle it." He turned to his brother. "Let's go see if the snakes are in the holly out front." And like a four-legged animal, they lumbered out.

I placed their wafers behind the altar next to mine and thought about poor Bova Poster. She'd been so desperate to do what she thought was right, she'd alienated three people who might have been her friends. *We'd rather be right than receive a miracle*. I hoped she heard the message in my sermon loud and clear.

I stuck to the concrete walk as I headed back to the parish house—the rain had left the air humid and the grass wet and I didn't want my good black shoes damp all day. I quickly printed my sermon in sixteen point font then sat for a last few minutes of quiet time. Preparing for a service was a lot like preparing for a soccer game to me—I wanted all of myself there to give.

A knock on my door and D.J. Brink appeared wearing his red and white acolyte robe over khakis and indoor soccer shoes. "Mrs. Alderink sent me to get you. She's starting the prelude."

I stood. "How's your leg?"

"Good," he said. "I'm fairly certain that I can move the sanctus bell today." Not for the first time I had to remind myself he was only eight. He often spoke more like a college kid than the college kids.

I wrapped my alb around me and tightened the cincture around my waist. "If your leg gets sore during the service, don't put the bell back. Just leave it out. People can walk around it during communion and I'll put it back after the service." Next door, the organ started.

"Come on, Rev Lon!" D.J. hopped in place. Like me, he attacked the service like a game. When he rang the bell during the Great Thanksgiving, he did it with the same gusto he put into his goal kicks.

I followed him, still fussing with the cincture. D.J. hopped down the stairs on one leg and the choir started to sing *O God, Our Help in Ages Past*. The Opening Hymn. "Come on!"

We half-jogged, half-hopped back to the church. D.J. grabbed a torch and fell in line behind the other acolytes just as the processional took off down the center aisle. I waited to follow the singers, then Bova and Eddie, letting the music flow around me. The pews held three dozen or so worshippers and at that moment, as every week, I really loved them all, despite our quirks.

I started down the aisle singing the fourth verse. *Talk about quirky. Fighting with my best friend. Making a pass at someone unsuited for me. Flipping a coin and lying about the results. To my father.*

I had a thought and my mouth froze open.

Flipping a coin and lying about the results. I should have seen it much before this because Eddie Zaloumi tried it with Bova at the last committee meeting. But I'd been so mad about how wrong-headed their battles were, so intent on getting them to behave the way I wanted them to, I'd missed it.

We'd rather be right than receive a miracle.

As I approached the altar and bowed electricity zipped up my spine and it all clicked together in my head.

Eli Borden had it all wrong. And so had I, for a long time. This wasn't terrorism. And it wasn't an attack on Cousin Donna.

It really had been the successful, well-planned murder of Guy Rittenga.

I knew who had done it.

Chapter Thirty-Four

I should have seen it at the coin flip.

I faced the congregation, all standing. "Blessed be God: Father, Son and Holy Spirit."

Eddie had flipped one then claimed he'd won, but wouldn't show the results to Bova or any of the rest of us. An elaborate joke, not really a serious attempt to get what he'd wanted.

"Almighty God," the congregation and I prayed together, "to you all hearts are open, all desires known, and from you no secrets are hid."

And I had flipped a coin and lied to my father to make him do what I wanted.

The organ picked up the tune and all of us sang the *Gloria*.

Josh had flipped a coin to determine whether he or Paul would get the tryst with Cousin Donna. Paul had felt sorry for Josh because he'd lost. After all, who wouldn't want to win this acclaimed sexual experience?

Someone who wanted to be alone in the prep kitchen, that's who. Who wanted to poison the salmon spread already chilling in the backstage refrigerator.

All he had to do was flip the coin and lie about the results. Paul would never suspect, because who would lie to lose?

"The Lord be with you," I said, trying to keep some part of my head in the game.

"And also with you," the people responded.

I started the collect of the day. "Grant to us, Lord, we pray, the spirit to think and do always those things that are right." My mouth kept going with the collect as my head ran in another direction.

We'd rather be right than receive a miracle.

Josh knew—everyone did—there would be a fish dish, something he could slip the pufferfish into without affecting taste. So he could have come to Frontline prepared. He knew about the prep kitchen and the security setup from helping Robbie and his mom. In fact, it was because he'd helped out with crowd control during ticket sales that he knew Rittenga would be at the show in the first place.

Bova rose to read the Old Testament lesson.

Josh probably figured that no matter who watched over the backstage kitchen, if he offered to give them a break—or flipped them for it—he could get himself alone with the food.

The whole plot couldn't have been hatched more than a few weeks ago, when the boys saw Guy buy that ticket.

I stood for the sequence hymn, "Love Lifted Me," and followed the acolyte bearing the gospel into the center of the aisle, where I read the gospel with part of my brain and struggled to focus the rest. I had a sermon to deliver, a Eucharist to preside over, people to serve. I could work this out later, call Red or Borden, explain it all.

I threw myself and all my nervous excitement into my sermon and it went well. They laughed when I mentioned old Wile E. Coyote and a "beep beep" from the pews assured me that Leon liked it. Though it was a dozen degrees cooler than it had been last Sunday morning, when I finished, sweat ran down my back. I'd been bouncing on my toes.

I took three deep breaths while the congregation recited the creed. *Focus, focus.*

"Let us confess our sins against God and our neighbor," I said, and led them in the recitation. "Most merciful God, we confess that we have sinned against you . . ."

It had been the raffle ticket that hung everyone up for so long. It seemed that the intended victim couldn't have been Guy because no one knew he'd win. But Josh had drawn it. He'd probably faked that too. We all had blank tickets. I remembered the messy handwriting on the winning ticket, but I knew now it didn't match Guy's, which I'd seen in the check register. Someone else had filled out the winning ticket.

I raised my hand for the blessing. "Almighty God have mercy on you," I said and thought, *and on all of us*. I concluded with the peace. I don't even remember what announcements I made and then, finally it was time for the Holy Communion. Wine, bread, prayers and we'd be done.

As if I didn't have enough on my mind, the wafers had disappeared from the patens again this week. I glanced at Bova who kept her eyes glued to the hymnal. Eddie Zaloumi watched me carefully. He could see that she'd done it again.

I could have let it go, of course. But I wanted the rest of the people of this congregation to get what they wanted, and not get bullied or manipulated into something by one troublesome, stubborn woman. Maybe it was juvenile. Maybe it was about being right. But by God, if the congregation wanted to choose between wafers and bread, I was going to offer them wafers and bread.

I reached under the altar cloth to my secret stash on the shelf and pulled out a third paten, shined by me special for the occasion, overflowing with communion wafers.

I heard Eddie stifle a snort.

I'd solved the case and gotten wafers into communion. It was a good day.

I made it through the Great Thanksgiving without losing track of my words and D.J. Brink rang the sanctus bell crisply at exactly the right four places. I held high the priest host baked by my best friend and broke it. The shimmer of energy that crossed my forearms almost made me squirm. Divine presence? Thoughts of my friend?

"Alleluia." In my heart, Marion stood here with me, present in her bread. As soon as I got out of here and called Red about the murder, I'd call Marion and fall all over myself apologizing. Friends like us shouldn't make things worse for each other. And so, using a goodly hunk of Marion's priest host, with a silent prayer of gratitude for all that had been revealed to me in the last hour, I gave myself communion and sipped the wine.

From his place at the communion rail, Eddie winked and raised his hand slightly, toasting our efforts to make things run right.

The communion hymn, "Precious Lord, Take My Hand," started on the organ while I gave communion to Eddie, who loudly cried, "Wafer, please," as he held out his gnarled hands. His eyes glowed as he took the wafer and placed it on his tongue. Bova's eyes glittered hard when I approached her. "Bread," she said and bread she received.

Next I served the acolytes and singers, and then we waited. Kitty Gellar had sat in the first row on the right and this early in the morning, she never moved very quickly. Just as she stepped forward, the choir began to sing.

A trickle of sweat ran down the side of my face. After I got things reconciled between me and Marion, I'd have to have a long heart-to-heart with Bova Poster. Surely I could help her somehow.

Kitty gripped the altar rail and kneeled. "Wafer, please," she said and I thought I heard a gasp from Bova. She probably took every request for a wafer as a personal affront.

And so it went until all forty-three of the communicants received the Lord's supper. The rest of the service sped by. I cleaned up the service ware while they sang the post-communion hymn. We prayed together that we might be sent out to do the work given us. I stepped forward to do the blessing, and wobbled.

Four hours of sleep is not enough, I thought, swallowing. I felt as if I'd run too hard at a game. Sort of like being overheated and standing up way too fast. Sparks went off in my head. I raised my hand and my fingers tingled. I hoped I wasn't going to pass out.

As the closing hymn started, I swallowed again and felt another runner of sweat on my face. I gripped my prayer book, then nearly dropped it and had to clutch it to my chest as I processed out. From her spot in the front, Kitty looked at me, clearly assessing whether I was okay. I swallowed, licked my lips. Tried to smile, but they felt cracked, as if suddenly sunburnt.

Thank heavens, everyone filed out quickly, hurrying to Sunday school and craving the cool of the parish house and coffee hour. I stood, leaning against the back wall until everyone had left, then went back to the pulpit to grab my sermon notes.

On the second step up to the altar, I tripped and had to grab the communion rail to keep from falling. But my grip didn't hold and the rail jarred into my armpit, my knee narrowly missing the brass cross sticking up out of the sanctus bell.

A punctured knee would end my soccer days. At the corners of my vision, darkness swam in. "No more all-nighters for me." My voice echoed against the stone of the sanctuary. I rotated and sat until I could catch my breath.

"You feeling okay, Rev Lon?"

My head lurched again, and I coughed, spitting everywhere. I swallowed.

Josh began to walk down the center aisle toward me.

Chapter Thirty-Five

I had to play it cool. I'd asked him to come back after all. To talk about Guy. "Hi, Josh. I didn't expect you so soon."

He dropped into a pew about halfway up the aisle. "You look a little peaked, as my mom would say."

A new hardness to his voice, a sharp edge to the set of his jaw—fear dazzled my head. I wasn't safe here alone with him.

Still, I pretended calm. "Let's go get some coffee. When things die down, we can chat."

"No." None of the teasing I'd heard so often lifted his voice. "We'll wait here."

"For?"

He shrugged. "No one can know about my papers."

Hands on thighs, I pushed myself up. My lips tingled and vision wavered. I tried to take a deep breath, but barely managed a half-gasp. I walked to the pulpit, willing myself to stay steady. I shouldn't have had that fourth cup of coffee.

"What about Paul?" I stood behind the pulpit, feeling a little safer. I glanced down at the printout of my sermon and it swam. "He knows."

"Geiger only knows about the first."

"First?"

His lip curled. "Don't screw with me. You said I'd done it twice, so don't pretend you don't know."

I'd meant lied twice. But he meant what? It was so hard to think through this damned sleep-deprivation fog.

"Besides, Geiger's not the one with a hell of a chance for a full scholarship to U Chicago Business School. He's not the one going to make more money than this berg has ever seen. He's not the one whose life is ruined if information about those papers gets out."

Papers. Twice. "You plagiarized twice. Why?"

Josh leaned forward, elbows on knees. "You sure you shouldn't sit down?"

I'd just begun to think the same thing because my feet had started to buzz, like they'd been asleep. I picked up my sermon and turned away, then looked down. I hadn't picked up the sermon at all. Puzzled, I tried again.

My fingers wouldn't work.

"They say the fingers and feet are first to go," Josh said from the pew. "That and the tongue. You salivating a lot yet?"

I froze.

Dear God! The poison!

In the time between when I'd set things up and the start of church, he'd come back and poisoned—what? *The wine? The bread? My parishioners?*

I stepped toward him, stumbled, but stayed upright. "Where was it?" I heard my voice rise in a panic, my words slur. "Where?!"

He stood, hands stuffed into pockets, shoulders hunched in an aw-shucks gesture. "You're doing pretty good," he said, "considering you've had it in you about a half hour now. Way better than Rittenga. You're even still on your feet. And talking." He smiled.

"Help!" I screamed, but barely as I couldn't get a decent breath.

And then I hit the floor, Josh's thick chest crumpling me, his long fingers clamping my lips closed.

"If I hold your mouth and nose shut," he whispered, "it will just look like the poison. So shut up if you want your last few minutes."

I nodded and he released his hand.

"I couldn't risk it, Rev Lon." I could smell fresh bread on his breath. "Maybe you'd tell about the plagiarism, maybe not. But if you knew that much you'd know the rest pretty quick."

He must've seen something in my face because now he grinned. "You did figure it out, didn't you? Since this morning? Shit, I was right."

I monitored my body for the symptoms I'd heard Don's doctors describe. If I didn't get help in about ten minutes, I was going to become paralyzed and remain conscious until my heart stopped. Josh was going to watch it all. He could say anything, do anything to me and I wouldn't be able to stop it.

In the back of my head, I heard the final verse of the hymn my congregation had just sung.

In the back of my head, I heard the final verse of the hymn my congregation had just sung, pleading with the Lord to linger with us during trouble.

Josh tipped off me. "Want your last few minutes to pray? While you can still kneel?"

"Josh, please. My congregation."

He blinked. "I'm not a monster. I only poisoned the priest host."

I swallowed and my mouth filled with saliva again. I lifted an arm and saw my hand flop at the wrist. Tingles traveled up and down toward my elbow.

"Please, don't."

"You act like I have a choice. Like I want to do this." He shook his head. "I worked hard for good grades, a decent chance and to get the hell out of here and off to business school. But that son of a bitch, Rittenga, he reneged on the deal."

"What deal?" A sudden pain knifed my stomach and I curled.

"If he caught you plagiarizing, you paid him to keep quiet and got a good grade. Geiger did it. I did it. Hell, lots of us did it. Most didn't get caught."

"You did it twice."

He shrugged. "So I paid him again. So what? But he didn't remember the deal. He went all wonky on me last spring. Said I'd proved I didn't deserve any more chances. That I'd disrespected the grace he'd offered me the first time. Said he was going to turn me in, but he'd give me the summer first, to figure out how to make it up to him." He scratched his head under his ball cap. "I offered him three times as much money, you know, but he said that wasn't enough. I didn't have more. He gave me until school started to work it out." He shrugged. "School starts week after next. I worked it out."

"Why?" I coughed.

"They expel you. My dad could probably stop that, he's a powerful attorney you know, but it still goes on your record. And then it goes to grad schools and employers and stuff. Forever. No way."

His voice whooshed in and out, weaving with the pain in my stomach. "Josh, you have to let me get help."

The congregation in my head sang again about life, gone.

Oh, God, I thought. *I'm going to die.*

"Yeah," Josh said. I must have spoken out loud. "Look at the suffering you'll avoid." He put his hands in my armpits and helped me into a sitting position on the stairs. I hung my elbow over the communion rail. My hands were no good, but I still had strength in my arms. "I saved Rittenga months of cancer eating him. You, you'll get to go meet Jesus soon. Isn't that what all you religious types want?" He squatted in front of me. "You got some drool, there, Rev."

I wiped my mouth with a flopping hand. All my skin had started tingling and I needed a bathroom. My lungs had started to wheeze against what little breath I had.

Before I knew I thought of it, I stuffed my hand in my mouth, hoping I had pointed a finger, hoping I could make myself gag.

"No!" Josh grabbed me, wrestled my hand from my mouth and held it between his. "No purging."

I yanked so hard I tipped into the rail again, but he didn't let go.

"We'll just wait like this," he said.

I wanted him to stop touching me. No one survived a big dose of this stuff. Even with quick hospitalization, only fifty percent lived. My chances dropped with every second.

Suddenly, more than anything else, I wanted to know what time it was. I tried to pull my hand from his, to see the watch, but couldn't.

Tears pinched my eyes. *The congregation in my head—or was it the approaching heavenly choir?—kept singing in circles, around and around, about the precious Lord and calls and holding hands, about letting me stand lest I fall.*

But I was falling, maybe not into hell, but certainly into death. I'd wind up a broken heap at the bottom of a chasm, like my friend the cartoon coyote. Only instead of holding up a sign that said "OUCH!" I'd be dead.

I thought of Linus and Marion and Red and Mom and Dad and Cassie and Annie. I'd never get to tell them how much I loved them.

Don't look down!

I heard the words from my own sermon. What a snotty, trite bunch of shit that had been. Easy to say don't look down, when you aren't the one walking on water afraid to die.

Don't look down, said the voice in my head.

"Fuck you," I told it. Nothing that sounded like much came out of my mouth.

"You want to pray?" said Josh.

Would you really rather be right than receive a miracle? asked the voice.

"Whatever you say," I tried to say but only "sssss," came out.

Josh took that as a yes. "That makes me feel better," he said, "knowing you're going straight to heaven." He helped me roll over and kneel beside the rail, then sat next to me, facing the pews.

I held myself up with my right arm on the edge, feeling my body for the tingling that would tell which part of me would die next. My stomach pain bit into my lungs again and again and I bent.

Be wrong. Take the miracle.

I remembered my prayer from last night. *Okay*, I thought. *I'm wrong*. About what, I didn't know, but whatever. I pushed myself straight up against the pain, waiting at the rail for the miracle to be delivered, like a wafer or bread.

Instead, my head lolled back, my neck weakening. I forced it upright again.

Oh, Christ, I'm dying.

Don't look down.

When Peter walked, he didn't sink. When the coyote ran, he didn't fall.

Something clicked in my heart. Or my head. Suddenly, I got it.

I'm wrong. I'm not dying. If I walk. Run. Move. I won't die.

I spit and moaned. *I'm going to live through this, even if it seems impossible*. Then the next wave of nausea and pain took me and knocked me over again. My hand slipped from the rail and went down, landing on, then slipping from, the sanctus bell.

D.J. hadn't put it back. His pulled muscle must have hurt too much. I shoved it a little. Heavy—maybe seven pounds—but my arms still worked. I had an idea. The injury that got me into this mess just might get me out.

Tears and sweat and drool ran down my face as I slipped my forearms under the bell. *Biceps, back, hips— time to walk on water.*

I imagined the coyote running so fast his legs blurred. *Move fast. Move hard.* I heaved and slammed the bell and my body as hard as I could at the back of Josh's head.

He toppled forward and his head clunked against the floor.

I tried to pick up the bell again, just in case. But it had landed on its side, its legs stuck out sideways. My hands wouldn't work so I couldn't get a purchase. And the black spots swam in from the edges now, clotting my vision.

Josh moaned, put a hand to the back of his bleeding head.

Run!

I used the first pew to pull myself up.

A roar of pain and fury ricocheted around the church as Josh flopped over and flung himself at me. He grabbed my right foot and I toppled onto the pew, my arms not fast enough now to stop the fall. My chin hit the back edge and I spit blood.

Behind me, Josh's fingers dug into my leg like flying shrapnel, pulling me back and down.

Images spun in my head—the coyote running on water, Simpsons kids singing karaoke, my dad hollering that we'd won, the sound of my own breath pumping, the thudding of my own feet hitting muddy turf as I ran through rows of blueberries after Linus. I yanked my leg, knocking myself off balance, but not breaking his grip.

Josh pulled himself to his hands and knees, still holding my ankle, blood dripping over his ear from the gash.

Heat, fear, adrenaline and anger pushed everything else from my mind except my free foot, Josh's head and the last gift of power coming to me from somewhere beyond myself.

I pulled my left knee to my chest and with every bit of soccer-loving blood left unpoisoned in my body, I drove my heel into Josh's forehead. His head snapped back as I fell off the pew, landing with a pain that shot up my spine and into my ears, knocking my vision blue and my body cold.

Josh moaned again, but I no longer felt his hands on my ankle. I could barely feel my legs. Hooking an arm over the end of the pew, I pulled upward again, waited while my head swam, breathing, tilting, hoping it would stop. It didn't. So I ran

258

anyway.

The floor undulated beneath me like a rope bridge over a ten thousand foot gorge. Vomit rose in my pipes as I careened down the aisle, my feet dead to me, flapping like scuba fins, threatening to trip up every step. I fell against the door and tumbled down the wooden steps, barely able to get my arms up in time to protect my face. Something cracked—I heard it, but didn't feel it.

"Reverend?" Someone yelled from somewhere. I stumbled up and ran like I was on an open breakaway and the Olympic goal would be ours if I only kept running.

I only made it a few steps then fell again onto the damp cool grass.

I spat more blood, watched the stars burst in my head and tried to breathe, to answer any of the shouts I heard in the distance. I tried to stand again, but instead flopped onto the ground half on my back. The sunlight seared my eyes with bright unfocused blue.

Something began to rattle, sounding like radiators in an old house. But we didn't have them in the parish house.

I wasn't in the parish house.

Someone knelt beside me. Not Josh. I couldn't see. Couldn't turn my head. Then Bets Alderink's face. My organist. A Belle. Asking me questions.

That rattle again. I couldn't get enough air. The rattle was my lungs. Drool escaped my lips, but my tongue wouldn't move to catch it.

"Fugu. Josh poisoned me," I tried to say. I couldn't hear what came out because of the rushing in my ears. The searing blue sky burned my eyes, but I couldn't close them. Even the dark spots didn't make the light go away.

"Nine-one-one," Bets yelled. I could barely hear her over the rushing sound in my ears. "And Marion Freeley. Wherever she is, find Marion, now."

With my last strength, I pulled my dead arm up and threw it toward the church.

Bets' eyes followed it. "Okay," she said. "We'll go look in the church."

Chapter Thirty-Six

I couldn't move my head. It was like having a heavy strap holding it in place, only no strap. No nothing. Suddenly, nothing seemed more important to me than being able to move my head.

My heartbeat skittered in my neck, inside my elbows, behind my knees.

The inky spots and flashing stars died away in the ambulance once they put oxygen tubes in my nose. The shiny metal ceiling reflected blinking colored lights. Occasionally a man's worried face appeared above me. Voices called out numbers. The siren split my head—I couldn't move my hands to cover my ears.

Next I saw the sky again, too bright and I couldn't blink. Then fluorescent ceiling lights sliced into my head. Red Carson appeared, looking down, curls falling forward, face shadowed. My eyes stared at her hairline—I couldn't move them to meet hers, to focus.

"You're going to be okay, Lonnie. We know what it is. They'll treat it."

Here comes the miracle.

The plastic tubes in my nose sat funny, tickling me. I thought I'd burst if I didn't scratch it. But I couldn't move.

"Pupils fixed," a man's voice said. "Her brain—"

"Eyes are affected by the poison," said a woman, smooth, calm.

I sensed my body lifted, manipulated as I listened to the floating voices.

"Flaccid paralysis," said the woman.

"Reverend Squires, can you feel this?" The man.

I couldn't answer. Couldn't even look to see who had spoken.

"Aphonia, Nels, remember?"

They rolled and pushed tubes inside me, held me while I heaved black sludge back up out of me. Gentle hands placed me on my back, my head straight up.

"Has anyone lavaged her eyes? She's not blinking." The woman.

Cool drops slid into my eyes, like an icy drink down a hot throat—a mercy.

"Heart rate is forty-nine and dropping!" said another woman.

"Where's the atropine?" The man.

"Did someone call her husband? Okay, parents?" The first woman.

God, don't call my mother. She'll flip out. Call Marion. Call Marion.

I felt woozy and numb in body but my spirit wanted to rise up, jump from my body and run, keep running, keep the miracle alive, the miracle of being alive.

"Respiration is disintegrating!" The man.

"Nels, calmer, please."

A shadow appeared at the corner of my eye until a dark-edged oval hovered in the center of my sight. "Reverend Squires, I'm Dr. Louise Lopez. We met the other day. I know that despite the neurotoxic effects of the tetrodotoxin, you know what's going on."

Let me out of here! My brain told my body to shake it off, rise up and go. When nothing moved, my heart stumbled.

I could feel my body dying around me.

Maybe I wasn't going to live, at least not on this earth. What made me think I knew what miracle would be in store?

"Your respiration is weakening," the unfocused oval said. "It's probable we'll have to intubate you, use a respirator to support your breathing until the effects of the poison pass. So we need to prepare. We're going to sedate you."

I knew from my own research that they could do nothing except try to keep my heart and lungs working while the poison ran its course.

"When you wake up, this will all be over and you'll be on the mend."

I wanted to say *Okay. Do your thing. Make me well.* To share in the brave public play. But I couldn't. Locked in my head, in a body that had become no more than a shell for my spirit, I could only respond to my own thoughts.

And suddenly, as I realized that I was about to lose consciousness too, most of my thoughts were shrieking and spinning in scarlet buzzing terror.

It's okay to die, one part of me told the screaming parts. *You'll go to sleep. It won't hurt. Either you'll wake up and you'll be better, or you'll die and you'll be better. No-lose situation, Squires. Like an empty net breakaway.*

The shadow above me melted away and another appeared. Even out of focus, I recognized Red.

"We found the boy. Josh. Banged up, but alive. He's not talking yet. But he will. The poison was in the priest host. No one else got any." She paused. "Borden's gone to get Marion now. She's bringing her here and while you fight this, we'll sort it out. I promise."

Tell her I'm sorry.

"We're starting the sedative now," said Dr. Lopez from the distance.

Tell her I love her and her family. I tried to lock eyes with Red who didn't move, who stayed right in the middle of my line of sight.

And tell my family too. I love them.

A wonderful warm rush like an enormous summer lake swooshed around my body. I imagined I could see Red more clearly than my unfocusing eyes would allow.

Tell them all to play hard, I thought. Then floated off into a warm dark lake.

Chapter Thirty-Seven

The next thing I knew for sure was that I had not gone to heaven.

My first clue: Brady Wesselynk's horsey laugh and my mother's tittering giggle overlapping in the space around me.

My second clue: when I opened my eyes, they landed on the clock on the wall, which instantly split into four spinning clocks. I couldn't tell the time.

I didn't know what heaven was, but this wasn't it. This was my life, no doubt about it. "Hey," I said. "What's up?"

After the hugs and tears and Brady's sweaty handshake, my mom ran from the room to call my dad and sisters.

"It's a miracle!" Brady said, easing himself into the square straight chair at the side of my bed.

Little did he know.

I spotted a Styrofoam cup to my left with a straw beside the bed and without thinking, reached for it. My arm moved, despite the tubes and wires, and my fingers stretched toward the cup. It was then I saw the cast for the first time.

"You just let me get that." Brady grabbed the cup.

"Did I break my arm?"

"Wrist." Brady held the straw to my lips. "Not bad, though. But they say you won't have your fine motor control back for a while yet. From the poison, not the break. Don't want you dropping ice all down the front of that pretty gown."

My throat moistened and I tried to speak. "Josh poisoned me. And Guy. To cover up—" Something caught, I coughed, sipped again.

"Tubes down your throat'll do that. And don't you worry, we've got the whole story, thanks to Star uncovering the relationship between Guy and Cousin Donna. Not to mention that woman's wicked past. Star even got Maris to search and find Guy's files of students. You know he had dozens he'd blackmailed over the years?"

I spit the straw out. "*Star* did this?" I coughed again.

Brady leaned back. "Oh, she's been generous with credit for you, telling all about how you urged her to keep her guest's confidence, to let the past stay past and to focus on the poison. Because, of course, who'd have thought Guy was the target what with that raffle and all. But Star just had to expose the snake so we could drive it from our little garden."

He glanced up at the blue beeping monitor beside me. "Whoa, there, missy. Heart rate's on the climb. Maybe we shouldn't talk shop just now." His big eyes flashed toward the door.

"Tell me." I cleared my throat. "Tell me exactly what Star did."

"Well." He looked at the monitor again. "After you beaned the boy in your sanctuary, he wasn't talking. So Star called that federal agent and spilled everything about that woman's wicked past. Then Donna herself accused Guy of blackmail and revealed the whole scam. That, of course, led the forces of righteousness straight to Josh's motive, so they followed up and sure enough, the boy had gone home to Ohio the weekend before the cooking show. Special-ordered a live pufferfish—wild caught, not captivity bred—on the Internet pretending he had a saltwater aquarium. Got the idea from the tanks up at the Five Points Science Center."

A live pufferfish! "He killed it?"

Brady nodded. "Killed it, cut it up, saved its most poisonous parts."

"Isn't it dreadful?" squealed my mother as she swept toward me. "Innocent little fish with such a cute little face." Her flyaway blonde gray hair frizzed out over a yellow blouse and tight jeans as she hugged me again. "Your father sends his love. Annie too. She called," my mom said in response to my surprise, "after we left a message on her phone that you might be dying."

"A loving sibling," Brady said, smiling.

"Nice to know something gets her attention," I said.

"Yes, dear," said my mother, who sat in the chair next to Brady and picked up giant purple plastic knitting needles and a wad of multifruit colored yarn.

"So, wait, Mom. How do you know what a pufferfish looks like?"

"Pastor Wesselynk and I have looked at more than a few pictures of them on my laptop WiFi, you know, down in the cafeteria."

The vision of my mother and Brady chumming it up over a shared wireless connection boggled my still none-too-clear mind.

"I think," said my mother, "that they all look like they should wear lipstick and false eyelashes and a fancy Sunday hat and carry a big old handbag, like your Aunt Katherine did. Remember, dear?"

The idea of Aunt Kate as a poisonous fish made me laugh so hard that a bunch of monitors started beeping and a nurse appeared to put an oxygen mask over my face.

I dozed and it wasn't until Red told me later that afternoon that I learned it was Tuesday—that I'd been out about three days and that it would probably be another day or two before I regained enough motor control to walk and use my hands normally. "Then they'll let you go home," she said.

She explained to me that Josh had kept the fish in the freezer at the house, thus his puzzling violence about not sharing his mother's lasagna with the rest of his housemates. Some of what they thought was lasagna was in fact enough poison to kill all of them and thirty more.

As she talked, I thought about what I'd learned about Guy, my theory for his graduation chapel service speech in support of inclusion, and how he may not have meant a word of it. But Red never brought it up. Maybe no one had figured it out but me. Or maybe I'd been wrong.

"I hear Star's taking all the credit."

Red's eyebrows arched. "Not all of it. She says she couldn't have done it without you, though she claims she's the one who hired you in the first place."

"How's Elyse taking that?"

"I'm not sure she cares." Red leaned forward. "Everyone knows you almost died trying to catch the killer. I think most everyone knows you really solved the case. If Star hooks up with you, she gets a little of that glory. Stealing glory is her gift. What can I say?"

"Glory? I have glory?"

Red nodded. "You do. You know how fast public opinion flip-flops around here."

I soaked that up. Then I caught myself itching my nose and grinned like a fool. Never again would I take itching my nose for granted. Never.

"How's Marion?"

Red's eyes slid toward the phone. "The Grind's full of hungry gossipers. And they're taking good care of Linus. So, good." Pause. "She was here, while you were sedated."

I nodded but didn't get a chance to ask more because my mother slid around the door singing, "Yoo-hoo, look who I found!" She led in a dazed looking Elyse Orion, staggering under the weight of the world's biggest bouquet of orange and yellow and green. Red rushed to clear cups and tissues from the bedside table so Elyse could settle her burden. Then she leaned in and kissed my cheek.

"You really are a superhero ecclesiastical sleuth," Elyse exclaimed, wiping an askew wisp of hair from her forehead. "The whole town's talking about you and Star Hannes teaming up."

Just like Holmes and Watson? Starsky and Hutch? Two of Charlie's three angels?

Elyse shrugged. "The Committee on Liturgy is worried there won't be enough room for people at church on Sunday."

The Committee on Liturgy! Good Lord, when I had last seen them Bova Poster had perpetrated yet another sabotage of the host. The Zaloumi twins and I had sabotaged her sabotage. And Marion's bread had been used to poison me. I closed my eyes. Woman at the Well may very well be in an escalated stage of Wafer Wars.

"That lovely Bova Poster stopped by," my mom said, pulling her knitting from a bag and plopping into the chair in the corner. "With your senior warden and two of the strangest old men. Brought me some astonishing honey whole wheat bread. And a bouquet of roadside weeds."

Not hard to guess who had brought which. "Were they being nice to each other?"

"Oh, yes," said Mom. "It was all lovely. They wanted to be sure I was fine in your cottage. Brought me a list of your messages, too, from the church." She began to rummage in her bag. "I have them somewhere."

"They're calling everyone to bring extra cookies for community hour afterward," Elyse said. "In case of crowds."

"I volunteered to make snickerdoodles," said my mom. "And Elyse has been lovely enough to let me use her kitchen, since yours simply won't do. I don't know how you feed yourself, dear."

Another miracle! My Committee on Liturgy working together!

"Maybe I need to nearly die more often," I said, my eyes drooping.

Red rose. "On that note, I'm gonna head out. One last report to file for Agent Borden."

"She still around?" I tried not to sound too interested.

"Leaving this evening," Red said. "Sent her regards to you. Wished you well with your soccer team."

I opened my eyes just in time to see her motioning to Elyse to leave as well. "Wait. What about Cousin Donna? And Mandy?"

"Gone," Elyse said. "Grateful to you, both of them. Donna apologized on her Web site and YouTube for hiding her plagiarism and promised to volunteer with youth to discourage cheating. She called upon all Christians for their mercy, and I suppose people will forgive her."

I waited, but no one said anything about Donna's rampant sexual behavior, so I didn't either. We were all very nice about it.

"And Mandy went with her, of course," Elyse continued. "Two peas in a pod there. I don't know what they'd do without each other."

I issued a quick prayer for Mandy Tibbetts, hoping she'd find the path that would lead her to her happiness, with Donna or without.

"And we made simply boatloads of money from the Culinary Ministries benefit!" Elyse clapped her hands. "The rec center is fully funded! Complete with an indoor soccer field. And did you hear? Mimi Manser's going to play for your team."

Great. *Star's prime henchman.* But without Marion, I still needed two more for the roster.

My mother clapped. "Isn't that wonderful dear? You can play year 'round!"

I smiled. "Wonderful."

If I only had a team.

Chapter Thirty-Eight

On Thursday morning I took my first unassisted walk down the hall, caught and threw tennis balls with near normal accuracy, and otherwise checked out well enough to go home.

I have to admit, my mom made things a lot easier, especially with my left wrist and hand nonfunctional. She picked up Linus from the Freeleys, stocked the kitchen with enough food for a month, and bucked me up when I mumbled about Marion not calling. "She's busy, dear. She lost an employee and the restaurant is overflowing."

But she did insist on bringing up my Aunt Kate about once every five minutes. Everything about Michigan reminded my mom of Kate and she ended each memory by pronouncing, "You were so lucky to spend all those summers here."

Eventually, I got too tired to remind her for the umpteenth time how much I'd hated being sent here, how the woman had treated me like her slave and verbal whipping post. Instead I just smiled, kissed her and waved her away so I could take a nap.

But I couldn't sleep. After worrying more about Marion, and worrying about my nonexistent soccer team, I worried about church. So I called Ashleigh. She sobbed when she heard my voice, glad I was alive, overwhelmed with work and questions from people about me and my state of health, freaked out about having dated a murderer, and grateful she'd gotten back together with Tom after the truth came out. After she purged, I asked her to double the order for bread from Marion and check the stock of wafers. To get the blood stains out of the sanctuary carpet. To check the sanctus bell and make sure I hadn't ruined it when I threw it.

"Done," she told me. "Some woman named Wanda sent carpet cleaners free of charge, and Bova and the Zaloumis took care of the communion stuff."

I couldn't be quite as happy as I wanted to be. I mean, all my efforts to reconcile the committee goes nowhere, but the minute I nearly die on the church lawn they bond?

"Mrs. Gellar called in a supply priest."

"Cancel him. I'll do the Sunday service."

"And Bishop Tappen called," Ashleigh said. "He extends his prayers for your recovery and wants to meet with you at your earliest convenience. Something about hosting a diocesan summit in October."

Great.

I still couldn't sleep, so I checked the readings for this week's service. Psalm 133 contained a line that made me laugh out loud. *Oh how good and pleasant it is when brethren live together in unity.* "Nice," I told God out loud. "Maybe I'll print that one out big and plaster it on the bulletin board! Or maybe, instead of a sermon, I'll just say that over and over again for ten minutes." Not a bad idea, actually. We could all meditate on that little mantra together.

My mom walked Linus and made meatloaf and scalloped potatoes and green bean casserole, the last things I wanted to

272

eat in steamy August weather. Still, I surprised myself by packing away double servings of all of it and gladly wrapping the rest to eat later.

Saturday I almost jumped out of my skin when my mom showed up with three brown bags of cleaning supplies, snapped on the rubber gloves and got down on her hands and knees to scrub my kitchen floor. "It's the least I can do," she sang when I protested, "after all the help you gave your father the other night."

"Then he ought to be the one on his hands and knees scrubbing my floor," I said.

She found this supremely funny and giggled for the next twenty minutes while she scrubbed. When she started on the bathroom, I fled the house for the lake, sitting on the sand for nearly two hours, just staring at the water and sky. Probably still the drugs running through me—as I sat, I disappeared, stopped thinking about anything and just soaked all of it in through my open pores. Drawing energy from the sand and water, grounded in Mother Earth.

Marion's Gaia.

She still hadn't called me.

I stood and slapped sand off my butt. Come hell or high water, I'm going over there tomorrow, I pledged. Right after church.

My mom cried a little when she left that night, but I could also tell she looked forward to getting back home. "Your father's eaten too many meals down at that sports bar this week. Lord only knows what that's done to his cholesterol." As she drove away she waved, shouting after her, "Don't forget, next month is Eighties night! You're still the phone-a-friend."

Sunday morning went without shenanigans. D.J. rang the sanctus bell with renewed fervor—or perhaps I just heard it that way, since the thing had saved my life. Afterward, everyone wanted talks, hugs, the inside scoop. D.J. and the other kids wanted a moment-by-moment account of what it was like to be "alive in a dead body."

"Didja know that stuff, that tetro-stuff you had, is the powder used to make zombies?" D.J. asked. "Real zombies?"

"No more unsupervised Internet for you, young man," called Colleen from the coffee table.

Bova Poster stood alone behind the goodies table, offering pink lemonade refills to everyone and assuring that each child took no more than one treat.

"Your committee did great work this week," I said. "What made you guys snap together like that?"

"It's one thing to squabble within the team," she said, her eyes locked onto Bets Alderink's children. "And it's another when someone from the outside comes after one of us. We aren't going to fold in a situation like that. Not on my watch."

Bova Poster? Talking about sticking together as a *team*?

"Bova," I said, not realizing what my words would be until after I said them, "if I can ever get a sponsor for the team, would you want to play soccer?"

What the hell? Did I just say that?

Her eyes turned to me, narrow, hard. I realized she thought I was joking.

"I still need one player," I said. Assuming I could talk Marion back into playing.

The lines at the corners of her face softened, but she didn't go as far as a smile. "The doctor does say I need to lower my blood pressure."

I could think of other ways she might do that—namely, simply being a nicer person—but I just smiled, half-horrified by what I'd just done.

"Besides, if it doesn't involve those nasty Zaloumi twins, it should be lovely!" The embroidered cardinals on her blouse rose and fell. "Yes. I'd like to play. But wasn't the deadline last week?"

I explained how Elyse had fixed it, that if I had players and a sponsor by Monday—tomorrow—I could still register my team.

I felt a bit like D.J.'s zombie when I finally snapped off my collar and changed out of the blacks into khaki shorts and an Episcopal Women's Caucus tee then walked the two blocks to The Windmill Grind. The street was jammed with cars and I grinned to see people clustered on the sidewalk, waiting to get in for brunch. They bolstered my courage a bit. If Marion didn't want to have anything to do with me, If Marion didn't want to have anything to do with me, she'd be too busy to have a huge fight. I'd been so wrong in how I'd treated her.

Maybe I should take this back to the car. I'd been so wrong in how I'd treated her. I squirmed with shame as I remembered accusing her of failing to support me. I turned away from the door. Why should I force her to talk to me?

You're so convinced you're right about this.

I smiled at the family seated on a nearby sidewalk bench and paused. I had to go in. I didn't know what would happen. But I had to.

The bell jingled when I opened the door, like always, and like always, every head in the place turned in unison to spot out who had just walked in. But unlike ever before, every face beamed when it met mine and someone in the back started to clap. Soon the whole place was applauding me like I'd just scored the go-ahead goal in a big game.

I didn't see Marion anywhere as I made my way to the counter, but then the kitchen door swung open so hard it banged into the wall and Marion appeared, purple gauze shirt blousing around her white apron, balancing a huge cake with blazing candles on a tray above her head, her whole body teetering dangerously on four-inch purple spikes.

"For," she sang loud and long until everyone joined, "she's a jolly good fellow."

She placed the cake on the counter in front of me.

Marion leaned forward to whisper under the laughter and applause. "The spirit guides told me you'd be in here today."

"You're connected to them again then?"

She nodded. "My karma is realigned."

I blew out the candles and everyone cheered when Marion announced it was a freshly made Boeterkoek, topped with almonds and pieces were on the house.

"Mare," I said, "I'm—"

"We both are." She wiped her forehead and blew out a big puff of air. "Good Gaia, these hot flashes!" She handed me a knife and placed a stack of side plates beside me. "Cut this for me." She pulled an ice bucket from under the counter and plunged her hands in up to the wrists. "Can you believe this is the only way I can kill the flash? No wonder I was so out of sorts the last few weeks. Ambushed by hormones on top of everything else!"

I pushed the knife into the warm, dense cake. "I need you to play soccer."

She blinked at me. "Well, thanks for the invite, but with all that bad chi behind us, I assumed I was. You couldn't keep me off the team, Squires. You aren't big enough."

I grinned. "If we have a team. Still no sponsor."

"Oh, I don't know," Marion said, a smile planting itself between her cheeks. "Business is looking up here. What if I sponsored the team? I mean, if the Windmill Grind did?"

"Seriously?"

"Would I ditch the Belles? Of course I'm serious."

I hugged her over the Boeterkoeke.

"Only one thing though," she said as she plunged her dripping hands back into the ice. "We can't call the team The Grind. What a loser name for an over-thirty women's soccer team."

"Plus, if we are losers, it might not advertise so well for the restaurant." I passed the first few plates of Boeterkoeke to the folks sitting at the counter. Kaylee showed up with a big tray to take the next few to tables.

"That too. We need something better," Marion said, pulling one hand out of the ice to grab a towel and wipe her brow again. "Something powerful."

I had an idea. "Something to make them run cold with fear at our soccer greatness, and hot with exhaustion when we whip 'em on the field?"

"Exactly." Marion watched Kaylee fill the tray up again. "A force that cannot be denied. And something associated with women. Too bad we can't use Gaia." She pulled her hands out of the ice and laid them against the sides of her neck. "When will these things stop? They keep coming and coming and every time, they just knock me flat."

Our eyes met and our grins grew. We knew what we would call the team. We laughed great belly laughs until Kaylee impatiently demanded to know if I was going to cut the rest of the Boeterkoeke or if she should do it.

On Monday morning, I drove to the dusty, bare drywalled offices of the new rec center and using Marion's money for sponsorship, signed up the new team to play in the lakeshore women's soccer league representing Middelburg.

I had loved the Well's Belles, but they belonged to another time.

As I signed the final papers, I looked down at the list of women under the new team name which I'd printed in all caps. I raised a toast in my mind's eye.

To us. Long live Middelburg's HOT FLASHES.